Black Guns

Black Guns

The MacHaven Legacy: Book 1

Bethany Croghan

Copyright © 2026 by Bethany Croghan
All rights reserved.

No part of this publication may be reproduced, distributed, or transmitted in any form or by any means, including photocopying, recording, or other electronic or mechanical methods, without the prior written permission of the author, except as permitted by U.S. copyright law. For permission requests, contact the author.

The story, all names, characters, and incidents portrayed in this production are fictitious. No identification with actual persons (living or deceased), places, buildings, and products is intended or should be inferred.

First edition 2026

Dedication

To 20 years of writer's block.
Ha! I beat you!

This novel contains dark, explicit, and potentially triggering material. Reader discretion is strongly advised.

- Graphic violence, including murder and bloodshed
- Sexual violence, exploitation, and coercion (not romanticized)
- Child abuse and long-term trauma
- Explicit sexual content and dark romantic themes
- Physical assault, captivity, and threats of harm
- Strong language, alcohol and tobacco use, and morally ambiguous characters

Prologue

The girl stared at the door, frozen in indecision, her green eyes wide as she measured the distance to the handle. Her thumb was shoved into her mouth, her blonde hair a wild tangle around her head, and her free hand clutched and unclutched the fabric of her nightgown as she weighed whether or not to open it. She could just reach the handle if she stretched up on her toes, though it would take both hands to pull open the heavy wooden door.

But that wasn't why she stood there, her small, grasping hand the only thing moving in the dark, silent room.

No. She stared at the door as if it were chained and barred instead of merely closed, because she wasn't supposed to open it. She was not to leave the room until her mother came to get her. Like the hundred times before, she had been told to lie down and sleep on the hard little couch while she waited for her mother to return and take her to bed.

She had never disobeyed before.

She had always done exactly as she was told, waiting and sleeping on the couch in the dark office. She hated waiting there alone. The dark was lonely and frightening, filled with strange noises, voices drifting from other rooms, banging, moaning. It was terrifying when you didn't understand what the sounds meant. To her five-year-old mind, the safest place in the world—the only place she wanted to be—was with her mother.

Her mother, whose bright smile and golden hair had become the child's sun.

In her mother's arms, she slept safely. Her mother would drown out the strange noises with a softly sung lullaby, her voice warm and sweet like honey against the girl's ear.

And just like every other night, her mother's honeyed voice had gently told her to stay in the room, to be a good girl, to go to sleep, promising she would return soon to get her.

Tonight, though, was different.

Tonight, she had forgotten her doll.

It was a pretty thing with a China face, blonde hair like her own, and a pale blue dress. The doll was her only comfort when she was separated from her mother. She couldn't sleep without it, and she had forgotten to bring it with her.

So, she stood at the door, torn between her need to please her mother and the fear of being completely alone in the dark.

Suddenly, a loud **BANG, BANG, BANG** slammed into the wall to her left.

She jumped, a small, frightened whimper slipping past her thumb.

Fear won.

She rushed to the door, yanking her thumb from her mouth with a wet pop, and stretched up to grab the handle. She pulled hard, her small arms straining, and the door swung toward her.

She rushed into the hallway without looking, her bare feet thudding softly against the cold wooden floor as she passed the rooms belonging to the other women. No one was there to notice her, and she didn't stop until she reached the door to the room she shared with her mother.

She reached for the handle, intending only to ask for her doll and then hurry back to the dark office.

But as the door swung inward, a strangled cry from inside made her pause.

That was her mother's voice.

Was something wrong?

Then she heard a gruff male voice. She couldn't make out the words, but the tone was harsh, unfriendly.

Warily, she pushed the door open, her small palms braced against the rough wood. She couldn't see the bed from the doorway; the indented wall blocked it from view. Taking a few steps forward would fix that.

Her bare feet shuffled ahead, her toes registering the change from cold wood to the softness of a rug. A pained whimper came from the direction of the bed, followed by a deep, ugly chuckle. The girl took another step, and then her eyes found the bed.

She froze.

Her mother lay helplessly beneath a man, her complexion drained of color, fear and pain etched into her face. Her green eyes were wild, fixed on the man straddling her. One of his large hands pinned both of hers above her head. The other held a long, dangerous-looking knife to her throat. Several vicious cuts crisscrossed her bare chest, shoulders, and upper arms, blood smeared across her pale skin. Tears streaked her face.

The man was fully clothed, the sleeves of his filthy shirt rolled to his elbows. Even his boots were still on, flaking dried mud onto the blanket. He had short, brown hair and a thick, solid build. The girl couldn't see his face.

Neither of them had noticed her.

A small whimper slipped from her lips. "Momma?"

Her mother's horrified gaze flew to her daughter. So did the man's, his eyes hard with irritation. The girl shrank back under that look, another whimper escaping her.

"Aura," her mother choked. Her eyes darted to the man, then back to her daughter. "Run back to the office," she said urgently. "Aura, run."

But the man's expression shifted—curiosity sparking there—and that frightened her more than the knife still pressed to her mother's throat. The woman gasped as he turned slightly, the blade slicing into her skin.

"This could be interesting," he murmured, his voice low and rough.

He looked back down at the woman, a wicked smile curving his lips. "Call her here."

"No!" the woman gasped, her body trembling. "Aura, go back to the office." She tried to harden her voice, but it shook.

"No?" The man tilted his head, studying her. His grip released her wrists and slid down her arm before wrapping around her throat. She gasped, struggling for air. He wasn't squeezing hard enough to choke her but hard enough to make breathing difficult. Her hands clawed at his wrist, but he didn't move.

He lifted the knife into her line of sight, twisting it slowly as lamplight gleamed off the blood. Then he flipped the blade in his hand and met her gaze again. "Call her," he said evenly.

There was no emotion on his face, only in his eyes. Excitement burned there. Pleasure. Impatience.

The woman saw it all, and her breath caught. She looked at her daughter, then back at him. He grinned, knowing she understood, and tightened his grip just enough to force a reflexive gasp.

"Momma?" the child whimpered, taking a hesitant step forward.

"No!" the woman cried, trying to scream. The man's hand tightened. She clawed at him desperately, but with the last of her air, she screamed, "Run, Aura!"

"Momma!" the child cried.

The man's arm lifted, then plunged the knife into the woman's chest.

He released her throat, but her scream dissolved into choking as blood filled her mouth. Crimson sprayed across the room, splattering the child. He pulled the knife free and drove it down again.

And again.

And again.

The child watched, frozen, as her mother's body jerked with each blow. The man's mouth stretched into a gleeful smile.

"Momma!" she screamed, throwing herself toward the bed.

As she reached it, the man lifted the knife again, slashing upward.

The blade caught her cheek.

She fell back, striking the wall before crumpling to the floor.

The man climbed off the bed, leaving the body behind him, and stood over the girl.

She hadn't felt the pain yet, but something warm dripped down her face. She looked at her nightgown, watching crimson drops spread across the fabric.

He crouched in front of her, angling the knife into her view.

"I'm going to kill you now, pretty child," he said calmly, as if remarking on the weather.

Then the pain came.

It flared hot and sharp along her face and she screamed, high and piercing. The man jumped back, swearing. She sucked in a breath and screamed again, her small body shaking with the effort.

He staggered away. “They may not have come for the woman’s screams,” he muttered, “but they’ll come for yours.” He glanced at her once more. “You get to live today.”

And then he was gone.

The child slumped to the floor, exhausted.

She barely noticed the gentle hands lifting her, checking her quickly for other injuries. A soft, sweet-smelling body cradled her, carrying her away from the bed.

“Momma,” she whispered, staring at the still form.

Her mother’s eyes were open, fixed on the ceiling, her face frozen in terror.

The child buried her face in soft black hair and cried.

CHAPTER 1

Aura Black rode her buckskin, Aries, slowly into the small town. Her body stayed loose in the saddle, posture relaxed, reins held easy, but her attention was sharp, outward facing. Time had taught her that appearances mattered. You were less likely to draw attention when you looked relaxed rather than when you arrived tense.

She couldn't remember the town's name. It didn't matter. Towns blurred together after a while. Faces, too.

Her pace was deceptively lazy as her green eyes swept the street beneath the lowered brim of her Stetson, cataloging movement, posture, threat. She let the hat hide her gaze from those who looked up at her with curiosity.

Dirty-blonde hair spilled down her back beneath the hat, untouched by ribbon or tie. Despite the mid-summer heat, she hadn't bothered to pull it back yet.

Her grip tightened on the reins as more people slowed or stopped outright to stare at her. She had been cursed with an extremely busty figure and a beautiful face, a combination that rarely failed to halt men in their tracks. Thankfully, the long scar that ran from just beneath her right eye to her jaw discouraged most from lingering too long or trying to approach her.

She supposed her clothing didn't help.

For comfort and ease of movement—necessities for someone who spent most of her time crossing the desert—she wore a simple black shirt and jeans. The shirt did little to disguise her breasts and made her narrow waist and flared hips impossible to miss. But Aura wasn't about to sacrifice comfort to spare a few people their curiosity, or judgement. It wouldn't help anyway. Even the tightly cinched gowns most women favored would only draw a different kind of attention.

Women did wear pants on the western side of the continent, but not often enough to avoid raised brows. Today, every woman she saw wore a decorative dress and bonnet. The fact that it was Sunday likely accounted for that.

She reined in before the town's only bar and dismounted, briefly noting the motorcycle parked nearby. She patted her stallion's neck but didn't bother to tether him. He was well trained and would stay until she returned or called.

Aura stared at the building.

Not at the peeling wood or grimy windows, but at a face only she could see.

She kept it sharp in her mind, drawing it up every time she entered a bar or brothel, hoping this would be the place her search finally ended. If not for the rare traces she'd followed over the years, she might have believed him dead.

She hoped not.

She wanted to be the one to put the bullet in him. To watch the light leave his eyes. To remind him who she was and why he was dying at her feet.

Her revenge.

It was the only thing that had kept her moving forward. The only reason she had endured the countless men who had paid for her body since she was thirteen. Every crude hand and drunken grope had been another coin toward her freedom. Toward leaving the brothel she had grown up in. Toward the price she had always known she would pay; money, body, soul alike.

Whenever disgust threatened to overwhelm her, she touched the scar on her cheek and remembered the night she'd earned it.

Resolve hardened.

Her fingers brushed that scar now, and before she realized it, she was moving. She pushed through the swinging doors and paused just long enough for her eyes to adjust to the dim interior. She scanned the room quickly, pausing on a trio seated at one table.

For one brief moment, she thought—

But no.

The resemblance was superficial. Brown hair, vaguely similar features but this man was too young. Too handsome. He couldn't be much more than thirty. The one she hunted would be closer to fifty by now.

She dismissed him and headed for the bar.

The bartender—round, graying—forgot the glass he was polishing as his gaze slid over her.

"Whiskey," she said before he could speak.

She slid several coins across the bar as she downed the drink without flinching. He refilled it immediately. This time, she let her fingers idle at the rim, watching him, letting silence work for her.

"I'm looking for someone," she said casually.

"Someone in particular," he asked with a hopeful grin, "or will anyone do?"

She raised a brow. "Hate to disappoint, but it's someone in particular."

"Pity."

She waited a moment longer, then said, "Goes by the name of MacHaven."

The bartender blinked. "Must be your lucky day. We've got three of them here right now."

Her calm shattered. "Where?"

He pointed behind her.

Aura spun, eyes locking onto the trio. She barely noticed the woman or the other man as she took in the first man again. Confusion replaced shock. The man she sought wasn't there, but shared blood might be just as useful. Had her luck finally turned?

She tossed the bartender a few more coins, drained the glass, and strode toward the table.

Up close, the resemblance sharpened. The eyes, the nose, the mouth too similar to ignore. If this man smiled, she was certain it would be the same smile she'd hunted for years.

Caution vanished.

Her gun slid free, the hammer's click snapping all three to their feet. Her focus never left the one in front of her. A rifle leaned nearby, untouched.

"MacHaven?" she snarled.

He nodded hesitantly.

"Good God, Trevor," the man beside him muttered. "What have you done this time?"

"I don't even know the woman," Trevor said.

Aura's gaze flicked to the speaker and caught.

Blonde hair, broad shoulders, hazel eyes, an infuriating grin. She cataloged him automatically—too automatically—and hated herself for it.

"Seems you've attracted another one, Donovan," the young woman sighed. Slim, with short black hair. She was younger than the others.

Heat rushed to Aura's face.

"So, is there a reason you're pointin' that gun at me, sweetheart? Or are you just the angel of death, come to deliver me into the arms of the Lord?"

Trevor's voice brought Aura's attention back to him and she quickly recalled why she was standing there with her gun trained on him. It galled her to think that a handsome face, no matter *how* handsome, had distracted her from her purpose for even a second.

"Oh, I'm the angel of death for someone," she growled at him, "but *that* one I'll be sending on to burn in hell and may he do so for eternity."

"That's a right shame," Trevor said with a lopsided smile. "But if I'm not the recipient of your heavenly wrath, then why are you pointing that gun at me?" He pointed a finger at the gun still in her hand.

"Because I've been informed you're a MacHaven."

"Bad day to be a MacHaven, Trevor," the one called Donovan said with a chuckle. Aura turned her head to glare at him.

"Hate to point it out," Trevor said, doing just that, "but you're a MacHaven, too, *brother*."

Donovan scowled at him. "So, why'd you point it out?"

"You a MacHaven, too?" Aura asked the woman—girl really—cautiously but firmly.

The girl shrugged. "That's kind of how siblings work."

"Then I hope, for *your* sakes, that one of you can answer my question," Aura said menacingly.

Donovan crossed his arms, unconcerned. "That gun really necessary for a question?"

"That depends on your answer."

"If you can't play nice, we won't play at all." In a blink, the weapon was gone, uncocked and airborne. Before she could react, its twin followed. He never touched her skin, but his proximity sent heat through her anyway.

Her pulse spiked but with recognition.

She hated that. She had learned long ago what men like this could take when they decided to. She had also learned how to survive them. What unsettled her now was that part of her wasn't reaching for survival at all.

Desire flared. Unwanted. Unwelcome.

"So, do I get to hit her now?" came the female's voice.

"And ruin such a pretty face? Have a heart, Janice," Trevor said with a chuckle.

"How boring," Janice said with a sigh. "You never let me have any fun."

Blinded by impotent rage now, Aura swung a closed fist at Donovan's grinning face. He sidestepped it, the grin never leaving him, and the momentum sent Aura spinning around. Donovan caught her arms as she came back around to face him and shoved her down into his vacated chair. Dumbstruck, all she could do was stare up at him in fury. He slid an untouched glass of whiskey across the table towards her. "On me," he said with a wink and turned to follow his siblings out the door.

Aura stared after him for several moments before growling at herself, downing the contents of the glass and jumping up to retrieve her guns.

Aura burst out of the bar and didn't slow until she reached her horse.

Janice and Trevor's horses were just turning a corner several blocks down to her right, but for some unconceivable reason, she looked for Donovan.

The motorcycle was already tearing down the far end of town, dust billowing up behind it in a thick plume. She swung into the saddle in one smooth motion and kicked the Aries hard into a gallop. He leapt forward eagerly, muscles bunching beneath her, hooves pounding as they hit the road.

The sound of the engine carried clearly in the dry air.

She leaned forward, urging her horse on, eyes locked on the shrinking figure ahead. Anger burned hot in her chest, at Donovan, at herself, at the way he'd disarmed her so easily, touched her without touching her, unsettled her without effort.

She hated that more than being disarmed.

The town fell away quickly behind them, replaced by open land and the pale stretch of dirt road cutting through scrub and dust. Donovan wasn't fleeing. That realization came with a fresh spike of irritation. He rode at an easy pace, shoulders relaxed, as if he had all the time in the world.

She closed the distance fast.

At the sound of hoofbeats behind him, he glanced over his shoulder and grinned.

That damned grin.

Aura snarled and drew her gun, steadying it with practiced ease despite the movement beneath her. She aimed carefully, calculating distance and speed in a heartbeat, and squeezed the trigger.

The crack of the shot split the air.

His hat flew from his head, spinning wildly before landing in the dirt.

"My hat!" he shouted over the roar of the engine.

He skidded to a halt, tires sliding as he swung the bike sideways and killed the engine. Aura reined in hard, dust clouding around them as her horse danced beneath her.

Donovan dismounted quickly and stalked toward the hat lying several yards away.

She reached it first.

With a sharp tug on the reins, she brought her horse to a stop squarely on top of it.

His outraged shout almost made her smile. Almost.

"Was that necessary?" he demanded, shoving at the horse's shoulder until the stallion shifted just enough for him to snatch the crushed hat free. He stared at it, horrified, brushing dust away and trying to reshape the ruined crown. "It's ruined! You owe me a new hat!"

She lifted a brow. "You owe me an answer."

He examined the neat bullet hole and snorted. "What—did you miss?"

“Hardly,” she said coolly. “Can’t get answers from a dead man.”

“You’re not getting answers from this live one either,” he replied, jamming the mangled hat back onto his head and turning away.

She nudged her horse forward, blocking his path. “Now wait a damn minute. I haven’t searched all this time just to get this close and walk away empty-handed.”

He rolled his eyes.

Then his hands were on her.

Fast. Too fast.

He grabbed her around the waist and dragged her off the saddle before she could react. She slammed against him, breath knocked from her lungs as her boots hit the ground. She shoved at his chest with an outraged cry, but it was like pushing against stone. He released her only because he chose to, not because she’d earned it.

“What do you think you’re doing?” she demanded.

“Making sure you don’t catch up to me again,” he said easily.

Before she could respond, he smacked her horse on the rump. The startled animal leapt forward and bolted back down the road. Aura spun after him in disbelief.

Donovan laughed—a deep, rich sound that curled unpleasantly low in her stomach—and turned back to his bike. The engine roared to life and he took off, leaving her in a cloud of dust.

Aura snarled.

Then she whistled.

Her horse skidded to a stop and wheeled back instantly, galloping toward her. She swung into the saddle without breaking stride and kicked him forward again.

“Oh, I’ll catch you,” she muttered grimly. “And this time I really will shoot you.”

…In the leg.

She leaned low over her horse’s neck as they surged after the motorcycle, intent on mayhem.

CHAPTER 2

Aura followed Donovan's tracks and caught up to him just after dark. They were easy enough to follow, and by the time night swallowed the ground completely, she was close enough to see his campfire. She followed its glow straight to him.

He let out a loud, exasperated sigh when she called out to announce herself.

"Not you again," he said sourly as she dismounted. He eyed her. "I could've sworn you'd be chasing that horse for hours."

She snorted as she stripped the tack from her stallion, then smacked him lightly on the rump, sending him off into the dark. She stared pointedly at Donovan for several long seconds before whistling. The horse returned at once.

Donovan grunted and turned back to the food he was cooking.

Aura rubbed the horse down quickly, patted him, then dropped onto the ground across the fire from Donovan, fixing him with an irritated look. He glanced at her and said nothing.

Several minutes passed.

Finally, he looked up. "You're not going to give this up, are you?"

"Did you really think I would?"

"I hoped." He sighed, leaned back on one hand, and gestured to her with the other. "Let's get it over with."

"It's not as painful as you're making it sound," Aura said. "At least, not for you. My emotions are another matter." At his raised brow, she waved it off. "Never mind. I just want to know if you've heard of someone I'm looking for."

"And this someone goes by MacHaven?"

She nodded, pulling off her Stetson and dragging a hand through her tangled hair.

"No first name?"

"No," she snapped. "MacHaven was the only name he gave."

"You realize it could be false."

"You think I don't know that?" she shot back. "All I can pray for is that it was real or that he's kept using it."

"That's not much to pray for," Donovan said mildly.

Her glare deepened.

"Is that really all you pray for, sweetheart?" he asked quietly.

"No," she ground out, fists clenched in her lap. "I pray he's still alive so I can kill the son of a bitch."

"You really don't like this guy, do you?" Donovan said curiously. "What'd he do to you?"

"That is none of your business," Aura snapped at him. "Just tell me if you know of him. Goes by the name MacHaven, looks quite a bit like your brother, and would be around his fifties by now."

"Sorry to disappoint you, sweetheart, but my siblings and I are the last of the MacHavens. If his name really is MacHaven—and I doubt it—he's no relation to me. And I haven't heard of anyone going around using the name, though, I might have to look into that. Can't have anyone besmirching my good name, now can I?"

"Damn!" Aura swore angrily. "Figures. The closest I've ever come to finding him, and it's another dead end." What the hell was she going to do now?

Misery crept in, heavy and unwelcome.

"Good God!" Donovan blurted. "You're not going to cry, are you?"

"Hell no!" Aura snapped. "I don't cry."

"Thank God." He shoved a plate at her.

She shook her head at it.

"Take it," he insisted.

"I don't want it."

"Take it anyway."

She sighed and took the plate, refusing to look at him while she ate. Accepting help was a weakness. Needing it was worse.

"Thank you," she muttered.

He didn't acknowledge it.

She ate quickly, washed the plate at the nearby stream, and returned it without comment. Donovan stared into the dark, and she found herself studying his face too closely.

She cataloged him the way she cataloged danger, structure, strength, reach.

The problem was that her body wasn't cataloging. It was reacting. And she didn't trust anything that answered without permission.

"If you keep staring at me like that," he said without turning, "I'm going to have ungentlemanly thoughts."

Heat rushed to her face. She looked away, furious with herself.

This man was dangerous.

Nothing had gone the way it was supposed to have today. She was quiet as she replayed all her actions of the day in her mind, and when sleep finally came, it was fitful.

***

Aura woke late the next morning. Donovan was gone.

She hadn't even heard him leave. How she had missed the sound of that damned motorcycle she didn't know. She whistled as she got up to gather her few belongings and her horse trotted quickly to her side. As she reached for the saddle, a piece of paper caught her eye. She quickly picked it up and scanned the note.

You owe me for 1 night's room and board, and a new hat.

Owing him sat wrong with her. Not because of the money but because a small, treacherous part of her wanted to see him again.

She let out a sound of disgust, crumpled the note and tossed it aside. Owed him, did she? Not if she had anything to say about it. If he had stuck around this morning, she would have replaced the food she had eaten last night. Now, well, too damn bad!

She saddled her horse and mounted. Ignoring the advice she had given herself last night to stay away from him, she followed Donovan's tracks south. She wasn't going to hurry this time. He wasn't really expecting her to follow him, so she'd catch up eventually. It really was ridiculously easy to follow the bike's tire tracks.

In the end, it took her over a week to catch up to him. Partly because he had passed through several small towns and Aura took the opportunity to ask around about the man she was really searching for. She led her questions with the description of the man before throwing out his name, which turned out to be a wise decision when she kept getting the response, “Well, we had a MacHaven through here, big blonde guy, though.” Unfortunately, the friendly townsfolk decided to enlighten her to the younger MacHaven’s actions while he was in each town.

In one town, he had apparently helped to raise a barn. In another, an elderly woman said he’d whitewashed her fence for her. In yet another town, a young boy claimed Donovan had re-shod the family’s horse. There were a host of lesser deeds as well, each person quite grateful for Donovan’s assistance and quite willing to pay what they could for the help.

She didn’t know what to do with a man who left places better than he found them. Men, in her experience, took. If they gave, it was because they wanted something back.

By the time she spotted him on a roof—shirtless, skin slick with sweat, muscles working—she was already irritated with herself for expecting anything else.

“What the hell are you doing?” she demanded a little too sharply.

“Having tea. Care to join me?”

Aura snorted at that ridiculous response. “And I am *not* buying you a new hat.”

Donovan grinned down at her mulish expression. “Woke up on the wrong side of the bedroll, did we?”

“Go to hell.”

Donovan laughed. He quickly hammered in two more nails, put his shirt back on, and swung off the roof to land before her horse. He quickly grabbed the Aries’ reins and stroked his nose to calm him.

She tried to get control of the reins back but failed.

“Let go,” she demanded stiffly.

“No,”

“Let go of my horse before I decide to put a bullet in your gut,” she snarled at him.

“I could have sworn I said no already.” He turned away and led Aries up the street.

“Where the hell are you going with my horse?!” Aura demanded, gripping the pommel

“To the restaurant,” he said, pointing ahead of him. “I’m famished and you’re gonna buy me lunch.”

"The hell I am!" she stated firmly as she slid from the saddle to try to take the reins again.

He stopped dead and turned around to face her, leaning close to her. "You owe me."

She wanted to hit him.

She wanted to kiss him.

She followed him instead.

He went to tie the horse to the hitching post outside the restaurant, but Aura said, "Leave it." He shrugged and did.

Once they were inside, Donovan said, "Come along, sweetheart."

As soon as they were seated, Aura said, though in a deceptively calm tone, "Don't call me sweetheart."

"Why not?" Donovan asked curiously.

"I am nobody's *sweetheart*," she replied, her tone turning hard.

"You look sweet enough to me," Donovan said offhandedly.

Aura tried to ignore the thrill the compliment sent though her, but she was stalled from replying when the waitress came over to take their orders. Donovan ordered for the both of them.

"I'm not hungry," Aura pointed out in annoyance as soon as the woman was out of hearing range.

"Do you ever eat?" Donovan asked her, brow raised. You weren't going to eat that night last week, either. Were you?"

"I eat when I'm hungry."

"And drink when you're angry?" he guessed.

"It's none of your business either way," she said sternly.

"Like I said. Sweet," he grinned.

Aura snorted. "I've never been sweet."

"Oh, I'm sure you were sweet at six," Donovan teased.

Aura's face suddenly contorted with rage. That was the year after her mother's death. She had suffered the entire year with night terrors, waking in the middle of the night, every night, screaming. There had been no reprieve from the violence in her mind, awake or asleep.

"I was too terrified to be a sweet six-year-old," she spat out. "And my life after that wouldn't lend to *anyone* calling me *sweetheart*."

Donovan's expression turned quickly to one of concern. "What happened to you?"

He didn't expect an answer.

She didn't give him one.

CHAPTER 3

Donovan watched his companion fume across the table, studying her with quiet focus. She fairly radiated pain; every expression, every sharp gesture giving it away. Someone had hurt her. Badly. And he had no doubt it was connected to the scar on her cheek.

He was determined now to learn her story, despite having been told—more than once—that it was none of his business. He was stubborn that way. And helpful. He couldn't ignore someone who so clearly needed it.

But not with her search. He was certain that path would lead only to misery and possibly even her death. But the woman herself was unhappy, and Donovan couldn't resist the challenge of trying to change that.

A woman who looked like her should be fending off suitors, not crossing deserts alone. The scar on her face didn't diminish her beauty in the slightest, though he suspected she believed otherwise. It certainly hadn't for him. The moment he'd seen her, desire had hit him hard enough to nearly knock him flat.

Luckily, her attention had been on Trevor at first, giving him time to collect himself before she turned that focus on him. He'd almost laughed when her reaction mirrored his own, fire leaping into her eyes as she took him in. With her interest so blatant, it had taken real effort not to respond in kind.

It was a shame Janice had interrupted. Still, he'd enjoyed the blush. Color had bloomed across Aura's pale skin, making her even more striking.

Her eyes were the first thing he'd noticed once she turned his way; emerald green, sharp and expressive, flaring with intensity when her temper spiked. Her nose was thin and straight, her lips full even when pulled into that constant frown. He'd caught himself watching them more than once, wondering—

He cut that thought short.

When she had noticed his scrutiny, he'd deliberately returned it, letting his gaze trace her the same way hers had done to him. It had been a point of pride, though it also gave him the chance to appreciate every dangerous curve. He wasn't sure how he'd managed to respond coherently to his siblings after that, but he had.

Disarming her had been… satisfying.

He could have done it immediately. She never could have stopped him. But curiosity had stayed his hand, particularly her strange reaction to Trevor. Women didn't draw guns on his brother.

His gaze drifted back to her as the food arrived. He thanked the woman without looking away from Aura. She'd calmed some. He regretted upsetting her earlier. He'd been trying, unsuccessfully, to make her smile.

She hadn't smiled once.

"You know," he said finally, spearing a piece of meat, "we never properly introduced ourselves. Donovan MacHaven."

He offered her a smile that usually worked.

She only raised a brow. After a moment's consideration, she said, "Aura Black."

"Nice to meet you, Miss Black—"

"If you're going to use my name," she cut in, "call me Aura. Miss Black is patronizing."

"Married, then?" he asked lightly. "Mrs. Black?"

She snorted. "Hardly."

"Why not?"

"I'm not marriage material."

"I hope that's not in reference to your temperament," he said mildly. "Being sour as a lemon doesn't disqualify you from marriage."

"That is *not* what I was referring to," she gritted out, glowering at him.

"Oh." He paused, then realization dawned. "Oh."

She wasn't innocent.

The knowledge landed hard. When she looked at him with hunger, she knew exactly what it meant and what it could lead to. Desire surged through him sharply enough that he had to look down and eat before he said something foolish.

Once he'd regained control, he ventured, "I'm headed toward a town known for collecting information. Kinsville. You're welcome to travel with me."

She stood abruptly, disgust barely masking anger. "We're done."

He was on his feet before she could leave, hand closing around her arm to turn her back to him. "What did I say?"

"You don't even like me," she snapped, "but the moment you find out I'm not pure, you offer to help."

He flushed. She wasn't wrong. At least not entirely.

"Yes, I want you," he admitted quietly, leaning in. "But the offer was genuine. I was considering it before that. I have access you don't. If you refuse, fine, but don't punish yourself for a misunderstanding. I wouldn't force myself on a woman. Ever."

Color rushed to her cheeks.

"Do you want my help or not?"

After a long moment, she nodded stiffly.

"Then sit," he said, guiding her back to her chair. "And eat."

She obeyed. Barely.

"Don't think I'll let you order me around forever," she warned, pointing her fork at him.

Donovan shrugged. God, she could be exasperating! But at least she'd agreed to accompany him. He couldn't very well help her if she wasn't around for him to help. After letting her eat in silence for several minutes, he said, "And I never said I didn't like you."

Her fork paused midair. "Nobody likes me."

"That's ridiculous. What about family?"

"I don't have any."

"Your father?"

"Died before I was born."

"And your mother?"

"That's none of your business."

There it was.

"And the scar?" he pressed.

She slammed her fork down. He grinned despite himself.

"Does that mean you aren't going to tell me?"

"No."

"No you aren't or no you are?"

Her glare could have killed. "No. I. Am. Not."

He laughed when she growled.

"You don't have much of a sense of humor, do you?"

Her angry expression relaxed into one of neutrality.

He had pushed too hard.

"You're right. I'll control myself better."

She stood, left the money on the table, and walked out.

Donovan followed quickly. She waited outside, mounted, gaze fixed ahead.

"It won't happen again," she said in reference to her temper. "Get your bike."

As he turned away, frustration twisted in his chest. He hadn't meant to push her into retreat. But nothing about her behaved as expected.

She was difficult.

Volatile.

A challenge.

And Donovan MacHaven had never walked away from one yet.

CHAPTER 4

They traveled until dusk before making camp. Aura pulled from her own supplies for dinner, despite having little appetite. She wasn't used to eating such a heavy lunch, but she suspected Donovan wouldn't tolerate her skipping another meal, so she planned to give him the larger portion. Big man that he was, he likely needed it anyway.

Donovan watched her quietly as she prepared the food. When she finally settled back to let it cook, he asked, "Is there anything else you can tell me about this man that might help?"

She didn't want to answer but she knew she would have to. "The only things I haven't already mentioned are that he's fond of whores and he's a sadistic, murdering son-of-a-bitch."

"That much I'd gathered." He hesitated, then frowned. "Did he rape you?"

Her jaw tightened.

"Is that why you're hunting him?" he pressed. "Why you think you're not marriage material?"

She didn't answer right away. That was a mistake. Horror crept across his face as he filled in the silence himself.

"Don't guess at things you know nothing about," she snapped finally. "You haven't come close to the truth, and I prefer it that way."

"It might help to talk about it," he said gently.

"I have," Aura replied stiffly. "The only thing that will help is putting a bullet in him."

"Who did you talk to?" His tone sharpened.

"The other women who were there."

"Did he hurt them too?"

"No!"

She was unraveling again she knew it. She just couldn't stop. This was why she stayed alone. People asked questions. He asked *too many.*

She gripped her head in her hands, her face screwed up as if in pain.

"But he hurt you?" Donovan had moved without her noticing. He knelt beside her, hands closing around her arms. "Aura—"

Stop asking. I don't want to remember. "Stop."

"Tell me what he did."

Don't make me! It hurts! "No."

He shook her once. "Tell me!"

"Nothing!" she yelled. "He didn't do anything to me compared to what he did to—"

She stopped herself too late.

"Let go of me!" She shoved him hard. When he released her, she stumbled back and swung blindly. Her fist connected, though it barely moved him.

She ran.

Aura mounted without saddle or reins and bolted into the dark. She heard Donovan shout her name, fear thick in his voice, but she didn't slow. She couldn't face him. Not now.

***

Donovan swore and paced the camp well past midnight.

She should have come back by now.

He should have gone after her.

He knew she was a skilled rider, but skill didn't save you from holes in the ground or a single bad step. All it would take was one misjudgment. No saddle. No reins.

He turned toward his bike, then stopped.

Chasing her might make it worse.

That thought sat heavy. He hadn't meant to push her that far. But once she'd begun answering—even vaguely—he hadn't been able to stop himself. Curiosity had turned into compulsion.

Guilt gnawed at him.

He barely knew her. Two days. If he didn't count the week between. She was right. Her past was none of his business.

At least she hadn't taken her belongings.

She would come back.

So, he waited.

When he heard hoofbeats at last, he forced himself into stillness, settling back by the fire as if nothing had happened.

Aura didn't speak. She rubbed down her horse, calm on the surface, and returned to the fire.

"I'm gonna have a bruise on my jaw tomorrow," he said lightly. "You've got a hell of a swing."

"Sorry."

The word was quiet. Flat.

"You burned dinner," he added. "Only saved a couple biscuits." He tossed her one.

"Sorry."

She didn't eat it.

"Don't you ever smile?" he asked.

"Not that I recall."

He blinked. "Really?"

She shrugged. "I imagine the only time I will is when I kill the man who ruined my life. And even then, it won't be a happy one."

"That's the saddest thing I've ever heard."

"It is what it is."

"Well then," he said decisively, "I'm not giving up until I make you smile. A real one."

She rolled her eyes. "Don't hold your breath."

He exaggerated a deep inhale and held it until her brow arched despite herself. When he finally exhaled, he grinned. "You're going to be difficult, I see."

She tossed the biscuit at his head half-heartedly.i

"That small bit of silliness you just displayed gives me hope that you're not a complete loss," he said, grinning at her. "Though, I am surprised you haven't blown up at me again."

Wait," she said simply.

"I could have sworn you said it wouldn't happen again."

"I lied," Aura said as she shrugged, rising her arms to fold them under her head.

Her movement pulled her shirt tight, and Donovan had to look away fast.

"I didn't mean it," she added after a moment of silence. "Not intentionally."

"I know."

She studied the sky, then asked, "Do you lie?"

"Only when necessary."

"Have you lied to me?"

"No."

"So, you think I'm sweet, do you?" She glanced at him again, her expression inscrutable.

Donovan scowled at her. "That was teasing. It was *not* lying. There *is* a difference." She stared at him, brow cocked, and after a moment his face revealed his shock. "Were you *teasing* me?!"

"No." Too fast.

He grinned. "You were."

She didn't respond.

Later, she asked quietly, "Why were you in that bar?"

He hesitated. "My siblings and I meet there once a year."

"For what?"

"To celebrate our parents' deaths."

"That sounds harsh."

"Not if you knew them."

She didn't ask more and he was grateful.

He had his own demons he wasn't ready to face.

CHAPTER 5

It took them two days to reach the next town. Another week, at least, remained before the town Donovan had mentioned.

During those two days, Donovan was careful not to ask questions that might upset Aura. Their coexistence was mostly peaceful if strained. Only two conversations stood out.

The first concerned the cameo she wore at her throat. Set against a green velvet choker, it drew the eye immediately. Donovan asked because it seemed out of place—too delicate for a woman who lived in the saddle—and because he had never once seen her remove it.

Aura's fingers rose to the cameo without her permission.

Lovely.

The word scraped. Men didn't get to decide what parts of her were worth keeping. She had sold everything else because she had needed to survive and survival didn't leave room for sentiment.

It's not for him, she reminded herself sharply. *It's for you. It's always been for you.*

Still, she didn't remove it.

"It belonged to my mother," Aura said carefully. "It was the only thing of hers I couldn't bear to sell."

"You sold her belongings?"

"Well, I couldn't exactly take them with me," she snapped.

He let several minutes pass before saying quietly, "I'm glad you kept it. It suits you."

He walked away before she could argue.

The second conversation happened the following day during a midday rest. Donovan leaned against his bike, watching Aura drink from her canteen.

She caught him looking. Studied him in return.

"Those are nice guns you carry," she said.

"Thank you."

"But I've never seen you use them. Do you even know how to shoot?"

The challenge was deliberate.

"Do you?" he challenged back.

Aura snorted and stepped back before pointing at three trees at different distances. Her gun cleared her holster and barked in quick succession as each tree was hit directly center.

She looked at Donovan pointedly.

He stepped beside her and his gun cleared leather a second faster than hers had. Each tree was hit and Aura had to move close to inspect them, only to discover he had put a hole directly on top of hers.

That wasn't luck.

She'd seen men shoot before. She'd seen confidence, bravado, even talent. What she'd just seen was something else entirely. Control so complete it bordered on indifference.

Nobody learns that without a reason.

And suddenly she was very aware that, for all her weapons and scars, she might not be the most dangerous one here.

By the time they reached town, the quiet had become unbearable.

The quiet should have been a relief.

Aura hated that it wasn't.

Silence usually meant safety. Silence meant no questions, no probing looks, no expectations. Yet every mile they traveled without speaking made her more aware of him, his presence at her back, the sound of his bike, the way her body tracked him even when her mind tried not to.

This is stupid, she told herself. *You've spent years alone without unraveling. He's just a man.*

Except he wasn't. Not to her nerves. Not to her body.

And that made him a liability.

As frustrated as Aura was, with herself and with Donovan, it was understandable that, as soon as she dismounted, she walked away from him. Donovan stared after her curiously, then quickly settled his bike so he could follow her. He fell into step just behind her as she strode down the boardwalk.

"I see a hat shop ahead," he said lightly. "You finally planning on buying me that hat?"

"I told you. I'm not buying you a hat."

"But you owe me one."

"I do not."

"You shot a hole in the last one. Then let your horse trample it."

"Tough."

"I've been without a hat for over a week. Look at me. My face is practically scorched."

She spun to retort and her foot slipped off the edge of the boardwalk.

She fell.

Donovan caught her.

His arm locked around her waist, pulling her hard into him. The impact knocked the breath from her lungs. The contact did the rest.

The world narrowed to heat and pressure and the solid reality of him.

No.

Her breath stalled. Her body betrayed her instantly, arching without permission, responding to the contact like it had been waiting for it.

This is wrong. This is dangerous.

She was too aware. Of his chest beneath her palms, of the strength locked around her waist, of how easily he could hold her there if he chose to.

And worse—

—how much part of her wanted him to.

His breath brushed her cheek.

"Aura," he said, breathless. "Are you hurt?"

She didn't answer.

He said her name again.

Reality snapped back.

"Let me go!" Panic flared sharp and hot, slicing through the desire. She shoved away hard, heart racing, disgusted with herself even as her skin burned where he'd touched her, only then realizing he'd positioned them so she wouldn't fall again.

She could feel it building, that familiar tightness behind her eyes, the pressure that came when emotions crept too close to the surface.

Don't rise to it. Don't engage.

She turned and stalked off, ankle aching from a fresh sprain.

Get distance. Now.

Anger was safer than want. Whiskey was safer than thinking.

Anything was safer than standing there long enough to forget why she ran in the first place.

"Where are you going?" he called.

"To get drunk!"

"Before noon?!"

"Go to hell!"

***

Donovan stood where she'd left him, pulse still thudding.

That was too close.

Not to sex. To disaster. He knew that feeling. The moment where instinct surged ahead of judgment, where strength answered before thought.

He'd spent years making sure that never happened.

And she had nearly undone that in seconds.

He didn't drink. Not because he couldn't, but because he didn't trust himself to. Losing control was never an option. He knew exactly how much damage he could do.

That knowledge followed him everywhere.

The contact replayed itself against his will. The way she'd fit. The way she'd gone still.

He shoved the thought aside.

This was dangerous. For both of them.

Wanting her wasn't the problem.

Acting on it would be.

Desire didn't excuse recklessness, and he refused to become another man in her life who took without asking.

If she comes to you, he decided, *it has to be because she chose it. Not because you pushed.*

He bought a hat. He planned to hide it later. Just to annoy her.

CHAPTER 6

Three men stood in a dark alley, watching the foot traffic along the boardwalk. Night had fully settled, and the shadows cast by the surrounding buildings kept them hidden from the lamplight spilling out of windows and doorways. The clunk of booted heels on wood, the restless whinnies from the nearby livery, and the raucous piano pounding from the saloons swallowed their low voices.

"How'll we know the man?" one of them muttered, scratching at his scalp and sending his greasy black hair into further disarray.

"'ow many blokes you know that tall, Jerry?" the portly man beside him sneered, wiping beneath his nose with the back of his hand. The third man shot him a look of disgust.

"There's that fella down in Henry," Jerry said, shrinking back.

"Yeah, but 'e ain't blonde, ya idiot," the big man snapped, stepping toward him.

"Ease off, Frank," the third man said calmly.

Frank immediately backed down. "Yeah… sure, Tommy."

Though only twenty-eight, Tommy was the unquestioned leader. Broad-shouldered, solid, and hard-eyed. He'd never lost a fight. The other two followed him without hesitation because hesitation earned you pain.

Tommy crossed his arms and studied the boardwalk.

"And the bloke who hired us said 'e'd be carryin' blue guns," Frank added, lowering his voice. "You ever seen blue guns before?"

Jerry shook his head quickly.

They'd been waiting since sundown. The job was simple: take the guns, deliver a message, get paid. Tommy had hesitated only briefly when he'd heard the man was as big as he was, but the instructions had been clear.

Keep it quiet. Don't let him fight back.

The alley would do nicely.

"What d'ya reckon he wants with 'em?" Jerry asked.

"Blue guns?" Frank scoffed. "Sell 'em. Rare as hell."

"What if he won't give 'em up?"

Frank sneered. "We ain't askin'."

Tommy stiffened.

There.

Tall. Broad. Blonde. Blue grips catching the lamplight at his hips.

He lifted a hand.

Frank's fists clenched eagerly. Jerry hefted the iron bar, grinning stupidly before smacking his own hand and yelping.

Tommy waited until the man passed the alley mouth.

Then he struck.

He grabbed the man's arm and yanked hard, slamming him face-first into the brick. Jerry followed with a brutal swing of the bar into the man's back. The man grunted, breath forced out of him, and Tommy drove him into the opposite wall. His head cracked against stone.

Before he could recover, Frank buried a fist in his gut, lifting him clear off his feet. Tommy struck next, clean to the cheek, sending him crashing to his knees. Jerry swung again. Frank kicked him in the ribs.

Too easy.

The man should have stayed down.

He didn't.

He seized Tommy's ankle and yanked. Tommy hit the ground hard, the breath torn from his lungs. The grip on his leg was crushing, unnaturally strong. Panic flared.

Don't let him punch.

Tommy kicked wildly, catching the man in the head. The grip broke. Jerry and Frank kept swinging.

The man rolled, came up fast.

Jerry's bar missed. His momentum carried him forward, straight into the man's fist.

The crack echoed off the brick.

Jerry flew back and didn't get up.

The man straightened.

For a moment he didn't move at all.

Tommy swore and drove punches into the man's kidneys. Frank hammered his face. The man elbowed backward, nearly catching Tommy, then went down again when Tommy kicked out his knee.

Frank grabbed him only to be hurled bodily across the alley.

Tommy barely dodged the flying mass before the man was on him again. A punch to the ribs cracked something deep. Tommy roared and swung upward, catching the man under the jaw.

He grabbed the iron bar.

The strike to the man's arm drew a cry this time.

Good. He bleeds like anyone else.

Frank was back, raining blows. Tommy drove the bar into the man's gut.

Finally, the man collapsed.

Tommy waved Frank off and crouched, gripping the man by the hair and lifting his head.

"You still awake?"

One swollen eye glared at him.

"Good. Here's your message." He nodded as Frank stripped the guns.

"'Blood's got them and you ain't gettin' them back. *'One woe is past; and behold, there come two woes more hereafter.'*"

Tommy let the head drop.

They were gone moments later, leaving the man bleeding in the dark.

***

The farmhouse lay quiet. Too quiet.

They entered without knocking.

Tommy almost didn't see the body until his boot caught on it. It lay sprawled across the entryway, blood already soaking into the rug beneath it.

He stepped over it without comment. So did Frank. Jerry hesitated just long enough to look down, then followed.

The air inside smelled wrong. Iron and something sour beneath it.

In the sitting room, the man who'd hired them sat before a cold hearth, calmly examining a blood-slicked knife as though it were nothing more than a tool in need of cleaning. In the corner, a woman lay bound and gagged, nightgown torn, skin carved with fresh cuts.

She was still conscious.

Tommy swallowed.

The man looked up.

Brown eyes. Flat. Interested.

"I trust you have my guns."

Tommy stepped forward and handed them over, careful to keep his hands steady.

The man took them one at a time, weighing each in his hand before turning it slightly, examining the lines, the balance. His attention sharpened, focused.

"You delivered my message?"

"Yes, sir."

"Good."

He paid them without counting.

Behind them, the woman made a small sound through the gag. A choked attempt at something—pleading, maybe.

The man didn't look at her.

As they turned to leave, Tommy hesitated. "What's so special about those guns?"

The man's mouth curved faintly. "They were made by the MacHaven Company. The last of their kind."

"Never heard of it."

"No." His gaze flicked up, precise now. "You wouldn't have. The company died with a son who wasted everything."

He looked back down at the weapon in his hand, running his thumb along the barrel as if confirming something only he understood.

"The man will be laid up awhile?"

"Broken ribs at least."

The man nodded once, as though that fit an expectation.

"Consistency matters," he said, almost to himself.

He tossed one of the guns back to Tommy without looking. "A bonus."

Tommy caught it on instinct and they moved quickly for the exit.

Behind them, the man laughed softly.

And the woman screamed into the gag.

CHAPTER 7

"Hey! I paid for those drinks! I *know* I paid you double for that last bottle!"

"Doesn't matter, lady," the bartender snapped from the saloon doorway. "You start throwing punches, I throw you out."

A small crowd of men lingered behind him, openly curious. They'd never seen a woman tossed from a bar before.

Aura tried to glare him into submission, but the boardwalk wobbled beneath her feet, refusing to cooperate.

"If that bastard hadn't grabbed my ass, I wouldn't have hit him!" Her words were only slightly slurred, her vision only mildly blurred. No one would have guessed she'd spent most of the day trying to get drunk.

Two and a half bottles of whiskey would have dropped a normal person cold. Aura had been drinking since she was ten.

Unfortunately, she wasn't drunk enough to forget Donovan, which was the entire point.

"Go sleep it off," the bartender barked.

Sleep it off, she scoffed. She wasn't that drunk. They just expected her to be.

Not drunk enough.

The thought burned with irritation as she walked down the boardwalk. She'd miscalculated. Again. She'd wanted the soft blur, the place where faces lost their edges and memories loosened their grip. Instead, everything still hurt too clearly.

You're losing your touch, she scolded herself. *Or your discipline.*

She frowned, then scowled.

Donovan.

"Donovan!" she shouted, expecting him to materialize before her. "Where the hell are you?"

When he didn't appear, she called for him again, scanning the boardwalk and the street.

He wouldn't leave without telling you.

She didn't know why that certainty lodged so deep when he still failed to appear, but once it did, the irritation drained fast, replaced by something tighter and colder.

"Donovan!" she called again.

A groan answered from the alley to her left.

She froze only a moment before she was moving quickly.

The haze vanished.

Fear snapped her sober faster than any cold water ever could.

He was slumped against the wall, blood drying dark beneath one eye.

"What the hell happened to you?"

"Don't remember," he muttered, head drooping.

Panic spiked.

"Donovan!" She shook him. Hard. "Stay with me."

"Ow, damn it."

"How badly are you hurt?" Her hands skimmed his shoulders, ribs, arms, searching for blood she couldn't see.

"Everything hurts."

"We need to get you to a bed. Do you have a room?"

"Boarding house… I think."

His eyes slid shut.

"No." She shook him again, gentler now. "You don't get to sleep yet."

She hauled his arm over her shoulders and braced herself as he staggered upright only to slam back into the wall with a groan.

She hissed as the brick scraped her arm.

"Come on," she growled. "Move."

They lurched forward.

"I'm supposed to be the one who needs help finding a bed," she muttered.

"You can find mine," he mumbled.

She ignored that.

Two blocks felt like twenty miles and when he went down, she barely managed to twist him so his face didn't meet the boards, landing hard on top of him instead.

"Damn you, Donovan!" she snapped. "Get up!"

He didn't.

She knelt beside him, furious and thinking hard.

"Need a hand there, little lady?" Two cowboys loomed behind her.

Relief hit so fast it nearly made her dizzy.

"Yes," she said quickly. "Please."

They got him to the boarding house and into his room and doctor was sent for.

Aura waited in the hall, pacing, ankle screaming as Donovan was examined.

It was mostly bruises and cuts but he had two broken ribs, doctor eventually informed her.

She exhaled, releasing some of her tension.

She should leave.

That was the smart thing. The safe thing. He was stable. He'd live. Her job was done.

Then why are you still here?

The answer sat heavy and unwelcome in her chest.

Back in the room, she stood at the foot of the bed and glared at Donovan's sleeping form.

Her search was on hold.

Because of him.

"Bastard."

***

CRASH! "God, *damn it*!"

Donovan cracked an eye, groaning as pain announced itself everywhere at once.

Aura stood across the room, barefoot, clinging to the dresser. A shattered vase lay between them.

Something was wrong.

Not the noise, the stillness. The way she was holding herself, like she expected pain and was braced for it.

That's not anger, he realized. *That's damage control.*

"Are you alright?" he asked.

"I'm fine," she growled.

She wasn't.

"What's wrong with your foot?"

"Nothing."

He pushed himself upright, ignoring the way his ribs protested.

"I wouldn't," Aura said, her tone a little softer now.

"Feels like I've been trampled by a herd of cattle," he complained, ignoring her advice and propping himself up anyway.

"You *look* like it, too," she commented.

Donovan tried to grin, but it hurt too much. "Teasing me again, sweetheart?"

She shrugged one shoulder. "Stating a fact." She stared at him a long moment before asking, "Are you in pain?"

"Some," Donovan admitted with another grimace, rubbing gently at his sore ribs.

Aura nodded to the table beside the bed. "There's stuff for the pain there. The doctor said take it as needed."

Donovan looked at the table then reached for the bottle. With a swift movement he knocked the bottle off the table and sent it rolling across the floor away from the bed. He turned pleading eyes back to her.

"No," she said firmly.

He clutched his ribs theatrically. "Oh! The pain!"

"Oh! For God's sake!" Aura cried in exasperation, pushing away from the dresser. She limped heavily over to the bottle, scooped it up, dropped the bottle in his lap and limped to the nearby chair to collapse into it.

"What the hell is wrong with your foot?"

"I sprained my ankle," she said stiffly. She carefully propped her injured foot on the footstool. He noticed a blanket scrunched up in the chair, too. Had she slept in the chair last night?

"How? When?"

"When I fell off the damn boardwalk yesterday morning," Aura snapped.

She'd been hurt and he'd leaned on her anyway.

You failed her, the thought accused. *And you didn't even know it.*

"I'm sorry."

She looked at him with a raised brow. "You're *apologizing* for getting your ass kicked? It wasn't exactly your fault, you know."

Donovan scowled at himself now. "It shouldn't have happened. I could have taken them, but…"

"What *did* happen?" Aura asked. "You couldn't remember last night, though the bumps on your head could account for that."

"I got dragged into an alley. Three men. They took my guns."

"Just your guns?"

"They were one of a kind. Made by my grandfather before the MacHaven company closed."

Aura shook her head. "I'm sorry, Donovan. Those men are probably long gone by now."

"They said something," he added. "Blood's got them. And I wasn't getting them back."

"Who's Blood?"

"No idea."

Donovan's hands suddenly shot to his head, then with a horrified look, he quickly scanned the room. "My hat's gone, too?!" he wailed.

"You didn't have a hat," Aura tried to remind him.

"I did! I bought one yesterday afternoon. That's it! When I find those guys, they're dead. Stole my guns *and* my hat!" His face fell to a dejected look and he mumbled, "Didn't even have it twenty-four hours."

He swiped up the bottle of medicine from his lap, took a swig of it, and lay back down to pout properly.

***

"Good, God! What are you doing?!"

Aura stopped dead and looked at Donovan wide eyed. "What?" she asked in confusion.

"What are you doing, walking around in *that*?" he demanded. "That" was the towel she had wrapped around herself after her bath.

She rolled her eyes at him.

"My clean clothes are in my pack," she explained, pointing across the room.

After three days stuck in the room with him, Aura had decided it was time to get out. She was nearly climbing the walls; she was so anxious to get out of the room. Out of the tight space and away from him.

Since she was little, she'd had a fear of dark rooms. She almost never stayed in a town long enough to have to spend the night there, preferring the wide open of the desert. The only reason she'd been able to stay in this one for so long was because Donovan had been here. Having someone else in the room made a lot of difference to her peace of mind. At least at night.

Being able to feast her eyes on Donovan during the day had turned into a battle of wills for her. She had never wanted anyone so much and it was driving her crazy. Which was why she needed the distraction of her search and distance between them.

Donovan stared as she walked across the room.

Aura almost smiled, knowing exactly what was bothering him. The same thing that was bothering her. And suddenly a devil was riding her, making her want to pay him back for all the desire she'd been fighting ever since first setting eyes on him.

So, she crossed the room and, without warning, dropped the towel.

His breath hitched audibly.

Something wrong?"

He folded over with a groan.

"I'm dying," Donovan mumbled into his knees.

"I could get your medicine," she offered sweetly.

"I swear to God, you're gonna be the death of me!"

She leaned over her pack.

"Do you have to do that?" he groaned.

She dressed slowly. Carefully.

She turned back in the brown leather vest, bare skin beneath it, and watched his restraint falter.

She felt only satisfaction.

She loathed the part of herself that responded to him – and punished him for waking it.

She left the room without looking back, abandoning him to the hunger she refused to own alone.

CHAPTER 8

It was a week later when Aura caught Donovan out of bed.

She stopped just inside the doorway, hand still on the knob, her body going very still. The room smelled faintly of soap and clean linen. That alone was wrong.

Donovan's back was to her. He hadn't heard her enter.

He was standing.

Not braced. Not careful. Standing like a man with nothing to hide.

I leave for three hours, she thought flatly, *and he forgets he's breakable.*

Anger flared first. Hot, immediate, familiar. It was safer than the other thing curling low in her stomach as she watched him stretch, arms lifted overhead, shirt pulling tight across his shoulders. He rolled his neck once, slow and loose, testing the motion.

Too loose.

Too easy.

That body should not move like that yet.

"How long has this been going on?" she demanded.

Donovan started, spinning around. He masked it quickly, but not fast enough. She caught the slight hitch in his movement, the barely-there wince he thought he'd hidden.

Good. You should hurt.

"Ah," he said, sheepish. "A couple of days."

Her jaw tightened. She shut the door with deliberate care and crossed the room, dropping into the chair she'd been sleeping in every night. The chair creaked softly under her weight.

"A couple of days," she repeated. "And you didn't think to mention that."

"I didn't want you fussing," he said lightly.

Fussing. As if she were some anxious wife instead of the only thing between him and his own stupidity.

"You should still be in bed," she said. "Another week at least."

He shrugged, unrepentant. "I feel fine."

That was the problem. Men who felt fine stopped listening.

"You don't look fine," she said, though her eyes betrayed her, tracking the easy line of muscle, the absence of stiffness. "You look…" She stopped herself.

Too good to touch, her mind finished treacherously.

Donovan turned his head, studying her with that infuriating half-smile. He knew when she caught herself. He always knew.

"Too good to what?" he prompted.

She shot him a glare sharp enough to cut and turned away. "I found out something while you were ignoring medical advice."

That got his attention.

"The men who jumped me?" he asked. "You found them?"

"They're still in town."

His eyes lit, sharp and eager, all boredom burned away. "You're sure?"

"As sure as gossip and whiskey make for trouble," she said. "They've been rotating saloons. Thought you'd be bedridden longer."

He laughed under his breath. "Idiots."

"No," Aura said flatly. "They were cautious. You're the idiot."

He grinned. "Then I'll correct that tonight."

She was already shaking her head. "No, you won't."

"Aura—"

"You're getting back into that bed."

He folded his arms. "I'm done lying down."

She rose slowly. Deliberately. Let him feel the shift. Let him see she wasn't joking.

"So help me," she said, voice low, "if you reopen those wounds—"

"I'll prove I'm fine."

The words barely left his mouth before his hands were on her. His palms framed her face and he kissed her.

The world detonated.

Aura didn't think. Couldn't think. Shock hit first, white-hot and blinding, followed immediately by something worse: recognition.

This is what I've been fighting.

His mouth was warm, firm, coaxing. Not hesitant. Not asking. Her body betrayed her instantly, leaning in, responding before she could stop it. Her hands rose of their own accord, fingers sliding into his hair, gripping hard like she needed to anchor herself to something solid.

God, he feels right.

The thought terrified her.

He pulled her closer, arms crushing her to him, mouth demanding. Desire roared through her, sharp and reckless and completely out of control. For a heartbeat, she let herself drown in it.

Then he whispered, breath hot against her skin, "God, I want you."

The words shattered everything.

She shoved him away hard enough to break the contact. His hands fell, surprise flashing across his face.

"You don't," she snapped, voice raw. "You don't even like me."

"That's not—"

"I'm convenient," she went on, anger surging to cover the fear clawing up her spine. "I'm here. You're bored. That's all this is."

She didn't wait for him to answer.

She ran.

***

Donovan didn't leave the room until dark.

The guilt sat heavy, unwelcome and deserved. He replayed the moment over and over. The way she'd melted into the kiss before snapping shut like a trap.

Idiot, he thought. *Absolute idiot.*

He should have known better. He did know better.

But he also knew this: that wasn't boredom. That wasn't convenience. That was want. Raw and mutual and dangerous.

And he had said the wrong thing.

Again.

He dressed carefully and slipped out into the night, intent on one thing he could fix. The guns. If nothing else, he could handle that.

Donovan entered the saloon with the practiced ease of a man who didn't want to draw attention to himself. And knew he could handle it if he did.

The air inside was thick with smoke, sweat, and whiskey. A piano clanged somewhere near the back, more enthusiasm than skill, while laughter rose and fell in uneven bursts. He paused just inside the doorway, letting his eyes adjust, his body settle.

Too many people. Too many angles.

He reminded himself—again—that he was not at full strength. Mostly fine wasn't the same as fine.

His gaze swept the room in a slow, methodical arc. Tables. Bar. Corners. Doorways. No sign of the three men he was looking for. No familiar slouch, no hulking frame, no greasy nervous energy that screamed trouble waiting to happen.

Not here. Not yet.

He moved to the bar, careful not to rush. The bartender eyed him briefly, then went back to wiping down the counter.

"Evening," Donovan said easily. "Looking for three fellows. Rough sort. One big as an ox, one built like he thinks he is, and one who looks like he might trip over his own feet if he walks too fast."

The bartender snorted. "Yeah, I know the ones."

Relief flickered, brief but sharp. "You seen them tonight?"

"Not tonight. Last night." The man leaned in slightly, voice lowering. "They been alternating. One saloon one night, the other the next. Keeps 'em from wearing out their welcome too fast."

So, they were creatures of habit. Good. Habits made men predictable.

Donovan thanked him, slid a coin across the bar more out of habit than necessity, and turned back toward the door.

He was already planning his next move—angle of approach, sightlines, how long he could afford to let this drag out—when a voice cut cleanly through his thoughts.

"What the hell do you think you're doing?"

He froze mid-step.

Damn.

He didn't turn right away. Took a breath. Let the irritation fade into something calmer. Something safer.

She was still mad then.

When he finally faced her, Aura stood squarely on the boardwalk, arms akimbo, her posture rigid with disapproval. The lamplight caught the sharp planes of her face, the glint in her green eyes unmistakably dangerous.

"Trying to get my guns back," he said plainly.

"No," she snapped. "That's what I'm doing. You're risking further injury by being stubborn."

He watched her for a moment, then smiled. Not wide. Not mocking. Curious.

"You were gonna get my guns for me, sweetheart?" he teased.

Her mouth tightened. "I know they mean a lot to you. And you're supposed to be stuck in bed." She crossed her arms, chin lifting. "But I wasn't about to let those men leave town before you could deal with it yourself. So yes. I was going to handle it."

There it was. Not pity. Not softness.

Practicality.

He liked that far more than he should have.

"And how was a little thing like you planning on getting my guns back from three big, mean men?" he asked lightly.

Her eyes flashed. "I'm not about to give you a demonstration here, but you know I'm no slouch with a gun."

She tapped the butts of the twin revolvers at her hips. Only then did he notice the snug brown leather of the shoulder holster beneath her jacket, the snub-nose resting neatly against her ribs.

How in the hell did I miss that?

"I've spent almost my entire life practicing," she continued, voice cool and even. "So, I don't miss when it counts. Do you really think I'd let a couple of thugs stop me?"

No. He didn't.

But teasing her was far too tempting.

"And if they take your guns?"

"I have a knife in my boot."

She said it like she was mentioning the weather.

Donovan barked a laugh before he could stop himself.

"You think of everything, don't you, sweetheart?"

"I try to," she said, frowning. "I don't like leaving things to chance. I also keep a small hand axe and a sawed-off on my saddle."

He laughed harder, sharp pain flaring at his ribs as he did. "Stop—damn it—stop! That hurts!"

Aura cocked a brow. "I don't see what's funny."

"No," he said between chuckles, "you wouldn't. But from where I'm standing, it's a hell of a picture."

"If you say this has anything to do with me being a woman, I'm going to hit you."

He grinned. "Figures."

He slung an arm around her shoulders, letting his weight settle into her just enough to sell the illusion. She stumbled a step, cursing under her breath, but he didn't release her.

"Have a heart, luv," he murmured. "Those men beat me half to death. How're you planning to stand a chance?"

"By not letting them get close enough to touch me," she growled, trying, and failing, to shove him off.

He steered her toward the street instead.

"Any man should be so lucky," he said lightly.

"Many men have been."

That stopped him.

"How many?" he asked, genuinely curious.

She didn't answer.

They reached the opposite boardwalk at the same moment the three men stepped out from a side street.

Everything went still.

Donovan felt it, the shift in the air, the way attention snapped tight like a drawn wire. His arm tightened around Aura automatically, posture slumping just enough to sell weakness.

It was them.

Tommy noticed him first. Recognition flickered, then hardened. His companions followed suit, stopping short as the distance between them closed to only a few feet.

"Well," Donovan said pleasantly, menace threading every syllable, "isn't this convenient."

"Those are the men?" Aura asked quietly.

"Yes," he murmured back. "Trust me but let me handle this."

Tommy smirked. "Didn't get enough last time?"

"I'm not the one hiding behind lackeys," Donovan replied calmly.

"Just behind a woman," Tommy sneered. "She gonna fight for you this time?"

Donovan squeezed Aura's shoulder gently. "Believe me, she could take the lot of you. The only reason I didn't finish things last time was because I couldn't see straight."

"Then it's a good thing we knocked the sense out of you," Tommy snarled. "And you're in no condition now to do anything about it." He never would have guessed that Donovan was as fit as he was. If he had, Tommy never would have been stupid enough to say, "And I think, that bein' the case, we'll take that wallet we never got around to lifting the last time. Get him!"

Frank and Jerry lunged.

Not together. Not cleanly. They rushed like men who expected momentum to win the fight for them.

Donovan moved anyway.

Pain flared instantly as he shifted his weight, a sharp protest from his ribs that reminded him too late that he was not healed. He ignored it. Pain was information, nothing more.

Frank came in fast from the left, fists already swinging, while Jerry hesitated a half-second too long on the right. That hesitation saved Jerry from something worse.

Donovan caught Frank first.

His hands shot out, fingers locking into Frank's skull just behind the ears. Bone. Pressure points. He twisted sharply and slammed Frank's head sideways at the exact moment Jerry surged forward.

The impact was sickening.

Skull met skull with a hollow crack, like splitting wood. Jerry's eyes rolled back before his body even understood it had been hit. Frank's knees buckled, his mouth opening on a sound that never fully formed.

Donovan released them both and stepped back as they collapsed in a tangle of limbs, unconscious before they hit the planks.

The whole exchange took less than two seconds.

Aura had already drawn.

She hadn't flinched. Hadn't shouted. Hadn't waited to see if Donovan needed help. The instant the men moved, her hands were on her guns, arms extended, stance low and locked. Both revolvers were trained squarely on Tommy's chest.

Her breathing was slow. Measured. As still as any hunter.

Tommy froze.

He'd been smiling, savoring the moment, right up until his friends hit the ground like sacks of grain. Now his eyes darted, assessing, recalculating. Too late.

Donovan turned slowly, deliberately, keeping his body loose, his posture casual. He was aware of Aura at his side in the same way he was aware of gravity. Constant, reliable, lethal.

"It's alright, sweetheart," he said softly, never taking his eyes off Tommy. "You can put those away."

Aura didn't move.

Not immediately.

She studied Tommy like prey, weighing distance, angle, intent. Her finger rested against the trigger guard.

Finally, she nodded once and holstered both guns.

Tommy's hand flashed to his waistband.

Donovan's missing gun came up fast, barrel snapping into place. Tommy aimed with shaking hands and pulled the trigger.

Click.

His face drained of color.

Click.

Donovan started walking toward him.

Slow. Unhurried. Each step deliberate, the sound of his boots loud against the sudden silence of the boardwalk. Pain tugged at his ribs with every movement, but he welcomed it.

Click.

Tommy fumbled with the gun now, panic stripping away bravado. He checked the hammer. The chamber. The ammunition.

Click.

"What—what the hell?" Tommy rasped. "It's broken!"

Donovan was close enough now that Tommy could see the faint bruising still shadowing his face, the calm in his eyes that was far more terrifying than rage.

Donovan reached out, faster than thought, and plucked the gun from Tommy's hands. He spun it once, smooth as breathing, and raised it, not at Tommy's head, but just to the side.

"It's not broken," Donovan said pleasantly.

He fired.

The explosion shattered the night.

The bullet tore past Tommy's ear, close enough that the heat of it burned. Wood splintered behind him. Tommy screamed and dropped to his knees, hands flying to his head as if trying to hold himself together.

He was sobbing now. Guttural. Uncontrolled.

Donovan crouched in front of him and tapped him lightly on the forehead with the barrel.

"Focus," he said calmly. "Where's the other gun?"

Tommy shook violently. "He—he has it."

"Who?"

"The man who hired us."

"Blood?" Donovan asked sharply.

"What? No! No, his name was MacHaven. I swear!"

Behind him, Donovan heard Aura suck in a sharp breath.

"Describe him," Donovan ordered.

Tommy babbled through it. Age, build, eyes, voice. Every word landed like a hammer. Donovan didn't turn, but he could feel the tension radiating off Aura now, tight and electric.

"When did he leave?" Donovan demanded.

"Days ago! He left after we got paid!"

"Where?"

"I—I don't know!"

Donovan straightened slowly, gun lowering.

"Get out of town," he said flatly. "Now."

Tommy didn't hesitate. He scrambled to his feet, nearly tripping over his fallen friends in his panic. As he turned to flee—

"One more thing," Donovan called.

Tommy froze.

Donovan's eyes narrowed. "Where's my hat?"

Tommy swallowed. "I—I think it blew away when we were—"

Donovan's hard glare finished the sentence for him.

Tommy ran.

"You owe me a new hat!" Donovan shouted after him, voice echoing down the street.

Aura stared at him for a long moment.

Then she snorted.

CHAPTER 9

Donovan turned to Aura.

She stood rigid on the boardwalk, as if the planks had grown up around her boots and pinned her there. Her eyes were fixed on nothing and everything at once. He said her name softly.

"Aura."

He didn't touch her. Not yet. He'd learned some instincts saved you, others got you hit.

"He was here," she said. Her voice sounded scraped raw. "He was here and I didn't even know it."

The words were flat, but the fury underneath them trembled like heat over sand.

"Come on," Donovan said gently. "Let's go back to the room."

He set his hand on her elbow, light, careful.

She jerked away like it burned.

Her face snapped up, eyes bright with something that wasn't quite anger, not quite panic. "It's your fault."

Donovan exhaled slowly through his nose. Here it came. He let it. Better it went into him than out into the street where someone might get hurt.

"If you hadn't been here," she went on, voice rising, "I would've found him."

He knew she didn't truly believe it. Not all the way. It was what she did when she couldn't bear the helplessness. She found a target and fired.

He kept his tone calm anyway. "Should I point out how many ways that's wrong?"

"No!" she snapped. "If I hadn't fallen off the boardwalk and sprained my ankle, I would've found out he was here instead of being stuck in that room with you."

Donovan rolled his eyes, then reached for her arm again—firm, but not hard—and propelled her down the street toward the boarding house. He ignored her attempts to wrench free.

"Aura," he said, patient as a priest. "You might not have been here at all if it weren't for me. You were following my direction."

"That doesn't—"

He stopped her with a look. "And even if you *were* here alone, do you think that man would've stopped? He had to find someone to hire. He had to wait for them to do the job. He had to pay them out. All without drawing attention to himself."

He tightened his grip only enough to keep her from bolting. "How long do you think he would've lingered if I wasn't around for his little plan to unfold?"

He felt her still thoughtfuly under his hand.

Finally, she said, quieter, "You're right." The apology followed like it cost her something. "I'm sorry."

Donovan glanced down at her. "I've never known anyone with a temper like yours who admits being wrong so fast."

Aura shrugged stiffly. "I lose control. I say things I regret. But I'm not so stubborn I can't admit when I'm wrong."

"No," Donovan said, grin returning. "You're only stubborn when you think you're right."

She shot him a look that promised bodily harm, then, unexpectedly, let her eyes rake over him from head to toe, slow, assessing.

"You really are healed," she said.

He lifted a brow. "I did try to tell you."

She looked away like the admission tasted bitter. "Then I'll concede I was wrong there, too."

They reached the boarding house. Donovan released her arm so she could take the stairs ahead of him.

"We'll see the doctor in the morning," she said at the door. "If he clears you, we can leave immediately. If that's… acceptable."

He smiled down at her. "As my lady wishes. Far be it from me to argue."

She snorted and entered the room.

Donovan chuckled, closing the door behind them.

Aura moved quickly to her chair, dropping into it like she could barricade herself there. Donovan watched her for a moment, then removed his gun belt and set it on the dresser.

Aura's frown deepened. He could see the question building in her like pressure.

She didn't make him wait long. "Why couldn't he shoot your gun? Was the safety on?"

"Something like that," Donovan said, dismissively.

"Donovan."

He sighed theatrically. "There's a standard safety, yes. But my guns have a second."

"And he couldn't figure out how to release it," she said, half statement, half challenge.

"He wouldn't have been able to even if he *had* known about it." Donovan sat on the edge of the bed, watching her eyes narrow. He waited, enjoying her irritation.

"Well?" she demanded.

"You're a terrible audience."

"Are you getting to the point or not?"

"It's called a dramatic pause, my dear."

Her glare sharpened.

Donovan relented slightly. "They're locked. The backup safety is keyed to blood."

Aura's brow furrowed. "Keyed how?"

"Only someone with MacHaven blood can fire them." His smile turned faintly proud. "My grandfather made them for his sons. My siblings and I took them after our parents died."

Aura crossed to the dresser with open curiosity. "May I?"

He waved her on.

She picked up the weapon, checked it like someone who respected what she held, then aimed away and squeezed the trigger.

Nothing.

Her mouth tightened. She set it down carefully, like it had earned her caution, and leaned back against the dresser, arms folding.

"It's a magnificent gun," she said casually, but there was real appreciation under it. "Makes mine look like toys. They're old. Practical. Not… refined."

Donovan's interest sparked. "Old? What model?"

"Forty-four caliber Army Micartas." She said it like a confession she didn't want to give. "They belonged to my grandfather on my father's side. The only thing I have of my father's."

Donovan held out his hand. Aura hesitated a fraction, then handed them over.

He inspected them with care, fingers reverent. "They're in damn good condition."

"They wouldn't do me any good if they didn't work," Aura said flatly.

Donovan grinned. "Only if you threw them at someone."

Aura's brow lifted.

"Had someone do that to me once," Donovan continued, delighted. "Ran out of bullets and chucked the gun. Hit me right here." He tapped the center of his forehead.

He expected a scowl.

Instead, Aura's head jerked away. Her eyes squeezed shut. Her hand flew to her mouth, and a strangled sound escaped through her fingers.

Donovan stared.

"Good God." He leaned forward. "Are you *laughing*?"

"No, I'm not," Aura snapped, dropping her hand.

But the corner of her mouth betrayed her, just a twitch, like the muscle didn't remember how.

"You were," Donovan accused, wonder lighting his face. "You were laughing."

Aura growled. "I need a drink." She turned for the door.

"You're allowed to laugh, you know," Donovan called after her, laughing himself now because he couldn't help it.

"I don't laugh!" Aura snapped as she yanked the door open.

"Oh come back! I'll tell you another funny story!"

The door slammed.

***

They got a late start the next morning.

Aura, up at dawn as usual, couldn't get Donovan out of bed until eight. When she finally did, he returned five minutes later to announce the doctor's office wouldn't open until ten.

By the time the doctor finished his exam and declared Donovan fit for travel, another two hours had bled away.

Aura spent the waiting time replenishing supplies, tightening straps, making sure there would be no reason for delay. She wanted out of this town. The air here felt… too crowded. Too close. Too full of him and what he did to her head.

When everything was ready, she waited outside the office, arms crossed, leaning against a post. Aries stood beside her, calm and solid as stone. He stretched his nose to her, and she scratched him between the eyes.

"Looks like we'll have company for a bit," she murmured to him. "I know you don't like his bike."

Aries snorted.

Her mouth quirked before she could stop it, then flattened again like she'd been caught.

What is wrong with me?

She rested her forehead briefly against the horse's neck. He was warm and steady and didn't ask questions.

"I don't think I've laughed in seventeen years," she said softly, more to Aries than to herself. "Not really. The women at the brothel… they were funny sometimes. But I couldn't. I never… let myself." She stroked down Aries's neck, feeling her throat tighten. "And he makes me feel like I want to."

That was the terrifying part.

Not the desire. Not the anger.

The softness it threatened.

"He riles me too," she continued, almost bitter. "His questions. His assumptions. His damned… *perception.* I don't know what I'm supposed to feel around him."

Aries nudged her shoulder. She scratched behind his ears.

"If I didn't need his help," she whispered, "I'd leave. But I'm out of ideas. And MacHaven—" She swallowed. The name tasted like blood. "There's always the chance he'll circle back to him. Like a vulture."

"Doc says I'm good to go."

Aura stiffened and turned.

Donovan stood a few feet away, expression mild, almost innocent.

"How long have you been standing there?" she demanded.

"Just stepped out," he said smoothly, that soft smile making her distrust her own senses.

Something in his eyes said he'd heard more than he was admitting.

"Shall we?"

She gave a stiff nod and turned to Aries, patting his neck harder than necessary. "Time to go, Aries."

Donovan started toward his bike, then paused. "Aries?"

Aura glanced back. "Yes."

"As in the war god."

"That's right."

He grinned. "Appropriate for a horse carrying you to revenge."

She mounted without comment, turning Aries toward the road. She didn't wait. The stallion surged into a gallop.

Behind her, the motorcycle roared to life.

***

They rode until dusk and made camp.

Aura settled Aries first then pulled dinner from her pack. Cold chicken and bread from the restaurant in town. It was meant for lunch, but the day had been eaten by waiting rooms and struggling patience.

She handed Donovan the bulk of it and sat beside the fire he'd started.

"Saves time cookin'," Donovan said, cheerful as ever.

Aura only grunted and picked at her portion.

Silence stretched. Their eyes kept finding each other, then slipping away like it burned.

Finally, Donovan leaned back and said, far too casually, "So. You don't know what to feel around me, huh?"

Aura's head snapped up. "You lied," she accused.

He grinned. "Not really. I only caught the tail end."

Her stomach dropped. Heat crawled up her throat. "Why didn't you make sure I heard you?"

"You were having such a deep conversation with Aries," he said, amused. "I didn't want to interrupt."

"And it was private."

"Was it two-way?" he teased. "Did he answer back?"

"He's a horse, you ass."

"Just checkin'," Donovan said lightly. "I'd hate to think I'm travelin' with a crazy woman."

"Don't call me crazy!" Aura shot to her feet. "I spend most of my time alone. Who the hell else am I going to talk to?"

Donovan's gaze tracked her, slow and steady, and she hated that her skin responded to it.

"Never said you couldn't," he admitted. "So long as the horse don't talk back." His smile shifted, softer. "But sometimes… someone who *does* talk back can be helpful. Care to tell me what you were talking about?"

"It's none of your damn business."

He sighed, exaggerated. "So that's what it was."

"What?" Confusion snagged her anger for a heartbeat.

"You say that when it's about your past."

Aura's jaw clenched.

He pressed, voice quieter now. "How come you'll tell a horse, but not me?"

"Because the horse doesn't talk," she snapped, each word sharpened. "He doesn't judge."

Donovan shot to his feet. The movement was fast, controlled, his cheerfulness evaporating. "Why the hell would I judge you?"

"Everyone judges me!" The truth ripped out of her before she could leash it. "Why should you be any different?"

"I'm not everyone."

"The hell you're not."

His hands curled into fists at his sides. "I'm not like them," he growled.

"Then why'd you kiss me?" Aura demanded—too loud, too sudden, too honest.

His eyes flashed. "Because I wanted to."

"Liar," she spat.

He was on her in two steps.

Donovan seized her arm, harder than he meant to, and she felt it instantly. Pain bloomed.

"Don't call me a liar again," he snarled.

Aura lifted her chin, defiant, yet terrified by how much her body still wanted him even now.

He shook her once, sharp. Her teeth clicked. She shut her mouth by force of will.

Donovan released her, stepping back, breathing hard like he'd barely stopped himself from doing worse. "I kissed you because I couldn't have done otherwise," he said, voice tight. "There's something between us. You know it."

"I know no such thing."

"It's not just attraction. I can understand your pain."

Aura scoffed, the sound ugly. "You understand nothing."

"I didn't say I understand what happened to you when you refuse to tell me. But I do understand pain," he said, jaw clenched.

"What do you know about pain?" Aura spat, rubbing her arm. She'd bruise. She knew she would.

Donovan's expression darkened.

Aura took an involuntary step back.

There it was. The thing she'd glimpsed in flashes: the shadow beneath the grin.

"You want to know how I know pain?" he said, low.

Her stomach tightened. Part of her wanted to run. The other part wanted to stay and watch because she couldn't help it.

Donovan moved in a blur.

Aura gasped as he swooped, reaching down, then straightened with her boot knife in his hand.

He stepped back, giving her distance, blade held with careless familiarity.

Knife in one hand, he raised his other forearm in front of him.

"I may be barely human," he said, voice rough, "but I know pain. The pain of parents who cared so little they put science before their children's lives."

He placed the blade against his skin.

Aura surged forward reflexively. "Donovan—"

He dragged it down his arm.

Aura froze.

The sound was wrong. Not the wet pull of flesh. Not the easy slice of skin. More like metal whispering against metal.

The skin parted… and what lay beneath caught the firelight in a dull, inhuman gleam.

No gush of blood. Only a thin trickle.

Her mind refused to name what her eyes were seeing.

"What…?" Her voice broke. "I don't—"

"My parents were scientists," Donovan said, and the words sounded like a verdict. "They used me and my siblings for their experiments." He didn't look at her. He couldn't. "Both my forearms. From the elbow down through the fingers. It's all metal and wires. Even the flesh is… made."

Aura's breath hitched.

That's why he moves like that. That's why he's so fast. That's why he can't—

"That's why… the strength," she whispered. "The speed."

"All of it," he said. "Enhanced."

"Oh my God." Her legs went weak. The world tilted. "How old were you?"

He answered without hesitation. "Ten."

The number landed like a fist.

Aura's vision blurred. Her hand flew to her mouth. Her knees buckled and she dropped to the ground like a puppet with its strings cut.

Donovan turned away, back rigid, waiting.

Waiting for the word he'd heard before.

Monster.

"You said… your brother and sister," Aura asked, voice small, "they're like you?"

He didn't face her. He didn't trust his expression. But he could give her the truth.

"Trevor, half his skull and face and one eye." His voice stayed even by sheer will. "Janice…" His throat tightened. "Both legs and hips. Both arms and shoulders. She was the last. The result of everything they learned."

Aura swallowed hard. "She's so young."

Silence stretched, heavy.

Then Aura's voice broke sharp through it. "Why?" she choked out. "Why would they do that to their own children?"

Donovan shrugged without looking back, because if he did, he might shatter. "Never got a chance to find out," he said quietly. "I assume it mattered more to them than we did."

He listened to her stand.

A strangled sound came from her, half sob, half choke.

"I'm sorry," she managed.

And then she ran.

Aura bolted for Aries, wild and fast. She mounted without saddle, without thought, and kicked him into the dark.

Donovan stood staring after her.

He didn't chase.

If she was going to leave, he wouldn't beg. He wouldn't trap her. He wouldn't make her stay long enough to hate him for it.

But the ache in his chest said he'd wanted her to.

When her hoofbeats faded, Donovan swore, low, vicious, then dropped onto his bedroll.

At least the town was only half a day's ride away. She could replace supplies. She'd survive. She always did.

It was better this way.

Better she ran now than stayed long enough to look at him with disgust.

He stared up at the stars, jaw clenched so tight it hurt.

He wished, not for the first time, that he was the kind of man who could drink himself empty.

CHAPTER 10

"What the hell are you doing here?!"

Aura cried out in surprise and dropped the tin of hot biscuits she'd been lifting from the fire. Several bounced free, landing in the dirt.

"Oh, great," she said flatly. "Those ones are yours."

Donovan barely registered the loss of breakfast. He was still reeling, still trying to reconcile the sight in front of him with the certainty he'd gone to sleep with the night before.

"Damn it, Aura," he snapped. "Answer me."

She stared at him like he'd lost his mind. "Where else would I be? I can't exactly get to Kinsville without you." She handed him two biscuits that hadn't touched the ground.

He didn't take them.

"But… you left."

"And I apologized for that."

"But you *came back*?"

Aura scowled. "Where the hell else would I go?"

"Back to town!"

"Why would I go back there?" she shot back. "We just left it."

Donovan scrubbed a hand over his face. "Alright. Stop. I'm missing something." He looked at her hard. "What exactly were you apologizing for last night?"

Color rushed into her face so fast it startled him.

"I—" She turned away. "I didn't want you to see me."

"See you *what*?"

She muttered something under her breath.

"What?" he demanded.

"I was crying!" she snapped, spinning back around.

Donovan stared at her, stunned. "You were… crying?"

"Yes." Her jaw set. "And I'd appreciate it if we didn't make a spectacle of it."

But he couldn't stop himself. "Why?"

She hesitated, fingers worrying the edge of her sleeve. "Because I felt ashamed," she said quietly. "For the things I said. For how angry I was. After hearing what your parents did to you… I realized that, at least for a little while, my mother loved me." Her voice tightened. "And I couldn't handle it."

Something in his chest loosened and something else twisted painfully tight.

"I didn't want you to see me like that," she finished. "So, I left."

Donovan stared at the fire, processing. She hadn't run from *him*. She'd run from her own vulnerability.

"Well," he said lightly, forcing casual into his tone as he finally bit into a biscuit, "I don't know why you didn't run screaming into the desert, but I'm glad you didn't."

Aura snorted. "Why would I do something that stupid?"

"Oh, the usual reasons," he said, then immediately regretted it. "I'm a monster. I'm not human. I'm a killer."

She snorted again, sharper this time. "You're none of those things."

His breath caught.

"What you *are*," she continued coolly, "is an ass. Frequently."

He grinned despite himself. "So, you're really not going to call me a monster and bolt?"

She gave him a flat look. "I've been called worse. And words don't make truth." She shrugged. "Everything you described fits the man I'm hunting. Since you're nothing like him, it'd be ridiculous to use the same words on you."

Something warm settled in his chest.

"Fair enough," he said. "Though now I'm curious. What worse names could anyone possibly call you?"

Her expression didn't change. "My favorite was *cold, obsessive, violent, bitch of a whore*."

His smile vanished. "Who said that?"

"The other girls."

"Girls?" He blinked. "They said that?"

"With love," Aura said. The corner of her mouth twitched.

Donovan froze.

That wasn't a smirk. It wasn't a snort.

It was barely a smile.

It softened her entire face. Made her look younger. Less guarded.

And it hit him like a blow to the gut.

God help him.

He watched her move around the camp for a long moment before risking the next question. "So… do you want to tell me what happened to you?"

She stilled.

Then she exhaled and turned back to him. "I think I do," she said quietly. "I just don't know how."

"Start small," he suggested. "Your father."

She frowned. "He was in the army. Married my mother, then got called back. He died before I was born."

"Noble," he said gently.

She nodded. "My mother came from back east. After he died, she worked in a brothel. It was the only way she could support us."

Donovan's stomach dropped. "You were… raised there?"

"I was born there," Aura said. "After she died, the girls raised me."

"How did she die?" he asked softly.

Aura curled in on herself, arms around her knees, rocking slightly. Her eyes unfocused.

"I was supposed to stay in the office. It was dark. I hated it." She swallowed. "I went to get my doll."

Donovan felt sick.

"He was on top of her. Knife already bloody." Her voice fractured. "Mama told me to run. He told her to call me closer."

Donovan moved instinctively but stopped when she flinched.

"She screamed for me to run. I froze." Her fingers tangled in her hair. "Then he stabbed her. Over and over. When I ran to her, he cut my face."

Her hand drifted to the scar.

"He said he'd kill me next."

Donovan knelt beside her, heart hammering. "Aura—"

"Please. Don't touch me."

He obeyed.

"The girls came. They bandaged me." She inhaled shakily. "They raised me. Taught me. When I was ten, I served drinks. Not long after, I started whoring."

"That young?" His voice broke.

"I needed money to leave," she said simply. "It was a job."

He stood abruptly, fury burning hot and helpless in his chest.

"It was your childhood," he said harshly. "And someone stole it from you."

He reached for her scarred cheek, thumb gentle against old damage. "I'm sorry," he said quietly.

Then he turned away, because if he didn't, he might break.

***

They did not speak much after that.

Not because there was nothing to say, but because what had been said now lived between them, heavy, fragile, and impossible to ignore. Words felt dangerous, as if the wrong one might shatter something that had only just stopped bleeding.

They traveled in near silence.

Mornings were practical. Donovan broke camp without his usual commentary, movements careful, quieter than before. Aura noticed he no longer startled her awake. He waited until she stirred on her own, offering coffee without remark, setting it within reach and stepping back as if giving her space were a language he was still learning.

She accepted it every time.

They rode longer hours. Fewer breaks. When they did stop, they worked around each other with an ease that hadn't been there before Never touching but never colliding either. Donovan no longer teased her into snapping. Aura no longer bristled at every glance. It wasn't comfort, exactly. It was truce.

At night, the silence stretched.

Aura still lay beneath the open sky, but she no longer placed her bedroll quite so far from his. Donovan noticed. He did not comment. He simply positioned the fire a little closer to her side of camp and made certain it burned low and steady until sleep finally took her.

She did not run again.

That mattered more than anything.

By the third evening, the quiet had changed shape. It was no longer sharp or defensive. It settled around them like dust after a long ride. Unavoidable, but no longer choking. When their eyes met, they held longer. When their hands brushed while passing supplies, neither recoiled.

One evening, as the fire burned low and the horse shifted quietly in the dark, Donovan broke the silence.

"You know," he said casually, staring into the flames, "there's someone you should probably be prepared for."

Aura glanced up from where she was cleaning one of her revolvers. "Prepared how?"

"My best friend," he said. "Tony."

She waited.

Donovan scratched the back of his neck, looking faintly amused. "He's… enthusiastic."

Aura's eyes narrowed. "About what?"

"Women."

The revolver cylinder clicked softly as she spun it back into place.

"And why," she asked slowly, "does that concern me?"

"Because," Donovan said with a resigned sigh, "the moment he sees you, he's going to try to charm you."

Aura snorted. "Charm me."

"He thinks he can charm anyone," Donovan said. "And to be fair, it works more often than it should."

Aura slid the revolver back into its holster.

"So, you're warning me that your friend is going to try to flirt with me."

"I'm warning you," Donovan corrected, "that he's going to flirt like a man who believes the world was invented for his personal entertainment."

Aura considered this.

Then she shrugged. "That sounds like most men."

Donovan huffed a laugh.

"True," he admitted. "But Tony does it louder."

Aura leaned back on one elbow, studying him. "Are you jealous?"

Donovan blinked.

"Of Tony?" he scoffed.

"Yes."

"No."

Her brow lifted.

"Absolutely not."

"Good," she said.

Donovan eyed her warily. "Why?"

"Because if he annoys me," she said calmly, "I'll just shoot him."

Donovan groaned and dragged a hand down his face.

"Please don't shoot my best friend."

"Then you'd better warn him."

"Oh, I will," Donovan muttered. "Repeatedly."

Aura settled back against her bedroll, satisfied.

Donovan stared at the fire a moment longer, shaking his head.

"God help that man."

Once, just before sleep claimed her, Aura realized she hadn't checked the darkness beyond the fire in hours.

The thought startled her more than the darkness ever had.

By the time the land ahead began to change—dry scrub giving way to wider stretches of open road, the distant promise of civilization rising on the horizon—they were no longer two people pretending nothing had happened.

Thcy were two people carrying it with them.

And whatever waited in Kinsville, whatever answers or violence or ghosts lay ahead, neither of them was traveling alone anymore.

CHAPTER 11

Kinsville was larger than Aura had expected.

Four main roads ran parallel to one another, crossed by three perpendicular streets, with narrower lanes threading between them. Two hotels, six restaurants, eight saloons, and a sprawl of other shops crowded the town. The size made sense once she realized Kinsville sat directly on the rail line. Towns like this didn't grow slowly They exploded.

Dusk was settling in, streetlamps flickering to life one by one. Aura's horse nearly unseated her when a truck engine roared nearby. She tightened her grip instinctively, heart jumping. She'd only seen a truck once before, two years ago. They were rare on this side of the country, mostly an eastern convenience, used for hauling goods.

Tony's place sat at the far edge of town, she was informed. The garage occupied the entire first floor, with living quarters above. A simple sign hung out front: **MECHANIC**.

Donovan cut the engine and Aura dismounted. She left her horse at the trough and followed him inside as he wheeled the bike through the wide doors. The garage was chaos, tools scattered, half-finished projects stacked in corners, scrap metal leaning against walls. They weaved through it toward the back, where the sharp hiss of a welding torch cut the air.

"Oi, Tony!" Donovan called.

The torch died instantly. A masked head appeared around a tower of tires. The mask flipped up, revealing a handsome young native man staring at them like he'd seen a ghost.

"Donny?"

He disappeared briefly, then reemerged, shedding apron and mask as he came around the tires. His grin was wide and genuine.

"What the hell are you doing here? I wasn't expectin' you for another month."

He pulled Donovan into a brief hug, clapping him on the back. Donovan grinned back.

"Ran into some business you might be able to help me with."

Aura stood partly behind Donovan until he shifted, bringing her fully into view.

Tony stopped dead.

His eyes locked onto her and did not move.

Slowly, deliberately, he took her in from boots to hair, his grin turning unmistakably sensual. Aura, long accustomed to being assessed, calmly returned the favor. He was leaner than Donovan but still broad-chested, shirtless, sweat gleaming on copper skin. Strong arms. Sharp features. Black hair tied back.

When he still didn't speak, Aura cocked a brow and glanced at Donovan.

You warned me, her look said.

Donovan returned it blandly. *Told you so.*

"Well?" Tony finally said, flicking a look at Donovan. "You gonna introduce us, or just stand there watchin' me admire her?"

Donovan rolled his eyes. "Tony, Aura Black. Aura, this is—"

"Tony Longtree," Tony cut in smoothly. "And not the thing that sways in the breeze but the thing that swings between my knees."

Donovan groaned.

Aura raised her other brow. "Optimistic."

Tony barked a laugh. "That's not optimism, sweetheart. That's confidence."

"You shouldn't make promises you can't keep."

His grin widened, unfazed. "If Donovan hasn't claimed you, I might make the effort myself."

"Try it," she said evenly. "See how far you get."

That caught him for half a beat.

Then he laughed again, softer this time. "Careful. You sound like a challenge."

"I don't repeat myself."

"That's enough," Donovan snapped, grabbing Aura's hand and dragging her toward the stairs. "Long week. You offering rooms, or not?"

Tony scoffed. "You know you're welcome anytime."

Donovan didn't slow.

"Nice meetin' you, honey," Tony called after them. "You'll have to come chat again. Or I'll come to you."

Aura glanced back just in time to catch Tony's wink.

"Well," she said once they were halfway up the stairs, "that was possessive."

Donovan growled. "He'd have had his hands all over you if I hadn't been there."

"Nothing I'm not used to."

"Don't remind me."

At the top of the stairs, Donovan opened a door. "This room's yours. Tony's upstairs. Kitchen too. Bathroom's at the end of the hall."

"It's bigger than it looks."

"He got a settlement after his father died. Doesn't need to work. He just likes it."

"He the only mechanic in town?"

Donovan smirked. "My siblings and I might've encouraged that."

Aura rolled her eyes.

She dropped her bags on the bed. Donovan lingered in the doorway.

"There're stalls out back. Feed's cheaper than the livery."

"Are we planning on staying long?"

"As long as it takes."

He nodded to her bags. "Get cleaned up. We'll have dinner soon."

After he left, Aura took in the room. Dark wood, warm colors, wide windows. Comfortable. Safe.

She stripped her weapons and boots, grabbed clothes, and stepped into the hall only to stop short.

Donovan was in the room across the hall, shirtless, rifling through a dresser.

She froze, eyes tracing the strength of his back before she caught herself and moved on.

The bath was hot and indulgent. She let herself linger, muscles loosening, tension easing. Still, she didn't forget her horse. She dressed quickly afterward and headed downstairs.

Donovan wasn't in his room. Tony wasn't in the garage.

She tended to her horse, rubbing him down, feeding him, grounding herself in the routine.

When she came back up the stairs, she nearly collided with Donovan.

"I was wondering where—"

He stopped mid-sentence.

His gaze swept over her in one slow, deliberate pass—black pants, white blouse, her hair pulled back neatly from her face. The look lingered just a fraction too long, something unguarded flashing across his expression before he caught it.

Hunger.

"Am I blocking the stairs?" she asked mildly.

He didn't answer right away. His eyes flicked back up to hers, sharper now, like he was trying to reset himself. "Where did you get that?"

"Down south. It's hotter there." She glanced down at herself, brushing an invisible crease from the fabric. "You don't like it?"

He groaned under his breath and dragged a hand over his face, like the question itself was unfair. "Tony's gonna have an aneurysm."

"Do you want me to change?"

He looked up immediately, hope lighting his expression before he could stop it. "Would you?"

"No."

His mouth twitched. "Damn," he muttered, then blinked, the shift catching up to him. "Wait. Were you teasing me?"

She didn't answer.

Tony dished out the chili and slid the bowls across the counter. "Eat," he said cheerfully. "Before Donovan starts glarin' holes in the furniture."

Donovan snorted and took a seat, though he still cast a warning look at Tony before settling back. Aura claimed the middle of the couch, folding one leg under herself as she accepted the bowl Tony handed her.

The chili was excellent. Rich, spicy, and filling in a way trail food never was. Aura hadn't realized how hungry she was until the first bite.

"Damn," she muttered before she could stop herself.

Tony grinned immediately. "That's the sound of approval."

"It's the sound of survival," she corrected. "You'd do well in a brothel kitchen."

Donovan choked on his bite. Tony, however, only laughed.

"Now there's a compliment I ain't never had before."

They ate in silence for a few minutes, the comfortable kind, punctuated by clinks of spoons and the low hum of the lamps overhead. Aura felt the tension in her shoulders ease, just a fraction. She hadn't realized how tightly wound she'd been until now.

"So," Tony said eventually, leaning back and eyeing Donovan. "What'd you break this time?"

"Arm," Donovan replied mildly.

Tony blinked. "Again?"

"Different arm."

Tony shook his head. "At this rate, I'm gonna start charging by the limb."

Aura glanced between them. "This happen often?"

"Too often," Tony said. "He's got a talent for trouble."

"Funny," Donovan said. "I was thinkin' the same about you."

Tony's grin widened. "Difference is, I enjoy mine."

Aura snorted quietly and caught herself before it turned into anything more.

Donovan noticed anyway.

Tony leaned forward slightly, elbows on his knees. "So, what brings you two through Kinsville together?"

Aura stiffened just a hair. Donovan answered before she could. "Mutual interests."

Tony's gaze slid to her, sharper now. "That so?"

"It is," Aura said evenly.

Tony watched her a moment longer than necessary, then leaned back again. "Shame. I was hopin' you were dragging him around for entertainment."

Donovan's eyes flicked toward him. "Careful."

Tony huffed a quiet laugh, unbothered. "Relax. I already like her." His gaze stayed on Aura. "Anyone who can keep you in line is worth keepin' around."

Aura raised a brow. "In line?"

"Or close enough," Tony amended.

Donovan exhaled sharply. "I should've known better than to bring you here."

"Yet you brought her," Tony said lightly.

Aura didn't move, her gaze steady on Tony.

Donovan didn't look at either of them.

Tony tilted his head, studying her more closely now. "You don't strike me as the sort who sticks around places long."

"I don't," Aura said.

"Then what's keepin' you?"

Silence stretched for a heartbeat.

Donovan felt it, tight, expectant.

"Purpose," Aura said finally.

Tony nodded once, sober. "That'll do it."

He glanced back at Donovan. "I haven't seen your siblings yet. Are they stopping by soon? Janice is due for her—"

Tony cut himself off mid-sentence, eyes flicking to Aura.

"She knows," Donovan said simply.

Tony blinked. Then, slowly, he smiled. "Well, damn. And she's still here?"

Donovan didn't answer.

Aura did. "Why wouldn't I be?"

Tony studied her for a long moment, then leaned back. "You're interestin', honey."

She shrugged. "I get that a lot."

"Yeah," Tony said. "But not like this."

The mood eased again as Tony launched into a story about a rail engine he'd once had to rebuild using scrap and prayer. Donovan countered with a tale of Janice blowing out a stabilizer joint during a race. Aura listened, amused despite herself, occasionally interjecting dry commentary that earned her startled laughter from Tony and long looks from Donovan.

Gradually, without realizing it, she leaned back slightly, the tension in her shoulders loosening another fraction.

Then Donovan leaned too far back.

The chair went.

The crash was spectacular. Wood cracking, metal shrieking, Donovan hitting the floor hard enough to rattle the walls.

Aura reacted before she could stop herself.

She turned away sharply, hands flying to her mouth as a strangled sound escaped, half snort, half breath. Her shoulders jerked once, twice—

—and then it broke.

Laughter.

It hit her all at once, sudden and violent, tearing out of her before she could contain it. It didn't feel controlled, didn't feel measured—it felt *wrong*, like something long-buried forcing its way to the surface.

She bent forward, breath hitching, the sound spilling out of her in uneven bursts. It hurt. Her ribs, her throat, her chest tightening around something she hadn't felt in years.

For a second—just a second—she wasn't in the room.

She wasn't here.

She was somewhere lighter. Warmer. Before.

The realization didn't come gently.

It snapped back into place all at once.

Donovan forgot how to breathe.

Tony stared at her like he'd just witnessed a miracle.

Aura barely noticed either of them. She was still laughing, helplessly now, eyes burning as tears blurred her vision, her body shaking with something she didn't know how to control anymore.

"Sweetheart," Donovan said quietly, almost in awe, "you've gotta do that more often."

The words landed wrong.

Not sharp. Not cruel.

Just wrong.

The laughter cut off like it had never been there.

Her body locked down instantly, every muscle going rigid as the moment snapped shut. Whatever had broken loose was gone just as quickly, buried again under something colder, tighter, safer.

"I don't like being made fun of."

Donovan was already shaking his head. "I wasn't."

She looked at him then—really looked—searching for it. Mockery. Amusement. Anything she could justify reacting to.

There was none.

He held her gaze, steady and unflinching.

Something in her eased. Barely.

After a long moment, she gave a single, controlled nod, lifted her beer, and drained it in three quick swallows.

Donovan exhaled slowly.

Tony cleared his throat, the moment settling around them. "Well," he muttered, quieter now, "there it is."

CHAPTER 12

It was well past midnight, but Donovan had no interest in sleeping.

The sound still hadn't left him.

He'd heard Aura make noise before—short, sharp snorts when something caught her off guard—but that hadn't been the same. This had been something else entirely.

It had hit him hard enough to knock the breath out of his chest.

He hadn't been expecting it. Hadn't been expecting *anything* like it.

And now he couldn't seem to shake it.

Across the room, she sat where she had been for the last hour, posture relaxed but never careless, one leg folded beneath her as she nursed her drink. There wasn't a trace of it left. No softness. No lingering warmth. If he hadn't seen it—hadn't heard it—he would've thought he imagined the whole thing.

His chest tightened at the thought.

Tony was still talking, filling the space with one story after another, easy and unbothered. Donovan let him. Normally he'd have kept pace, but tonight his attention kept slipping, dragged back again and again to the woman on the couch.

Something had changed.

He didn't know what to do with that.

Aura tilted her head slightly at something Tony said, the corner of her mouth threatening the ghost of a reaction before she smoothed it away. Controlled. Always controlled.

Except she hadn't been.

Not then.

The memory hit again, sharp and immediate. The sound of it. The way it had torn out of her like she didn't know how to stop it. The way it had filled the room.

The way it had gone through him.

He shifted in his seat, jaw tightening as he dragged his focus back to the present.

He needed to get a handle on that.

Tony leaned back slightly, studying her in a way that had nothing to do with his story now.

"So," he said mildly, nodding toward her cheek, "can I ask about the scar?"

Donovan didn't hesitate.

"No," he said, sharper than he intended. "You can't."

Aura blinked, turning toward him. The look she gave him wasn't anger. It was surprise. That caught him off guard more than anything else had.

She shifted her attention back to Tony, her voice calm, but not quite as steady as she probably meant it to be. "It's alright. I think… I think you were right, Donovan. Talking about it helped."

Donovan studied her carefully, searching for any sign she didn't mean it.

"Only if you're sure," he said, quieter now.

She nodded once, then looked back at Tony. "I got the scar when I was five. From the man who killed my mother."

Tony winced. "Sorry I asked."

Donovan didn't let the silence sit long this time.

"It's why we're here," he said. "Aura's looking for him. He's been using the name MacHaven. Whether he's related or just borrowed it, we don't know yet. I was hoping you might've heard something."

Tony's expression sharpened immediately. "Why would someone use the MacHaven name? It's rare enough to draw attention."

"That's what I want to find out," Donovan said grimly. "Assuming Aura lets him live long enough for me to ask."

Aura arched a brow. "Oh, I'll give him plenty of time to recognize me before I send him to hell."

Tony let out a low whistle. "Remind me to stay on your good side, honey."

"Don't kill people I love," Aura said evenly, "and you'll be fine."

Tony laughed. "Guess that leaves me free to shoot Donovan, then."

Donovan shot him a look. "Do you know anything, or not?"

Tony sobered. "No. But I'll ask around."

"We will too," Donovan said. "Tomorrow. I'm hoping John or Theo's heard something. I don't like my family name being dragged through blood. Especially not by a man who's stolen one of my guns."

Tony sat bolt upright. "He stole your gun?"

Donovan relayed the story. By the time he finished, Tony's expression had darkened.

"They damn near killed you," Tony said.

Donovan shrugged. "She would've kept me in bed longer if she could've."

Aura's gaze snapped to him. "You never explained how you healed that fast."

"Nanotechnology," Donovan said easily. "Keeps my implants running and accelerates organic healing." He removed the bracer from his arm, revealing the partially healed cut. "Tony, I was hoping you could finish patching this."

"Of course."

Tony stood, already moving toward his tools without another word.

Donovan leaned forward slightly, resting his forearms on his knees as he watched him go, grateful for the shift into something practical. Something he could focus on without thinking too much.

Across the room, Aura hadn't moved.

He could feel her there anyway.

He didn't look. Not yet.

***

Donovan woke slowly, the way he always did. Alert first, eyes opening second.

The habit held.

The rest didn't.

Something lingered at the edge of his awareness, not quite a thought, not quite a memory. Just enough to keep him from settling fully into the moment.

His body catalogued the room before his mind fully engaged: the quiet hum of the building settling, the faint metallic scent of oil drifting up from the garage below, the distant rattle of a train moving along the tracks.

Then something didn't line up.

There was a presence beside the bed.

Not on it—*beside* it.

His gaze slid downward and found Aura curled on the floor, wrapped tightly in a blanket, her pale hair spilling across the pillow beneath her head. One bare hand rested near her face, fingers curled loosely, as if she'd dropped into sleep the moment she'd stopped moving.

For a long moment, he didn't breathe. Didn't move.

The dark. Being alone. The way she tensed when a door closed behind her.

"Damn it," he muttered softly.

He should've thought of that.

She'd chosen the floor over being alone in the dark.

Carefully, so carefully, Donovan swung his legs off the bed and stood. He dressed quickly and quietly, movements controlled, eyes never leaving her. She looked smaller like this. For a moment, he saw it again. Not like this, not quiet and still, but alive.

Unrestrained.

He shut the thought down immediately.

He crouched beside her, hesitating.

Would waking her frighten her? Would she snap awake ready to fight, like she sometimes did from nightmares?

He slid his arms beneath her slowly and lifted.

She stirred the moment he lifted her.

A sharp inhale, then her fingers caught in his shirt, gripping hard enough to stop him for a fraction of a second.

Donovan stilled.

The grip shouldn't have meant anything.

It did.

"Didn't want to wake you," she murmured, voice rough with sleep, her hand tightening as she pressed closer instead of pulling away.

Something tight and unfamiliar twisted in his chest, sharp enough to make him pause.

"You didn't," he whispered. "Go back to sleep, sweetheart."

She sighed—soft, trusting—and tucked her face against his chest as if that were where she belonged. The warmth of her body seeped through him, grounding in a way that had nothing to do with physical need and everything to do with belonging.

Donovan carried her to the bed and lowered her gently onto the mattress he'd just vacated, pulling the blanket up around her shoulders.

She curled instinctively toward the warmth left behind.

For one quiet, dangerous second, he considered staying.

Not touching. Not moving.

Just… staying.

The thought hit harder than it should have.

Not like this, he told himself. Not when she doesn't know. Not when she's trusting me to keep her safe.

He stepped back, fists clenching once at his sides, then turned and left the room before he could change his mind.

***

The shriek of a train whistle tore Aura from sleep.

She bolted upright, heart hammering, senses scrambling to orient, and froze.

This wasn't her bed.

The scent was wrong. Oil and clean metal and something warmer beneath it. The blankets were heavier, the mattress firmer. Morning light spilled in through unfamiliar windows, painting the room in shades of teal and shadow.

Realization dawned slowly.

Donovan's room.

Heat rushed to her face as memory returned in fragments: the dark pressing in, the restless pacing, the way her thoughts had circled until exhaustion drove her across the hall without conscious choice.

She rubbed a hand over her face, groaning softly.

I slept in his room. On his floor.

Worse. She'd let him move her without waking.

The idea should have made her angry.

Instead, it left her unsettled in an entirely different way.

She swung her legs over the side of the bed and stood, shaking off the lingering warmth. Whatever comfort she'd taken, she wouldn't dwell on it. Comfort was dangerous. Comfort made you careless.

Voices drifted up through the floorboards. Laughter. Male. Familiar.

She dressed quickly and headed downstairs.

The garage smelled of oil, metal, and hot coffee. Donovan and Tony sat cross-legged on the concrete floor amid the disassembled remains of Donovan's motorcycle, both dressed in blue jumpsuits streaked with grease. Donovan had one arm braced against his knee as he laughed, head tipped back, utterly at ease.

The sight hit her harder than expected.

This—*this*—was Donovan unguarded. Relaxed. At home.

"Mornin', sweetheart!" he called when he spotted her.

"Aren't you a sweet sight in the morning," Tony's grin widened. "Enough to make a man want to—breakfast, anyone?"

Donovan's low growl cut him off.

Aura leaned against the wall, arms crossing loosely. She was suddenly very aware of her rumpled clothes, her tangled hair and equally aware that neither man seemed to care.

"Does breakfast include coffee?" she asked, stifling a yawn.

"Wouldn't be breakfast without it," Tony said, hopping up. "Maybe after breakfast I could join you in the shower."

Donovan moved faster than Aura expected.

One moment Tony was grinning. The next, Donovan had yanked him flat onto his back. What followed was a chaotic wrestling match punctuated by curses and laughter, until both men lunged toward her at once.

Aura barely had time to gasp before Donovan scooped her up, slinging her over his shoulder like she weighed nothing.

"Donovan!" she shouted, shoving uselessly against his back. "Put me down!"

"Not until you're safe from Tony's machinations," he laughed.

Tony followed close behind. "You gonna marry her? 'Cause that's the only way you're keepin' her from me!"

They reached the third floor before Donovan set her down.

Aura spun, ready to unleash fury—

—and both men burst into laughter.

She followed their pointing fingers with dread and twisted, just enough to see the black, greasy handprint smeared across the back of her pants.

Her face burned.

"You son of a bitch!" she yelled, swinging at Donovan.

Donovan caught her wrist easily, holding it just long enough to stop her momentum.

"Easy, sweetheart," he said, his voice still thick with laughter. "It's nothing to get upset over."

"The hell it isn't," she snapped. "I don't own that many clothes, Donovan. You can't go around ruining them."

"If that's what you're worried about, I'll buy you more."

"I don't want you to buy me more."

He sighed and released her hand, rubbing the back of his neck. "You are the oddest woman I've ever met. Most would be glad of a new wardrobe."

"I'm not most women," she reminded him sharply.

Tony, wisely sensing the shift, cleared his throat and retreated toward the kitchen. "Coffee," he announced. "Before somebody dies."

Aura stalked to the counter and seized the mug the moment it was set down, wrapping both hands around it like an anchor. The warmth grounded her. The bitterness steadied her.

Donovan watched her over the rim of his own cup, saying nothing.

The laughter ebbed, leaving something heavier behind.

Not tension exactly, something quieter. Charged.

Unfinished.

She took a long swallow of coffee and finally said, without looking at him, "Thank you. For last night."

He blinked. "For what?"

"For not waking me."

His expression softened, just a fraction. "You didn't want to be alone."

She stiffened, then exhaled slowly. "No."

He nodded once, accepting that answer without pushing further.

And somehow, that restraint unsettled her more than if he had.

CHAPTER 13

Donovan and Aura spent the rest of the day questioning people in town, to little success. Nobody seemed familiar with anyone matching the man's description. Donovan had been hopeful that one or two of the saloon owners might recognize him, but each conversation ended the same way; with polite confusion or vague recollections that went nowhere.

By late afternoon, frustration gnawed at him. He leaned against a post along the boardwalk, scanning the street while he tried to think of other angles. An older couple passed and greeted him by name, and he returned the greeting absently, his thoughts still circling.

"You seem to know a lot of people here," Aura said suddenly.

He turned to look at her. She'd been mostly silent all day, her expression distant, watchful.

"I know just about everyone," he said. "This is the closest thing I have to a hometown."

"That explains why everyone's been so cooperative."

"A little kindness goes a long way," he smiled faintly. "You should try it sometime."

"I don't have that kind of time," she muttered, folding her arms and looking away.

"Good thing I already invested it," he replied easily. He pushed away from the post. "Come on. One more place. I'm not as friendly with the owner, but one of the girls there will talk to me."

He didn't see her stiffen as he stepped past her.

Dusk was settling in, streetlamps flickering to life one by one. This would be their last stop before dinner. Tony would be waiting for them.

They cut down a narrow side street that ran the length of the bank building. No lamps. No windows. Just a strip of darkness between two lit roads.

Aura was a few steps behind him when she cried out.

Donovan spun.

The man was already there, tossing Aura's guns asside.

One arm locked around Aura's throat, forcing her head back, fingers tightening slowly, deliberately. Her hands clawed uselessly at his wrist. His other hand held Donovan's stolen gun, aimed squarely at Donovan's chest.

He took a step forward without thinking.

"Move," the man said calmly, smiling, "and I kill her."

His grip tightened. Aura's face went white, her breath breaking into thin, panicked gasps.

Donovan stopped.

Every instinct screamed at him to act, but the angle was wrong. The man had positioned himself perfectly, directly behind her, her body shielding his. Donovan knew he could kill the man if he had the chance. He just couldn't do it fast enough to save her throat.

"What do you want?" Donovan growled.

"Just paying my respects, boy," the man said mildly. "And I wanted a look at this girl who's been asking after me."

His cheek brushed Aura's hair. She struggled harder, nails scraping skin, but his hold never faltered.

"She's prettier than I expected."

"You've seen her," Donovan said through clenched teeth. "Now let her go."

"But now I'm thinking I want to keep her," he replied calmly. "For a while."

"You won't leave here with her."

The man's smile widened. "I think a bullet in your heart would say otherwise."

Donovan forced himself to breathe. "You can't fire that gun."

The man laughed.

The sound went through him like ice, sharp and wrong in a way he couldn't immediately place.

"You think so?" the man said, almost amused. "You expected the genetic lock to stop me?"

Donovan went cold.

No one outside the family—besides Tony and Aura—should even know that existed.

"How did you bypass it?" he asked carefully. He'd been considering drawing, but now he wasn't sure. If the man could fire the weapon—

"No need," the man said lightly, as if the question itself bored him.

Donovan's eyes narrowed, something far sharper than suspicion taking hold. "Who are you?"

The man's mouth curved again, that same unsettling amusement. "Don't recognize family, boy?"

"My only family is my siblings."

"You're wrong, boy."

"Stop calling me boy!"

"Tsk." The sound was soft, almost indulgent. "Temper. Just like your father."

Donovan felt something in his chest drop out from under him, the ground shifting in a way he couldn't correct for. "How do you know my father?"

The man tilted his head slightly, studying him like something familiar he hadn't seen in years. "I should know my own brother."

The words didn't just land. They detonated.

For a second, Donovan couldn't process them. Couldn't make them fit into anything that made sense.

"You're not—"

"Luc MacHaven," he supplied, as casually as if he were introducing himself at dinner.

"Luc is dead."

"Not quite."

"It's not possible."

"I assure you it is."

Luc's attention shifted back to Aura, his grip easing just enough to let her draw a shaky breath before tightening again when she tried to move.

"So, tell me, boy," he said lightly, almost conversational, "why is this pretty thing looking for me?"

His thumb traced along her jaw, slow, deliberate—testing, not affectionate.

He didn't look at her. He looked at Donovan.

"I assume she had a reason for it."

Donovan saw the tremor in her body beneath Luc's grip. Fear held tight under something harder.

She wasn't breaking.

The sight hit him hard.

"Ask her yourself," Donovan said. "Let her go. Give her back her guns."

Luc chuckled. "Revenge, then. I thought so."

Every muscle in Donovan's body tightened.

"And what are you going to do?" Donvan asked.

Luc considered. "She lives… today."

He shoved Aura forward a step, his hand still locked at the base of her skull, controlling every inch of her movement.

"But a warning is in order."

He raised the gun.

"*I will laugh at your calamity,*" Luc said calmly. "*I will mock when your fear cometh.*"

The gunshot cracked through the narrow street.

Donovan was already moving.

Too late.

Aura folded, thc impact stealing her balance as the sound echoed off stone.

Luc's laughter faded into the dark.

Donovan hit the ground beside her, already tearing his shirt free. Blood soaked through her shirt—entry and exit both visible.

Too deep.

"Aura," he said fiercely, pressing hard against the wound. "Stay with me."

She screamed once—raw, shocked—and went still.

He tied the makeshift bandage tight, his hands shaking despite himself. Her breathing came shallow but steady.

No blood at her lips.

Maybe—maybe the lung was spared.

He scooped her up and ran.

"Don't you dare die on me," he muttered, sprinting toward Tony's. "We're not finished."

CHAPTER 14

Doctor Roger Fernandez—"Doc" as the townsfolk affectionately but unimaginatively called him—had been Kinsville's only doctor for the past thirty years.

Before that, he'd served back east during the war. He'd joined at twenty, new to medicine and still naive enough to believe he could make a difference. The war had taken that from him. It had given him the rest.

When it was over, he headed west, looking for quiet, and found it here. A small town. One doctor. Predictable days.

He'd been there ten years ago when two teenage boys rode into town together. Donovan MacHaven and Tony Longtree, clearly without family, yet not marked by it.

Someone had to keep an eye on them.

Jovial. Capable. Loyal to each other in a way that suggested shared history rather than coincidence.

They never caused trouble. In fact, they did the opposite. Donovan's speed with a gun and Tony's uncanny aptitude for machines had solved more than one problem for the town over the years.

Doc had taken to checking on them out of habit. His wife had too. Sunday dinners became routine. Over the years, he'd watched them grow into men he respected.

So, when Tony burst into his office the bottom dropped out of Doc's stomach.

It was only when Tony started talking that panic sharpened into urgency. A girl. Shot. Bleeding.

Doc grabbed his bag and followed.

The wound wasn't life-threatening.

That was the first determination—and the only one that mattered.

The bullet had passed cleanly through the young woman's shoulder, missing the lung by a miracle and only grazing bone. Painful. Dangerous, but survivable. She'd lost blood—enough to matter, not enough to kill her if she rested.

Doc worked quickly, methodically, hands steady despite his years.

The morphine kept her under.

Donovan, however, was anything but steady.

Doc had never seen him like this—not even when Tony had broken his leg years earlier.

Pale. Rigid. Hands slick with blood, refusing to let go.

It took both Doc and Tony to pry him loose.

"Donovan."

He didn't let go.

"Donovan," Doc said again, sharper this time. "You're not helping her."

That cut through.

Donovan's grip faltered.

"Let me do my job," Doc added, quieter now, but no less firm.

Slowly, reluctantly, Donovan released her.

Doc didn't waste time acknowledging it.

He simply moved.

Donovan refused to leave the room.

Tony tried to stay, but a single groan from the girl sent him bolting out, face ashen. The door hit the frame harder than it should have.

Donovan dropped into a chair beside the bed, knuckles white as he gripped the armrests.

Doc glanced at him once before setting to work.

He worked in silence, cleaning and stitching the wound with steady precision.

When he finally looked up, Donovan hadn't moved.

"You're not going to faint on me," Doc said dryly. "I need you to turn her."

"Oh, God," Donovan muttered, but he stood and helped.

When Doc finally finished and packed his bag, he paused a moment, looking between them.

The girl was lucky.

Not for the bullet, but for the men in the room.

He'd seen enough to know she had a chance.

He left instructions. Bandages. Medication. Warnings.

And he left knowing she wouldn't be alone.

***

Donovan remained seated long after the doctor left, elbows braced on his knees, head buried in his hands.

The room smelled faintly of antiseptic and blood.

Aura slept, morphine-heavy, chest rising steadily. Doc said she'd be fine. Said it calmly. Confidently.

Donovan didn't believe it. Not yet.

Not until she woke up and told him to go to hell.

He deserved that much.

He could have shot Luc.

The truth gnawed at him. He'd had chances. Clean ones. He hadn't taken them. Not because he couldn't, but because Aura had been in the line of fire. Because fear had crept into his certainty for the first time in his life.

He'd hesitated and hesitation had cost her blood.

Dark bruises were already blooming around her throat. Purple. Angry. Evidence of how close Luc had come to killing her.

Donovan clenched his fists.

Uncle Luc.

The name tasted bitter. He'd grown up on stories of the family's black sheep—cruel, brilliant, sadistic. Dead, supposedly. Trevor would need to know. Janice too.

Later.

Donovan's gaze returned to Aura.

When had this happened? When had she stopped being a traveling companion and become… this?

The thought of her dying had nearly stopped his heart. He'd barely breathed while she bled beneath his hands, waiting for Tony to return with the doctor.

He'd never known fear like that.

Tony returned quietly with a cup of coffee, setting it into Donovan's hands.

"Are you going to tell me what happened now?" he asked.

Donovan stared at the bed. Silence stretched before he said quietly, "The man we were looking for found us first."

Tony frowned. "Did you find out who he was?"

Donovan swallowed. "My uncle. Luc."

Tony went still. "Luc's dead."

"So, we thought."

Tony cursed under his breath. "Do Trevor and Janice know?"

"I'll tell them later." Donovan's jaw tightened. "He shot her with my gun."

"Doc says she'll be fine," Tony said carefully.

"That doesn't mean anything until she says it herself."

Tony exhaled sharply. "You blaming yourself?"

"With how many chances I had to stop it? Yes."

"That's bullshit."

"If I'd kept her closer—"

"If Luc wasn't a calculating bastard, you'd both be dead," Tony cut in. "You didn't cause this."

Donovan's jaw clenched. "Get her guns?"

"In the garage. Undamaged."

"Thanks."

Tony hesitated. "I'll sit with her if you want food."

"Don't you dare leave me."

Donovan was on his feet instantly.

Aura's eyes fluttered open. "Tell me you didn't kill him."

"No," Donovan admitted. "I was worried about you."

"Good," she muttered. "I want him alive so I can kill him."

Donovan helped her sit, pillows supporting her carefully. "How do you feel?"

"Like I've been shot."

Tony snorted. "You want to try eating?"

"I'll try."

Tony left.

"Rest," Donovan urged.

"Who are you, my nursemaid?"

"Apparently."

She glared. He glared back.

"Die on me," he snapped, "and I'll never forgive you."

She paled. "I'm not dying."

"No. You're not," he quickly reassured her.

He moved to leave, intent on a shower and a change of clothes now that she was awake.

"Donovan."

He turned.

"Don't leave me."

He saw the panic in her eyes and understanding struck hard.

He turned back immediately, sitting beside her, drawing her carefully against him.

"I'm here," he murmured. "I won't leave."

She clutched him, breath ragged. Slowly, she calmed.

He held her until sleep claimed her again.

When Tony returned, Donovan only motioned silently for him to set the tray down.

CHAPTER 15

"He could shoot my gun. What more proof do you need, Trevor? … Janice, shooting first and getting the blood test later doesn't tell us how he's still alive. … No, I want to know why the hell we were told he was dead when he's not. … Well, I'd like to know if my psychotic uncle is going to randomly pop up and start shooting people."

Aura woke to Donovan's raised voice, and pain.

Fire tore through her chest and back as she tried to roll over, a groan ripping free before she could stop it.

"Lie still, sweetheart," Donovan said immediately, appearing at her side and pressing a steadying hand to her shoulder. "Easy."

"Goddamn, it hurts," she grit out.

"I know." He guided her carefully onto her back and pressed a small cup into her hand. "Drink this."

She cracked one eye open. Medicine. He slipped an arm behind her shoulders, lifting her just enough to help her swallow, then eased her back down again.

She lay there for a moment, breathing shallowly. "Who were you talking to?"

"My siblings," he said. "I told them about Luc. They're coming."

Her brow furrowed. "Coming… here?"

"In about a week."

"Was that really necessary?" she asked.

He leaned against the window frame, exhaustion etched deep into his face. "This stopped being just my problem. Or yours. They deserve to know."

"Bullshit," Aura muttered. "I'm still killing him."

A faint smile tugged at his mouth. "I figured."

She studied him more closely then. He looked awful, same clothes as yesterday, wrinkled and stained with blood, dark stubble shadowing his jaw, deep circles under his eyes.

"You sleep at all?" she asked.

"A little."

She shifted slightly and hissed in pain. "I'll be alright for a bit if you want to go clean up."

"No," he said without hesitation. "After last night? Not a chance. I promised I'd stay."

She huffed.

He ignored it. "Doc'll be here soon."

"Can you help me sit up, then?"

He nodded and carefully eased her upright, arranging pillows behind her until she was supported.

"Better?"

"Yes. Thank you."

A knock sounded at the door and Tony poked his head in. "Well, look at that. You're awake," he said cheerfully. "Doc's here. And I was about to make eggs. You hungry, honey?"

"Starving," Aura said, a little too quickly.

Tony grinned. "I like her."

He disappeared just as the doctor entered.

"Well now," Doc said, approaching the bed. "How are you holding up?"

Aura scowled.

"Don't," Donovan warned.

She shot him a look, but he turned back to the doctor. "She's in pain. No fever," Donovan said, already ahead of the question.

"That's the important part," Doc said, winking at Aura. "The no-fever bit, not the pain."

He reached for his scissors. "Mind if I take a look?"

She hesitated, then gave a short nod.

He removed the bandages gently, examining the wound with practiced efficiency. She winced when his fingers pressed near the stitches.

"Have you taken anything for the pain?"

"I have."

"Good." He nodded. "You'll need a sling for a few weeks. And you should stay in bed a week at least. You lost more blood than you think."

Aura frowned, clearly displeased.

"I'm going to clean up," Donovan said. "Doc, don't leave her alone."

Aura gasped. "Donovan—"

Doc chuckled. "Is she a flight risk?"

Donovan opened his mouth.

"Don't," Aura snapped. "If I wanted my shortcomings shared, I'd do it myself."

He smiled calmly. "Wasn't planning to."

She glared as he left.

He didn't look back.

Doc turned back to her with curiosity but didn't press. "Roger Fernandez," he said. "But everyone calls me Doc."

"Aura Black."

"Nice to meet you, Aura."

"Have you known the boys long?" he asked.

"The boys?"

"Donovan and Tony."

"A few weeks," she said carefully.

"They bring you through town?"

"Not exactly," she said, not elaborating.

Doc hummed. "I won't need to box their ears, will I?"

"No," she said quickly. "They're… helping."

"Good," Doc said. "They're good boys."

He finished bandaging her shoulder. "You'd do well somewhere safe for a while."

She flushed, irritation flashing through it. "It's not like that."

"Of course," he said, not sounding convinced.

Tony reappeared with a tray. "Eggs, bacon, toast, milk."

Aura eyed the milk suspiciously. "No beer?"

"No alcohol," Tony said firmly. "Drink your milk."

She scowled but ate anyway.

Donovan returned freshly showered, clean clothes replacing yesterday's. He nodded goodbye as Doc left and leaned in the doorway, arms crossed.

"Thanks for being civil to Doc," he said quietly.

She looked away.

"He's family," Donovan continued. "One of the few people who ever made us feel like we belonged."

Tony nodded. "Damned good man."

"I'll continue to behave then," Aura said stiffly.

"That's my girl," Donovan said, smiling.

CHAPTER 16

Three days later, Aura was finally allowed out of bed, but Donovan refused to let her leave the room.

She was supposed to be *taking it easy*.

After a week of confinement, she was ready to scream.

Her temper had frayed to nothing. Every encounter with Donovan ended in an argument. He hovered, scolded, and watched her like she might shatter if she breathed wrong. Despite that, he had dragged a cot into the room and slept there every night. For that, at least, she was grateful.

During the day, however, he kept his distance, avoiding her to prevent more fights.

The result was torture.

By the tenth day, she was pacing like a caged animal, her shoulder still aching but functional enough to remind her she wasn't helpless. Tony tried to distract her—dropping by with jokes, flirtation, and food—but even he eventually retreated, recognizing a storm he couldn't charm away.

That morning, Aura decided she'd had enough.

She dressed slowly, jaw clenched, teeth bared at every stab of pain from her shoulder. Then she marched down the hall, fury carrying her the rest of the way.

She slammed Donovan's door open hard enough that it rebounded off the wall before she kicked it shut again.

"Donovan—"

She stopped dead.

He stood at the dresser, freshly bathed and completely nude, a pair of pants halfway out of a drawer. A damp towel lay abandoned over the chair. Water slid down his bare skin, tracing muscle, dripping from his hair.

Desire hit her like a blow to the gut.

For one traitorous second, her knees nearly buckled.

"What the hell are you doing?" he demanded, color flooding his face as he grabbed the pants to cover himself.

Her eyes hardened instantly.

"I'm done with your damn babysitting," she snapped. "I'm going for a ride."

"The hell you are!" he roared. "You can barely use that arm!"

"I don't need two hands to sit a horse."

"And how do you plan to saddle him?"

"I'll ride bareback."

"You're not riding at all!" He advanced on her, anger eclipsing modesty. "It's too dangerous!"

She backed toward the door, fingers closing around the knob. "If I stay locked in that room any longer, I'll start breaking things. Tony won't appreciate that."

"You're being childish!"

"Childish?!" she shrieked. "How dare you. If my arm didn't hurt, I'd hit you!"

"If it hurts, you shouldn't be riding!"

She screamed in frustration and yanked the door open—

Straight into Tony.

He stood there with a towel slung low around his hips, hand raised mid-knock.

"Heard the yelling," he said mildly. "Thought I'd—"

"Close the damn door!" Donovan shouted.

Aura slid sideways, planting Tony squarely between herself and Donovan. "I'm going," she said flatly. "You won't stop me."

"Tony! Grab her!"

"What?" Tony blinked.

Aura kicked.

Hard.

Tony yelped as he crashed into Donovan, both men going down in a tangle of limbs and swearing. Aura spun to bolt—

—and slammed into a solid chest.

She barely had time to register the obstacle before a hand closed around her upper arm. Not rough, but unyielding.

"There something you want to explain, Donny?" Trevor asked mildly.

She found herself staring up at a tall man with Donovan's eyes and none of his humor. Trevor. His expression was calm, assessing, already taking stock of the scene: Tony on the floor, Donovan half-dressed and furious, Aura bristling like a cornered animal.

Behind him, Janice leaned against the wall, her grin slow and sharp. "Well," she drawled, "this looks… domestic."

"Let me go," Aura snapped.

Trevor glanced down at her, then back to Donovan. "You want her restrained?"

"No," Donovan said immediately. "I want her *here*."

"Same thing, different justification," Janice said lightly as she pushed past Trevor and perched on the edge of the bed, swinging one leg. Her gaze slid over Aura without apology. "So, this is her."

Aura stiffened. "This is *me*."

Janice smiled wider. "I like her already."

"Don't," Donovan warned.

Trevor put Aura forcibly in the chair and Donovan leaned over her, bracing his hands on either side of the chair so that she was boxed in, his face only inches from hers. She could smell soap and clean skin beneath the faint metallic tang that always clung to him. His jaw was tight, eyes dark, breathing controlled only by effort.

"You are going to sit here quietly," he said slowly, each word deliberate, "while I talk to my siblings. After that, you and I are going to talk. Do you understand me?"

Her spine went rigid. Every instinct in her screamed at being cornered—at being *told*—and yet she didn't look away. She lifted her chin instead, eyes flashing up at him.

"You don't get to decide what I do," she said coldly.

His nostrils flared. For a heartbeat, he looked like he might snap. Instead, he straightened abruptly and turned away, pacing once across the room before scrubbing a hand through his hair.

"Damn it, Aura," he muttered. "You don't make this easy."

"I never said I would."

"What's the little bitch still doing alive anyway?" Janice asked, her expression blank despite the insult.

Aura growled at her.

Janice only grinned.

"That's none of your damn business, Janice. And watch your language," Donovan snapped at her.

"Of course it's my business," Janice turned her grin to him. "If the slut's got her hooks in you, I want to know about it."

"You bitch!" Aura exploded from her chair.

"Sit *down*, Aura!" Donovan ordered sharply. She dropped back into her chair quickly. "And, Janice, you insult her again and I'm kicking your ass, little sister or not."

"Love to see you try it, big brother," Janice grinned at him, motioning him forward.

"Shut up or get out," he snapped.

Trevor interrupted them.

"Start talking, Donny. You don't usually lose control like this."

Aura barked a laugh. "Not from what I've seen."

Donovan shot her a look, then dragged a hand through his hair. "She's supposed to be resting."

"And she's trying to escape," Janice observed. "Bold choice, injured and angry."

"I was going for a ride," Aura said coldly. "Your brother doesn't get to cage me."

Trevor tilted his head, studying her more carefully now. "You don't scare easily."

"No," Aura said. "And I don't submit, either."

Janice snorted. "Oh, she's definitely trouble."

"That's enough," Donovan snapped. "She stays out of this."

"Too late," Janice said. "She's already in it."

Trevor's gaze sharpened. "Luc?"

Donovan nodded once.

The room shifted. Even Janice sobered.

"So," Janice said slowly, "the ghost's real."

"And armed," Donovan said. "And dangerous."

Trevor exhaled through his nose. "Then this isn't just unfinished business. It's our business."

Aura surged forward. "No. It's *mine*."

All three siblings turned to her.

Trevor spoke first. "You're injured."

"And you're not," Aura shot back. "I don't see how that gives you priority."

Janice laughed outright. "God, I really like her."

Donovan moved then, positioning himself subtly between Aura and his siblings. "Enough. We'll handle Luc."

"No," Aura said. "*I* will."

Silence followed.

Trevor broke it gently. "That's not how family responsibility works."

"I don't care how *your* family works," Aura said. "He killed my mother."

That hit hard.

Janice's smile faded. Trevor's jaw tightened.

Donovan closed his eyes briefly.

When he opened them, he said, "Get out. Both of you. We'll talk later."

Janice blinked. "You sure?"

"Yes."

Trevor studied him a long moment, then nodded. "Dinner."

"Dinner," Donovan echoed.

Janice hopped off the bed and sauntered toward the door, pausing beside Aura. "Careful, angel," she murmured. "You don't survive men like Luc without scars."

Aura met her stare. "Good thing I don't intend to survive him."

When his siblings finally left—Janice's laughter still echoing faintly down the hall—the room felt smaller. Quieter. Charged.

Aura was still standing by the chair when Donovan came up behind her. He didn't touch her at first. Just stood close enough that she could feel the heat of him at her back, the careful restraint in the way he held himself.

"You survived Janice," he said lightly, though his voice hadn't fully lost its edge.

"She's a piece of work," Aura said after a moment.

A soft huff of laughter brushed her ear. "That's the polite version."

He rested his hand on her shoulder then and the gentleness of it caught her off guard more than any roughness would have. Her breath hitched despite herself.

"You don't have enough to do," he went on, quieter now. "You're healing, bored, angry… and you don't like feeling helpless."

Her fingers curled. "I don't *feel* helpless," she snapped. "I *am* being treated that way."

His thumb shifted, warm against her skin. "That's not what I'm trying to do."

"Then what *are* you doing?" she demanded, turning to face him.

For a moment, he just looked at her.

Not the casual glance she was used to. Something sharper. More deliberate.

It lingered longer than she liked.

"I'm trying not to cross a line," he said quietly.

Her laugh was sharp. "You crossed a line days ago."

Something dark flickered in his eyes. Before she could react, his hand came up to the back of her neck firmly. Possessive. Intentional.

"I want you," he said, voice rough. "That part's not complicated. What *is* complicated is that I don't want to take something you'll regret later."

Her pulse thundered. "You think I don't know what I want?"

"I think," he said, pulling her just close enough that their foreheads nearly touched, "that you've spent so long surviving that wanting feels dangerous."

That struck too close. She inhaled sharply and that was all the opening he needed.

His mouth came down on hers, hard and unrelenting. No teasing. No patience. Just heat and control and hunger he'd been holding back for days. Her protest died instantly, replaced by a low sound she didn't recognize as her own as she melted into him.

Her good hand fisted in his shirt. His arms locked around her, crushing her against him like he needed to feel her solid and real. The kiss deepened, his control slipping just enough to show how badly he wanted her.

And then—just as suddenly—he stopped.

He pulled back, breathing hard, hands still on her arms like he didn't quite trust himself to let go. His eyes were dark, conflicted, furious with himself.

"Damn it," he muttered.

He released her abruptly and stepped away, turning his back before she could speak.

"This isn't how it should start," he said tightly. "Not like this."

Before she could find her voice—before she could decide whether to strike him or kiss him again—he walked out of the room.

The door clicked shut behind him.

Aura stood there for a long moment, heart racing, lips still tingling.

"Son of a bitch," she whispered into the empty room.

CHAPTER 17

Aura sat in the middle of Donovan's room for nearly three hours, exactly where he had left her.

She wasn't waiting for him to come back. She told herself that repeatedly. If she'd been waiting, she would have been angry. She would have paced, or cursed, or stormed out. Instead, she sat there, motionless, staring at nothing, her thoughts tangled so tightly she couldn't find a way through them.

He hadn't come back.

That was good. It made it easier not to decide anything.

He had told her to think hard before she answered him.

That was the problem.

She wanted him. There was no point pretending otherwise. Not after the way her body had reacted to him, not after the way her pulse still raced when she remembered his mouth on hers, the weight of his hands, the heat of him pressed so close she'd nearly forgotten how to breathe. He knew it, too. If she told him she didn't want him, they would both know it was a lie.

But saying she *did* want him felt worse.

Every man she'd ever been with had come with a price attached. Sex had never been something she chose; it had been something she endured. Something mechanical. Get through it. Get paid. Don't feel anything. Don't think about it afterward.

Donovan didn't fit that shape.

That scared her more than any man ever had.

Good men were dangerous. They made promises without meaning to. They made you hope. And hope was a weakness she couldn't afford. She had learned that lesson young and learned it well.

Finally, she moved. Her shoulder throbbed as she headed down the stairs and out through the back of the garage. She didn't look around to see if anyone noticed her leave.

Aries greeted her softly, stretching his neck toward her. She rested her forehead briefly against his, scratching his nose without really thinking about it. She didn't want to ride—not tonight—but the horse needed the exercise, and she needed something to do.

She opened the paddock gate and let him out, then slid down to sit against it once it was closed again. Aries bounded across the enclosure, kicking up dust, tail high, clearly pleased with himself. Despite everything, she smiled faintly.

The distraction didn't last.

Her thoughts drifted right back to Donovan, to the choice she couldn't make.

Lie to him and keep herself safe. Tell him the truth and risk wanting more than she could control. Or do nothing at all.

Doing nothing felt safest.

If she stopped fighting him, if she simply let him come to her, maybe she wouldn't have to decide yet. Maybe she could let her body answer the question her mind refused to touch.

Aries returned and nudged her shoulder gently. She leaned into him, breathing in the familiar scent of horse and leather. When she finally looked up, the sky had darkened.

Dinner would be starting soon.

She didn't care.

The sudden slam of the stall gate startled both her and the horse. Aries bolted away as the wood struck her shoulder and clipped the back of her head.

She cried out, pain flashing sharp and bright.

"What the hell—"

Donovan loomed over the gate, his anger evaporating the moment he saw her on the ground.

She rubbed the back of her head and glared up at him. "What the hell did you do that for?"

"Why are you hiding behind the gate?" he snapped.

"I wasn't hiding. I was keeping Aries company."

As if summoned by his name, the horse trotted back and snorted directly in Donovan's face. Donovan recoiled, clearly offended.

"He did that on purpose!"

Aura huffed out a laugh despite herself. "You startled him. He was letting you know."

Donovan offered her a hand, hauling her to her feet more quickly than she expected. She clucked softly, guiding Aries back into the stall and slipping past Donovan before he could block her. He had to wrestle with the horse to shut the door, then jog to catch up with her as she crossed the garage.

"Would you slow down?" he demanded.

"What do you want, Donovan?"

"I was worried you'd gone for that ride."

"Whether I did or didn't isn't your business."

"I'm making it my business. Until I say otherwise, you're not riding."

Her temper flared hot and fast. "You don't give me orders."

His frustration showed plainly. "I'm trying to keep you from getting hurt."

"By caging me?"

She was already irritated when she glanced toward the back of the garage, and froze.

Janice sat calmly in a medical chair, one arm detached at the shoulder while Tony worked with focused ease.

Aura went cold.

"He—he took her arm off," she whispered.

Donovan's hands closed around her shoulders, forcing her to look at him. "Aura. It's maintenance. She's fine."

Her stomach rolled. "I think I need to lie down."

He didn't argue. He guided her upstairs, his hand steady at her back, and for once she didn't pull away.

***

Donovan hovered at the edge of the bed longer than he needed to.

Aura lay propped against the pillows, color slowly returning to her face, her breathing finally even. He watched the rise and fall of her chest with more focus than he was willing to admit. The sight of her pale and shaken in the garage had lodged somewhere deep and ugly in his gut, and he hadn't been able to shake it since.

"How's your head?" he asked, brushing his fingers lightly against the back of her skull. He felt the small swelling there and frowned. He'd shoved that gate harder than he'd meant to.

"It's fine," she murmured.

He didn't believe her. He rarely believed her when she said that.

"You wouldn't tell me if it wasn't," he said quietly.

She finally opened her eyes and looked up at him. "Probably not. But it really is fine."

He searched her face another moment, then let out a breath he hadn't realized he'd been holding. "Promise?"

She rolled her eyes. "Yes, Donovan. I promise."

Good.

The thought barely had time to settle before something in him snapped.

He bent and kissed her.

There was no plan to it, no careful consideration, no restraint. Just the sudden, overwhelming need to feel her mouth under his, to confirm she was real, alive, here. He expected resistance. He was half-prepared for it.

It never came.

Her lips parted beneath his, her hand fisting in his shirt as if she'd been waiting for it. The response hit him hard, a jolt straight through his spine. He groaned into her mouth, sliding his hands to her face, thumbs stroking her cheeks as he deepened the kiss.

God.

She tasted like heat and want and something far more dangerous than either. When her tongue met his, tentative at first and then eager, his control frayed completely. His hand slid down her neck, fingers brushing her collarbone, then lower—

Her soft sound of pleasure went straight to his groin.

He shifted closer without thinking, his mouth leaving hers only to trail across her cheek, her jaw, her throat. Her skin was warm beneath his lips, sensitive. When his thumb brushed her nipple through the thin cotton of her shirt and she arched into his touch, any remaining restraint shattered.

He wanted her.

He had never wanted anyone like this.

Her hand tangled in his hair, holding him there, and he knew—*knew*—that if he kept going, he would not stop. He would take her, right here, consequences be damned.

Someone cleared their throat.

Once.

Twice.

Donovan swore viciously and dropped his forehead against Aura's chest, his breathing heavy, his entire body buzzing with barely checked violence and frustration.

"I could kill you right now, Trevor," he growled.

Only then did he lift his head and saw the moment awareness snapped back into Aura.

She went still.

Everything that had been there a second ago. Gone.

Buried.

He pushed himself back instantly, forcing distance between them.

Aura was already moving.

She straightened against the headboard, pulling herself upright in one controlled motion, every trace of what had just happened locked down behind her expression.

The shift hit him hard.

Trevor leaned against the doorframe, smug and entirely unapologetic.

"Door," Trevor said mildly, knocking on the frame.

Donovan shot him a glare that promised future retribution, then glanced at Aura. She didn't look at him.

She slid off the bed and moved past Trevor without a word.

The distance hit harder than the interruption.

Trevor stepped aside to let her pass, watching her go with open curiosity before turning back to Donovan.

"We're not done talking," Donovan said.

Aura didn't slow.

"We are," she said from the hallway, her voice steady and final.

Donovan didn't call her back.

By the time he moved, she was already gone.

Trevor's grin widened. "Serves you right for leaving the door open."

Donovan dragged a hand down his face. “You have the worst timing of anyone I know.”

“True,” Trevor agreed easily. “But you’re the one who forgot where you were.”

Donovan exhaled sharply, his body still humming with unspent desire. “Get out.”

Trevor only chuckled as he pushed away from the door. “You want her.”

“That obvious?” Donovan snapped.

“Painfully.”

Donovan stared toward the stairs, jaw tight. “But I don’t want to push her.”

Trevor sobered, just a little. “Then don’t rush her.”

Donovan didn’t answer.

He’d already pushed too far.

He just didn’t know where the line was.

CHAPTER 18

When Donovan joined the others, they were already settled around the low coffee table, plates balanced on knees and forearms, the room warm with lamplight and the lingering scent of food. Tony's place always felt lived-in. Soft shadows thrown by mismatched lamps, dark wood worn smooth by years of use, the faint hum of machinery still echoing up from the garage below.

Donovan dropped into the seat beside Aura, close enough that his thigh brushed hers, and picked up his plate. He eyed the pale pink fillet of poached salmon with faint suspicion, prodding it once with his fork.

He lifted a brow toward Janice. "I take it you picked dinner?"

She lounged back against the couch cushions, one boot propped casually on the edge of the table, twirling her fork between her fingers. "Tony promised me salmon the next time I came by."

"Anything to make my girl happy," Tony said cheerfully, leaning back in his chair. "You know I miss you when you're gone, sweetheart."

Janice didn't miss a beat. "More like you miss the fun of playing with my parts."

Aura's gaze flicked between them, brow knitting. "So… are you two lovers?"

The response came fast and loud from multiple directions.

"Hell no!"

Aura started, shoulders jumping. "I'm sorry! The way you two talk, I assumed—"

"Ugh," Janice cut in, wrinkling her nose. "Tony's like my brother. That's disgusting. Leave it to a slut like you to think otherwise."

The room tightened instantly.

Aura's fork stilled halfway to her mouth. Slowly, deliberately, she lowered it to her plate and turned her head toward Janice. "With the way *you* talk," she said coolly, "I'd think you were a whore yourself."

Janice's grin sharpened, eyes glittering. "I don't turn men down when they want me."

"Even sluts can have standards," Aura shot back. "It sounds like you don't."

Donovan felt the tension spike like a pulled wire. He knew that look on Janice's face, bright, intent, enjoying the clash.

"How old are you anyway?" Aura added flatly. "Fourteen?"

"Eighteen," Janice replied without blinking. "Which makes you what—twenty years older than me?"

"I'm four years older than you," Aura growled. "And if your eyesight's that bad, I could wring your neck so you get a better look."

Janice laughed outright, the sound sharp and delighted.

"That's enough," Donovan said, voice hard.

Janice glanced at him, all feigned innocence. "What? I'm just talking."

"Then stop."

She rolled her eyes but turned back to Aura, undeterred. "So why aren't you married, if you're so worldly?"

Aura's expression went flat, closed.

"It wasn't an option."

That stopped Donovan cold.

Janice leaned forward now, elbows on her knees. "Too unpleasant for men to ask?"

"No." Aura's voice was even, detached. "I've had plenty of offers. Since I was thirteen." She paused, eyes unfocused for a moment. "I never took them seriously."

For the first time, Janice didn't smile.

"Why not?"

Aura set her fork down carefully. "Because the women I knew married to improve their lives. I didn't want to improve mine. I wanted out."

Silence settled over the room like a held breath.

"I wasn't going to chase Luc with a husband telling me what to do."

Janice studied her now, gaze sharp, curious. "None of them would travel with you?"

"Even if they would have," Aura said quietly, "they couldn't. Most were dirt-poor farmers. Old enough to be my father. Or older."

She shuddered, barely perceptible, but Donovan caught it.

"And younger men?" Janice pressed.

Aura's jaw tightened. "No decent man would have me."

Something twisted painfully in Donovan's chest.

Before Janice could respond, Trevor reached out and yanked her hair.

"Ow!"

"That's enough," he said calmly.

Aura stabbed at the salmon with more force than necessary, her bad arm steady despite the sling. Donovan shifted closer, instinctively.

"Want help?" he asked softly.

"No."

He let it drop.

Tony cleared his throat, trying to lighten the mood. "I'll make stew tomorrow. Easier to manage."

Aura pushed her plate onto the table. "I'm not hungry anyway."

Donovan slid an arm around her shoulders, pulling her gently against his side, pressing a soft kiss to her temple. She stiffened at first, then didn't pull away.

"We'll behave," he said mildly, then more firmly, "Won't we, Janice?"

Janice blinked, then smiled wide. "Angels."

Tony spoke up suddenly. "Donovan, I heard Alice is gone."

Donovan stiffened. "Gone?"

"Missing a week. Parents think she left."

"That doesn't sound like her."

Tony hesitated, glancing at Aura. "She might've given up."

"Who's Alice?" Aura asked.

"No one," Donovan said quickly.

Her gaze sharpened. "Then why are you worried?"

He exhaled. "We were involved. She wanted more. I didn't. After I ended it, she tried to hurt herself. I found her here."

Aura absorbed that quietly.

"She's gone now?"

"That's what it sounds like."

"Then I hope she's done with you," Aura said flatly.

Donovan smiled faintly. "You don't need to be jealous."

"Jealous?" Aura snapped. "Don't flatter yourself."

He squeezed her shoulder, amused, while Tony and the siblings laughed.

"Pick me," Tony grinned. "I'll never give you a reason to be jealous."

"Because I'd never expect fidelity," Aura shot back.

"Ouch."

"Enough," Donovan growled.

"I think she should kiss him," Janice added.

"No," Donovan snapped.

Tony laughed. "You're so possessive lately. You'd think you were in love already."

Donovan shot him a warning look.

Aura shook her head, a reluctant smile tugging at her mouth. "I pity the woman who falls for your charm, Tony."

"I should hope so."

Donovan rolled his eyes, but his arm stayed firm around Aura's shoulders.

CHAPTER 19

It was after two in the morning when Donovan walked Aura down the stairs to her room.

It had become his habit to give her a few minutes of privacy to ready herself for bed before returning to claim the cot, but tonight he lingered in her doorway, one hand braced against the frame, his expression tight with thought.

When the door didn't close, Aura turned to look at him. She was tired, he could see it clearly now, the faint shadows beneath her eyes, the subtle sag of her shoulders. It had only been a week since she'd been shot. He should have sent her to bed hours ago.

Instead, he stood there, selfish and indecisive, weighing whether to start a conversation he knew would cut deep.

What she'd said at dinner—what she'd *believed*—had lodged under his skin like a splinter.

When he still didn't speak, her brow arched.

"Did you want to watch me undress tonight?" she asked lightly.

It wasn't a genuine invitation. It was a challenge.

He knew damn well that if he said yes, she'd strip without blinking.

Donovan scowled. "Don't do that."

"Do what?" she asked innocently, leaning against the dresser, head tipped to the side.

"Don't play the whore for me. You don't need to."

Her eyes hardened. "I *am* a whore, Donovan."

"Circumstances forced you to grow up in a brothel," he said, stepping fully into the room. "That doesn't make you one."

"For four years I slept with men for money," she snapped. "What else would you call that?"

"Did you enjoy it?"

She blinked. "What?"

"Did you enjoy sleeping with them?"

Her surprise shifted quickly into irritation. "No. Of course not. What does that matter?"

"Because if you *had* enjoyed it," he growled, "then you'd be a whore."

"That's not how the world sees it."

"Damn the world." His voice rose. "Why do you care what they think?"

"Why do *you*?" she shot back.

The question landed. Hard.

"You're right," he said quietly. "I don't. I only care what *you* think."

"Well, I think you're an ass. Satisfied?"

"No." His gaze sharpened. "Why did you say no decent man would have you?"

Aura exhaled slowly and sank onto the edge of the bed. "I'm too tired for this conversation."

"Too bad." He crossed his arms. "Answer me."

She glared, then laughed without humor.

"Because once people know what I am, that's all I'll ever be to them. A few hours in the dark? Fine. Daylight? I don't exist."

Her voice steadied as she spoke, but every word cut.

"Men think a whore belongs to them. That she won't object. That she won't fight back." Her jaw tightened. "And the few who are decent enough to know better run the other way."

She looked at him squarely. "So yes. No decent man will have me."

Silence crashed between them.

Then Donovan moved.

The door slammed shut behind him as he crossed the room in three strides, catching her hand and hauling her upright. She gasped as she hit his chest, his arms locking around her.

"Then I must not be decent," he growled, mouth crashing down on hers.

The kiss was fierce, punishing, possessive. Nothing tentative about it. He forced a response from her, his grip ironclad, his breath hot against her skin.

"I want you," he muttered against her cheek. "Not for hours. Not in the dark. For as long as you'll have me."

She melted into him, hands clutching at his back, her body betraying every doubt she'd voiced.

The door opened.

"Donovan, Trevor wants you. Now."

A vicious snarl tore from him. "I swear to God, Janice—"

"Kill Trevor," she said cheerfully. "He's the one summoning you."

Donovan dragged a hand down his face. "Stay with her," he ordered.

"Stop telling people to babysit me!" Aura snapped.

"Are you suddenly cured?" he shot back. "Should I move back to my room?"

Her silence answered him.

He didn't wait.

Janice stayed.

Aura changed slowly, pain blooming with every movement. Removing her jeans one-handed was an exercise in quiet frustration.

Janice finally sighed. "Want help?"

"Yes," Aura muttered. "Please."

Once changed, Aura sat back against the headboard, shoulders sagging as the adrenaline finally drained out of her. Her pack lay open beside her, clothes half-spilled across the bed where she'd abandoned the effort to be neat. Janice returned to the doorway, arms crossed, watching her with open interest.

"You look like hell," Janice observed mildly.

"Charming," Aura muttered, tugging at the hem of the loose shirt she'd pulled on. Her injured arm throbbed, the ache deep and insistent. She shifted, trying to find a position that didn't aggravate it. "If you're going to stand there staring, at least tell me why."

Janice tilted her head. "I'm trying to figure you out."

"Join the line."

A corner of Janice's mouth quirked. "You don't strike me as the type who lets herself be ordered around. And yet—" her eyes flicked toward the cot in the corner, "—you let my brother camp out in here every night like a loyal guard dog."

Aura stiffened. "He offered."

"That's not the point."

She sighed, rubbing her temple. "It's temporary."

"Uh-huh." Janice pushed off the doorframe and perched on the edge of the dresser. "So, what is it, then? Pain? Bad dreams?"

Aura hesitated.

Just for a second but Janice caught it.

"Well?" she pressed. "What's got Donovan playing nursemaid instead of sleeping like a normal human being?"

Aura's jaw tightened. "It's nothing."

"That's a lie."

"I don't owe you an explanation."

"No," Janice agreed easily. "But you're giving me one anyway."

Aura stared at the wall, weighing her options. Deflection was a reflex. Anger, sarcasm, insults, those were easy. This wasn't.

Finally, she muttered, "I don't sleep well at night."

Janice blinked. "That's it?"

Aura shot her a glare. "Don't make that face."

"What face?"

"That one. The one that says you're about to laugh."

Janice studied her more carefully now. "You don't sleep well *in the dark*… or you don't sleep well *alone*?"

Aura's fingers curled into the blanket. "Does it matter?"

Janice's tone shifted subtly, but noticeably. "It does."

Silence stretched.

Then Aura exhaled, sharp and irritated. "Fine. Alone in the dark."

Janice stared. Then—inevitably—she laughed.

"Seriously?" she said. "You're terrifying. You shoot people. You hunt monsters. And you're scared of the dark?"

Aura's head snapped up. "I said don't."

Janice cut herself off when she saw Aura's face. Closed. Walled off.

"Oh," Janice said slowly. "That kind of dark."

Aura swallowed. "It's not the dark itself," she said stiffly. "I don't care about night. I sleep outside just fine. I've slept in deserts, forests, open plains—"

"But not in rooms," Janice finished quietly.

Aura didn't answer.

Janice nodded once. "You're afraid of being trapped."

Aura's breath hitched, barely noticeable, but Janice saw it.

"Being shut in," Janice continued. "Alone. No exits. No witnesses."

Aura's voice came out rough. "Stop."

Janice raised her hands, palms out. "Alright. Alright." She paused. "How long?"

Aura stared at the bedspread. "Since I was five."

Janice's expression changed, not softened, exactly, but sharpened with understanding.

"That's why he's sleeping on a cot in here instead of in his own bed," she said.

Aura laughed humorlessly. "I don't know why it matters."

Janice was quiet for a long moment.

Then she grinned.

"Well," she said lightly, pushing off the dresser, "that explains a lot."

Aura frowned. "Explains what?"

"Why you're such a pain in the ass," Janice said cheerfully. "You're always braced for something to happen."

Aura scowled. "If you're trying to be comforting, you're failing spectacularly."

Janice shrugged. "I'm not comforting. I'm cataloging."

She took two steps toward the door, then paused, glancing back over her shoulder.

"So," she said casually, fingers brushing the light switch, "what happens if you're alone in the dark for too long?"

Aura's heart slammed.

"Janice," she warned.

Janice's grin widened. "Relax. I'm just curious."

The light clicked off and Janice slipped out of the room.

The darkness slammed down on Aura like a physical blow.

Her breath stuttered. The room shrank. The walls pressed inward, close enough that she could feel them, even though she knew, rationally, they hadn't moved at all. The air felt wrong. Thick. Stale. Her pulse roared in her ears, drowning out thought.

She was five again.

No—*now*. This was *now*. Her body didn't care about time.

Get out.

The command screamed through her, sharp and wordless.

Aura launched herself off the bed, stumbling as her foot caught the edge of the rug. She slammed shoulder-first into the door, pain flaring hot and bright, but she barely registered it. Her hands fumbled wildly for the knob, fingers slick with sweat, shaking so badly she missed it twice.

Too long. Too long.

Her vision tunneled. Blackness crawled in from the edges.

Open. Open. Open.

Her hand finally closed around the knob. She wrenched it down and yanked the door open with a sob she didn't remember making and ran.

She didn't see him.

She ran straight into something solid and unyielding and would have bounced off if strong hands hadn't closed around her upper arms, stopping her dead. She gasped, a sharp, panicked sound tearing out of her throat as her body recoiled, already fighting—

"Aura?"

Her name cut through the noise.

She looked up, eyes wild, breath coming in harsh, broken pulls, and found Donovan staring down at her. His face was tight with shock and immediate concern, his hands steady but gentle where they held her.

The world lurched.

She sagged forward with a broken sound and clutched at his shirt, fingers digging in as if he were the only solid thing left in existence.

Donovan swore softly under his breath and wrapped his arms around her without hesitation, pulling her fully against him. One hand slid up her back, broad and warm, anchoring her there. The other cradled the side of her head, pressing her face into his shoulder.

"It's alright," he murmured, low and steady. "I've got you. You're safe."

Her body didn't believe him yet.

She shook violently, breath hitching, her fingers locking tighter into his shirt as if letting go might drop her straight back into the dark. Her legs felt weak, unreliable, and she leaned into him without thinking, letting his weight hold her upright.

Behind them, Janice let out a small, startled laugh that died almost immediately.

"Oh," she said quietly this time. "Shit."

Donovan didn't look away from Aura, but his eyes hardened.

"She lasted longer than I thought," Janice added, attempting levity that rang hollow now.

Donovan's head snapped up.

"If you ever," he said, voice low and dangerous, "do something like that to her again, I will personally make sure you regret it."

Janice opened her mouth then closed it. For once, she had no retort.

Aura made a small, broken sound, her grip tightening reflexively as Donovan shifted his stance to brace them both. He felt the tremors running through her and cursed again, softer this time.

"Easy," he said, smoothing a hand down her back in slow, repetitive strokes. "You're not alone. I'm right here."

Her breathing gradually slowed, still uneven, but no longer tearing. She pressed her forehead into his collarbone, eyes squeezed shut, fighting the lingering echoes of terror that refused to fade completely.

"I'm sorry," she whispered hoarsely.

Donovan immediately tipped her chin up with two fingers, forcing her to meet his gaze.

"No," he said firmly. "Don't you dare apologize."

Her eyes were glassy, unfocused. "I didn't mean to—"

"I know," he cut in gently. "And you don't have to explain."

He glanced past her shoulder, pinning Janice with a glare.

"Get out."

Janice hesitated. "Donovan—"

"Now."

Janice raised her hands in surrender and backed away, her expression stripped of humor for once. "I'll... yeah. I'll go." She paused at the stairs, glancing back at Aura. "I didn't know," she said quietly.

Aura didn't answer.

Donovan didn't either.

The moment Janice disappeared down the stairs, Donovan turned his attention fully back to Aura. She was still shaking, though less violently now, her fingers flexing unconsciously against his chest as sensation returned to her limbs.

"You okay to walk?" he asked softly.

She shook her head, still unsteady, though the motion was barely perceptible.

He didn't argue. Scooping her up without warning, he lifted her into his arms and carried her back into the room. She started briefly, then melted against him again, instinctively curling into the security of his hold.

He kicked the door shut behind him and crossed to the bed, setting her down carefully in the center of it. She immediately drew her knees up, arms wrapping around herself as if to hold the remaining fear inside where it couldn't spill out again.

Donovan stayed close.

He reached up and turned the light on, bathing the room in warm illumination, then crouched in front of her so he was eye level.

"You with me?" he asked.

She nodded again, swallowing. "I hate this," she said quietly.

"I know."

She looked at him then, really looked, at the concern etched into his face, the way his hands hovered near her as if ready to catch her again if she so much as wobbled.

"I know it doesn't make sense," she said.

"It doesn't have to."

He straightened and reached for the light again.

"I'm going to turn this off," he said calmly, watching her closely. "But I'm not leaving. I'll be back before your body has time to decide anything bad is happening. You trust me?"

Her fingers curled into the blanket.

"Yes," she said, even as fear flickered in her eyes.

The light went out.

Darkness rushed in but this time, it didn't have time to take hold.

Donovan was back at the bed instantly, shrugging out of his shirt as he moved. He sat down hard on the mattress so she could feel the shift, the proof of his presence, then kicked off his boots and leaned back against the headboard.

He opened his arms.

Aura didn't hesitate.

She crawled into him, pressing herself against his chest, her head finding the hollow of his shoulder as if it belonged there. His arms closed around her, firm and unyielding, one hand splayed warm and steady against her back.

Her trembling faded quickly now, replaced by bone-deep exhaustion.

"That's it," he murmured, kissing the top of her head. "I've got you."

Her breathing evened out. Her grip loosened. Within minutes, the tension drained from her body as sleep claimed her completely, leaving her heavy and slack against him.

Donovan adjusted them both carefully, settling her more comfortably into his side, his arm tightening just enough to keep her there. He rested his cheek against her hair and let out a long, quiet breath.

She slept.

And for the first time that night, so did the fear.

CHAPTER 20

It was another three weeks before Aura could use her arm with any real comfort. The constant ache had finally faded, though sharp movements still sent a warning twinge through her shoulder. Her draw with that arm would be slower for a while yet, but even with her left hand she was dangerous. She had trained it deliberately, long ago, in case she ever needed it.

Preparedness had kept her alive.

Donovan's siblings had left after a week. The plan was simple enough: Trevor and Janice would search for signs of Luc and report back, while Donovan stayed with Aura until she was healed enough to travel.

Aura thought it was unnecessary. She understood needing to stay put herself, but Donovan could have been out hunting instead of hovering. The fact that she had told him she would sleep in the stable with her horse while he was gone may have influenced his decision. He seemed convinced she had never slept properly before meeting him.

After the night Janice had frightened her on purpose, Donovan had moved back to the cot.

The next morning's fallout had been… memorable.

Aura had barely finished assuring Donovan that daylight made her perfectly safe before he stormed down the hall in nothing but his jeans, bellowing Janice's name. Aura heard a door slam open several rooms away, followed by Janice's startled scream. She was out of bed and at the door just in time to see Janice tearing down the hallway, Donovan close behind.

He caught her at the stairs, hauled her over his shoulder, and marched her toward a closet at the far end of the hall. Janice kicked and shouted the entire way. He opened the door, tossed her inside, and slammed it shut.

"And you can stay there and think about what you did!"

"The hell I will!" Janice shouted just before the door splintered outward.

"Hey!" Tony called from the bathroom. "Quit breaking my house!"

Janice launched herself at her brother and they went down in a tangle of limbs, rolling across the floor. Aura stared, slack jawed. Janice appeared to be winning.

Trevor arrived silently behind her, surveyed the scene with folded arms, and said flatly, "You're both going to hell."

The fight stopped immediately.

Aura had barely managed to shut her own door before laughing so hard her ribs hurt.

It was only one of many moments that left her stunned. She had never seen a family like this. Loud, physical, infuriating, affectionate. And though she mostly watched from the edges, they included her without hesitation.

Even Janice, in her way.

By the time Trevor and Janice left, the garage felt strangely quiet.

Tony remained an incorrigible flirt, especially when Donovan was nearby. Donovan remained close—too close, sometimes—but she had stopped fighting him over it. They were all doing their best to keep her mind off Luc.

Which was why it caught her attention when she came down to the garage that morning and heard his name.

Tony and Donovan stood near the front of the garage, seated before a network terminal Aura hadn't noticed before. Tony traced something on the screen with one finger as he spoke.

"There's a pattern," he said. "Same sequence in every town. These points aren't random."

"But why leave so many bodies?" Donovan asked. "Why risk it?"

"Breadcrumbs," Tony replied. "He wants you to follow."

Aura stopped behind Donovan. "Who wants you to follow?"

Donovan turned. His expression hardened. "Luc. He's been leaving a trail."

"How do you know it's him?"

"He's leaving a trail of bodies. All women," he said. "Mutilated. Raped. Shot between the eyes." He hesitated. "They were all whores."

Aura's jaw tightened. "He remembers me."

"And the bullets," Donovan added. "They're from my gun. He's calling us out."

"Then let's not keep him waiting," Aura said. "Where does the trail lead?"

Tony shifted the display. "Across the mountains to the east."

Aura frowned. "Why that way?"

"That's what we're going to find out," Donovan said. "There's a city near the last murder. I've got a contact there. I'll send my siblings to look into these others."

Aura leaned closer, then froze. "Except that one."

Donovan followed her gaze. "Why?"

"It's the town I was born in."

He nodded once. "Then we'll check it ourselves."

"What was her name?" Aura asked quietly.

Tony pulled up the file. "Sylvia Tanner."

Aura closed her eyes.

She had known Sylvia. Kind. Too kind for the life she'd been forced into.

Donovan's fingers brushed her cheek. "Are you alright?"

"I'm fine," Aura said. "When do we leave?"

"Two days," he replied. "We need supplies. And we have dinner with Doc."

"That's fine. Give me a list."

He hesitated. "There's something else. The train passes through your town. It would be faster. You could leave your horse here."

Aura considered it.

"That makes sense."

His smile was brief, surprised. "You keep doing that."

"Being practical?" she asked.

"Agreeing with me."

He leaned down, kissed her quickly, and headed upstairs.

Tony chuckled behind her. "Never seen him like this."

"Like what?"

"Protective. Affectionate."

Aura scoffed. "He's been ordering me around since we met."

“That’s not who he usually is,” Tony said. “But around you, the weight lifts.”

She stared at the empty stairwell thoughtfully.

CHAPTER 21

After five long years, Aura was home.

She hadn't realized how much she had missed the town until she was standing on the station platform, staring at the familiar buildings while a tightness settled in her chest, making it difficult to breathe. She didn't have friends here—not really—but when you spent most of your life in one place, attachment crept in whether you wanted it or not.

Townsend was nearly as large as Kinsville and just as busy. Even at this hour, the streets were crowded, shops open, voices carrying easily through the air. Aura groaned quietly when she realized how fast news of her return would spread. The town might have shunned her, but they all knew her.

You didn't forget a beautiful whore with an attitude and a gun.

She had hoped to reach the brothel before anyone noticed her, but that hope died the moment a man on the platform stopped short, stared openly, then hurried off to whisper to someone else. One look turned into two. Two into many.

Damn it. What was taking Donovan so long?

He had gone to retrieve his bike from farther down the line, and Aura was about to go find him when she spotted him rolling it toward her, scowling heavily.

The reason became clear when she saw the front tire.

"Damn rail workers gave Billy a flat," he muttered when he reached her.

"Billy?" she asked, brow lifting.

He blinked. "Didn't I ever tell you? Bike's name is Billy."

"You named your motorcycle Billy."

"Named after the man who gave it to me."

Aura shook her head as he rolled the bike past her toward the ramp. "I get naming a horse. But a motorcycle?"

"It seemed appropriate at the time."

They walked in silence, Aura acutely aware of the stares following them. Donovan noticed too.

"Do I have mud on my face?" he muttered. "Why the hell is everyone staring?"

"They're not staring at you," Aura said quietly. "They're staring at me."

"Why?"

"This is my hometown. Everyone knows who I am."

"And?"

"And I doubt they ever expected to see me again."

"Still rude," he grumbled, glaring back at the crowd.

She huffed. "I wasn't infamous for no reason."

A cowboy lounging outside a saloon called out loudly, "You comin' back to work, darlin'? If you are, I might just visit tonight."

"She's booked!" Donovan barked.

Aura stared at him. He scowled back.

"Move," he growled, pushing the bike faster.

The brothel doors swung open to a world unchanged, deep reds, purples, laughter, smoke, music. Women leaned into men, cards slapped tables, couples disappeared upstairs.

Then someone shrieked.

"Aura!"

A petite blonde launched herself at her, hugging her fiercely. Aura stiffened, then returned it reflexively.

"I've missed you," the woman gushed. "Candice! Look who's back!"

Another woman hurried over, and Aura was hugged again.

They hadn't forgotten her.

That didn't make sense.

Then Maggie appeared.

Not rushing at first—stopping a few steps away like she needed to see her properly.

"Aura…"

Her voice broke on the name.

Then she closed the distance fast, pulling Aura into her arms, holding on like she wasn't sure she'd get another chance.

"You're really here."

Aura went still in Maggie's arms, something in her chest tightening in a way she couldn't place.

She swallowed hard, her hands tightening briefly in Maggie's shirt before she forced them to relax.

She didn't pull away.

Something shifted—quiet, disorienting, and far too close to mattering.

She swallowed it down before it could take shape.

Maggie finally pulled back, wiping her eyes. "I'm making a spectacle of myself." She turned to Donovan with practiced charm. "First time here, young man?"

"Uh—yes," he said cautiously.

"Well then, make yourself comfortable. My girls'll take good care of you."

"I'm with her," he said quickly, nodding toward Aura.

"Oh?" Maggie blinked.

"Go ahead," Aura said mildly, amusement flickering. "Maggie and I have catching up to do."

"I'm staying," Donovan said quietly, leaning closer.

She smiled thinly. "I'll come get you."

He hesitated, clearly unconvinced.

"I'm not leaving this room," he said finally.

Maggie laughed. "We'll see about that."

Two women appeared at his sides like they'd been waiting for the cue.

Donovan tensed immediately. "No—no, that's not necessary—"

They each took an arm.

"Absolutely necessary," one of them said sweetly.

"Aura—" he started, shooting her a look that was half warning, half accusation.

She didn't help him.

He was pulled out of the room anyway.

Aura watched him go, shaking her head.

Maggie's smile vanished the moment the door to her office closed.

"Why didn't you ever write?"

Aura swallowed. "I'm sorry."

"For five years."

"I didn't think—"

Maggie waved it off. "Never mind. I'm just glad you're here."

Aura studied her for a moment.

Then—

"Sylvia?"

The shift was immediate.

Maggie's expression tightened. "You heard."

"No… I didn't."

Maggie exhaled slowly. "The guards never came back. We found them outside town."

Aura's jaw tightened. "Both of them?"

"Both of them."

"And Sylvia?"

Maggie's gaze dropped for just a second. "Out back."

Aura went very still.

"She didn't have time to fight back," Maggie added quietly.

Silence settled, heavy and close.

The door burst open and Donovan stepped in, shirt half-pulled loose, hair a mess, eyes sharp with something much closer to panic than he'd probably admit.

"Aura."

She took one look at him and understood immediately, something had gone very wrong for him.

"Do not let those women near me."

Aura blinked, then a smirk tugged at her mouth despite herself.

"They're animals," he muttered, already moving toward her, lowering his voice like it might make a difference. "Someone took my wallet."

There was no humor in him at all.

"And your hat," she added.

He stopped cold. "What?" His hand went to his head.

Aura didn't answer. She just watched him for a second—the rigid control barely holding, the calculation already shifting into something more immediate. Whatever had just happened out there, he was done with it.

He reached for her hand without hesitation.

"We're leaving."

From the hallway—

"Donovan!"

He flinched, the reaction quick and unguarded, then exhaled sharply like that settled it.

"Now."

***

The hotel lobby was all clean floors and polished brass, the air faint with cigar smoke clinging to velvet drapes. Aura felt it immediately: the difference between this place and every other door she had ever been pushed through.

Respect lived here. Or at least, the illusion of it.

The restaurant host took one look at her and stiffened.

His eyes flicked first to her boots, then to the revolvers at her hips, then—too obviously—to her face. Recognition dawned, followed quickly by disapproval so practiced it might as well have been rehearsed.

"I'm sorry," he said, lips tightening before Donovan had even opened his mouth, "but—"

"Dinner for two," Donovan cut in flatly.

The man hesitated, gaze sliding back to Aura, lingering long enough to make his judgment unmistakable. Aura smiled sweetly and shifted her weight, letting the movement draw attention to the gun at her side.

The host swallowed.

"Very well," he said quickly, turning on his heel. "This way."

Donovan leaned in close as they followed. "You alright?" he murmured.

"I've had worse looks," Aura replied softly. "Most came with a proposition."

His jaw tightened, but he didn't comment.

Dinner passed with murmurs and glances, eyes tracking Aura like she was something dangerous and fascinating all at once. Donovan ignored it all with stubborn focus, but Aura saw every look. She always did.

They ate a quick dinner and when they finally approached the front desk for a room, the hotel manager—a thin man with ironed sleeves and a superior expression—didn't even bother hiding his disdain.

"I'm afraid we have no rooms available," he said smoothly.

Donovan glanced around the lobby. "Your hotel looks half empty."

"Policy," the man replied. His eyes cut briefly to Aura, then away. "Certain… individuals are not permitted lodging here."

Aura's lips parted, already prepared to dismantle him.

But Donovan spoke first.

"And my wife and I fall into that category?"

Aura turned slowly to look at him. He didn't look at her. His posture had changed, shoulders squared, chin lifted, voice cold and precise.

"Your wife?" the manager echoed skeptically.

"Yes," Donovan said sharply. "Is that a problem?"

Aura recovered instantly.

She slid her hand into Donovan's arm, fingers curling possessively. "Now, dear," she sighed, voice smooth as silk. "Let's not do this again."

The manager's confidence wavered.

"I—sir, I don't—"

"My husband has a temper," Aura continued lightly. "Coupled with money, it's a terrible combination. You should have seen what happened in Reddington."

Donovan scoffed. "I now own three hotels I don't have time to visit."

Aura patted his arm soothingly. "You barely remember owning them."

The manager's face went pale.

Aura smiled at him kindly. "Lawrence, isn't it?"

He stiffened. "Yes… ma'am."

"We'd hate to inconvenience you," she went on. "But if this becomes… unpleasant, my husband may decide he wants a change in management. He gets that way when he's tired."

Donovan leaned forward. "I am extremely tired."

A bead of sweat formed at Lawrence's temple.

"I—I suppose a room could be arranged. Just for the night."

"I should hope so," Donovan snapped, snatching the key. "And a bellhop. Unless indignity is part of your service."

Lawrence waved frantically.

They didn't say a word until they were halfway down the hall.

Donovan's hand stayed on Aura's shoulder, firm and unyielding, steering her away from the lobby as if he expected someone to grab her back at any moment. She tolerated it for exactly six steps before shrugging him off.

"You didn't have to do that," she muttered.

"Yes, I did," he said flatly, not slowing.

She huffed a breath and followed him anyway, boots clicking against the polished floor. "You enjoy making scenes?"

"I enjoy putting rude people in their place."

"They weren't insulting *you*."

"That's irrelevant."

She shot him a look. "You always decide that for everyone else?"

He stopped at the stairs and turned on her, brows lowered. "Do you *want* to go back down there and argue policy with that smug bastard?"

"No."

"Then let it go."

She glared, but climbed the stairs ahead of him, shoulder aching with every step. She was painfully aware of the looks trailing after them. Recognition, curiosity, judgment. Familiar faces pretending they weren't staring.

At the top of the stairs, Donovan caught up and reached for her again. This time she didn't shake him off.

"They're watching," she said quietly.

"Let them," he replied.

At the door to their room, he unlocked it quickly and ushered her inside, closing it with a decisive thud. The bolt slid home with a sharp click that echoed louder than it should have.

Aura let out a slow breath she hadn't realized she was holding.

Too tight. Everything felt too tight.

She crossed the room and pulled the curtain aside just enough to look out. The street below was busy, lamps casting yellow light over familiar storefronts and familiar faces—people who hadn't changed, who hadn't left, who hadn't needed to.

"Nothing's changed," she said.

Donovan set their packs down near the bed. "You expected it to?"

"No," she said shortly. Her fingers tightened against the curtain before she forced them to relax. "That's the problem."

Because if nothing had changed—

then neither had she.

He leaned against the wall, arms crossed, watching her reflection in the glass. "You don't have to prove anything to anyone."

She snorted softly, though there wasn't much humor in it. "That's exactly what they think I'm doing."

"Then they're wrong."

She turned to face him, the movement sharper than she intended. "You don't get to decide that."

His jaw tightened. "I get to decide what I tolerate."

"And I don't need you stepping in for me."

"I'm not stepping in," he said evenly. "I'm shutting people down before they get stupid."

She frowned. "By telling them we're married?"

"It worked."

"That's not the point."

"It is when it keeps them out of your way."

Her irritation sharpened, something deeper threading through it now. "And if I hadn't gone along with it?"

"You did," he said calmly.

She scoffed, folding her arms like it might hold the feeling in place. "Confident."

"Observant."

Aura shook her head, pacing once toward the bed and back again. The room suddenly felt smaller than it should have. "You don't get to make decisions like that for me."

"I didn't make it for you," he said. "I made it for them."

She stilled.

"That's worse."

His expression didn't change. "It's effective."

"You don't own me."

"I know that."

"Then stop acting like it."

He pushed off the wall and stepped closer, his voice dropping just enough to carry weight. "I'm acting like someone who doesn't like watching you get cornered."

Her throat tightened, anger and something sharper twisting together before she could separate them.

"Well don't," she shot back. "I can handle myself."

"I know you can."

"Then let me."

A beat stretched between them, thin and taut.

"No," he said.

The word landed solid. Unmovable.

Aura stared at him, something in her chest shifting in a way she didn't like—didn't understand.

Silence settled between them, thick and uncomfortable.

She broke it first.

"I need a bath," she said, turning away before he could read anything else in her face.

Distance. She needed distance.

Donovan hesitated, then nodded. "I'll go find a mechanic."

She paused at the washroom door, her hand resting against the frame. Something pulled at her—sharp, unexpected.

"You're not staying?"

The question slipped out before she could stop it.

"Not unless you ask me to."

That answer was immediate. Steady.

She didn't.

Didn't trust what would happen if she did.

He watched her a moment longer, like he was waiting for something she wasn't going to give him, then turned for the door. "You'll be alright?"

She gave a tight, almost wry smile. "I think I can manage."

He nodded once and left, closing the door softly behind him.

Aura stood there long after he was gone, the quiet settling in around her, her pulse still unsteady.

Nothing had changed.

That's what she'd said.

But something had.

And she didn't know what to do with it.

CHAPTER 22

Aura stood at the window, staring down at the dark street below. The city was quieter at this hour, the lamps casting long, distorted shadows across the pavement. She had finished bathing over an hour ago and now wore a soft cotton shirt that brushed her thighs when she shifted her weight. Her hair was nearly dry, falling in loose waves down her back, catching the lamplight so that the darker strands looked almost golden.

She would have liked to go to bed, but she couldn't until Donovan returned.

Partly because of the fear — the old, irrational kind that tightened her chest when she was alone at night — and partly because there was nowhere else to sleep. No chair. No couch. The floor was an option, but she thought she should at least discuss it with him first.

He'd been gone nearly two hours.

She frowned at her reflection in the glass. They'd had the worst luck since meeting. Donovan beaten half to death. Her shot and nearly killed. Trouble seemed to follow them relentlessly. And yet, because of him, she had found Luc. Because of him, she had laughed again. Something she hadn't done in years.

She had never allowed herself to imagine a life after Luc. Never planned beyond killing him. Now she couldn't think of that end without Donovan intruding into it, uninvited and persistent.

The door opened behind her.

She didn't turn.

"I take it you're alright, then?" she asked casually.

"I think that's a matter of opinion."

She turned and crossed her arms, leaning back against the window. The cool glass sent a shiver across her skin, but she didn't move away.

"Oh?" she asked mildly.

"Had to push my bike clear across town. Got sent in three different directions. The place was closed when I finally got there."

Her brow rose. "So, you pushed it all the way back?"

"Hell no," he muttered. "I was so irritated by that point I dragged the owner out of bed and left it there with instructions to fix it tomorrow."

She smiled faintly. "I'll bet he appreciated that."

"It's amazing what the promise of a large tip will do."

"Threats of violence work just as well and don't cost as much."

He cocked a brow at her. "Used them often, have you?"

"Only when necessary."

Donovan sighed. "I'm really going to have to teach you how to play nice, sweetheart."

"Oh, I know how to play nice," she said, her tone turning deliberately sultry.

He groaned. "That just begs for trouble."

"It's usually the men begging by the time I'm done."

"Dammit, Aura! Don't do that!"

She frowned. "Don't do what?"

"Don't talk about them like that."

"It's not a big deal, Donovan. I'm a whore. It would be hypocritical to pretend otherwise."

He crossed the room in a few hard strides and grabbed her arm, pulling her away from the window. His grip wasn't painful, but it was tight.

"You think I like knowing about those other men?" he snarled. "Knowing how they used you? It rips me apart every time I think about it. Every time you bring it up."

"They didn't use me," she snapped back. "I used them. I got what I wanted, money, information. I've been using men since I was a child. My body was a small price to pay."

"It is not a small price," he growled, his face inches from hers. "It's something precious that should have been for one man."

"Maybe for the wealthy," she shot back quietly. "But people like me don't have that luxury."

He shoved her away and turned, raking a hand through his hair. “Would you prefer I was poor, then? Or cruel? Would that make me acceptable?”

“Rich, poor, cruel or kind,” she said flatly. “It makes no difference to a whore.”

“Stop calling yourself that!” he shouted.

“Why the hell do you care?!” she shouted back.

He stalked into the bathroom. “I don’t.”

The door slammed.

Aura stood there shaking with anger. What the hell was his problem? She had never hidden what she was. If he couldn’t handle it, that was his issue, not hers.

When he finally emerged an hour later, his hair was damp, curling slightly at the edges. He stood shirtless in the doorway, pants unbelted, water still glistening on his skin.

Her resolve evaporated instantly.

God, he was magnificent.

She hated that she needed him. Hated that desire made her weak. She clenched her jaw as he sighed heavily.

“I’m sorry,” he said. “I shouldn’t have yelled.”

“You’re damn right you shouldn’t have,” she snapped. “Especially since I don’t even know why you were yelling.”

“I don’t want to fight.”

“Then stop acting like I’m something you can’t stand.”

He frowned. “That’s not what I meant.”

“Do you want the floor or the bed?” she asked stiffly.

He stared at her. “Is there a reason we can’t share it?”

“I didn’t think you’d want to.”

“Dammit, Aura! I’m not going to touch you.”

“Oh, I know,” she sneered. “Just like the others.”

The light went out and they got into the bed from opposite sides.

Darkness settled over them, thick and immediate, pressing in from all sides. Aura lay rigid on her back, arms folded beneath her head, staring into nothing. She could feel Donovan beside her without touching him, his heat, his weight, the controlled stillness of a man holding himself in check.

Every inch of space between them hummed with tension.

She wanted him.

The admission came sharp and unwelcome, cutting through her anger and pride alike. Damn him for making her want him like this. Quietly, achingly, without permission. Damn him for lying there as if he weren't just as aware, as if he weren't struggling against the same pull.

She could hear his breathing. Slow. Measured. Too controlled to be accidental.

Time stretched. Seconds passed. Maybe minutes.

Her body betrayed her first, muscles tightening, breath growing shallow as awareness coiled low in her belly. She shifted once, just enough that her thigh brushed his.

He swore softly.

The sound was rough, scraped out of him like a surrender.

He rolled toward her, one arm coming over her waist, his hand gripping her hip firmly, decisively, pulling her flush against him. The contact stole the breath from her lungs. She tensed for the briefest moment—habit, instinct—but she didn't pull away.

She didn't resist.

His mouth found hers, hungry and unapologetic, the kiss nothing like the restraint he'd tried to maintain. It wasn't gentle. It was desperate, edged with frustration and want, as if he'd been holding himself back for far too long.

Her body melted into him.

All the sharp edges dissolved as she clutched at him, fingers tangling in his hair, her lips parting without thought. The anger faded, the fear blurred, replaced by heat and need and the simple relief of no longer pretending she didn't want this.

His hand slid up her side, firm and possessive, anchoring her there as if he were afraid she might disappear if he let go. She gasped against his mouth, the sound swallowed by his kiss, and arched into him without meaning to.

For a moment—just one reckless, breathless moment—nothing else existed.

The beeping cut through the dark, sharp and insistent.

Donovan swore under his breath and rolled partially away from Aura, bracing himself on one elbow as he lifted his wrist to his ear. His body was still tense, breath uneven, as if the interruption had torn him violently out of something he'd barely allowed himself to want.

"I'm going to murder you," he growled into the communicator. "And I mean that in the most affectionate way possible."

There was a pause, then Trevor's voice came through, faint but unmistakably amused.

"Did I interrupt something?"

"Yes," Donovan snapped. "Something important. Now unless the world is ending, this could have waited."

"It couldn't," Trevor said, the humor draining from his tone. "That's why I called."

Donovan stilled. Aura shifted slightly beside him, drawing her knees up as she listened, her earlier heat cooling into alert focus.

"What is it?" Donovan asked, already knowing this wasn't going to be good.

"I went out to the compound."

Donovan's jaw tightened. "Why?"

"A hunch," Trevor replied. "One I didn't like ignoring."

Donovan exhaled slowly. "And?"

"It paid off."

Silence stretched between them. Donovan sat up fully now, one hand dragging over his face.

"Someone's been there," Trevor continued. "Recently."

Donovan's eyes flicked toward Aura for half a second before he looked away again. "That place is a graveyard," he said. "Collapsed tunnels, sealed doors, half the structure buried. Why would anyone go back?"

"That's exactly what I asked myself," Trevor said. "But the signs are there. Fresh tracks. Disturbed debris. Power rerouted."

Donovan frowned. "Power shouldn't even be running."

"It is," Trevor said. "Not everywhere, but enough. More than there should be. Someone's been redirecting it."

Donovan's mouth thinned. "Luc."

"I don't see who else it could be."

Donovan leaned back against the headboard, eyes unfocused now, memory pulling him somewhere far colder than the dark hotel room. "He knew the compound," he said quietly. "Spent enough time there when we were kids. He wouldn't have forgotten it."

"No," Trevor agreed. "And that's what bothers me."

"Why go back?" Donovan muttered. "There's nothing left there."

"I don't know," Trevor replied. "But, there are areas I couldn't reach. Doors still sealed. Sections buried but intact. And whatever he's doing, he's not just passing through."

Donovan's hand clenched into the blanket. "You think he's using it?"

"I think he's preparing something," Trevor said. "Or revisiting something."

Neither of them said what that something might be.

Aura felt a chill creep up her spine. She didn't know the compound, but she could hear it in their voices, the weight of what it represented. Not just a place, but a beginning. A wound that never really healed.

"Have you heard from Janice?" Donovan asked finally.

"Yeah. Nothing useful yet. She's following one of the other trails, but it's cold."

Donovan nodded once. "Stay sharp out there, Trevor. If Luc is circling back to old ground, he's doing it for a reason."

"I know," Trevor said. "That's why I'm staying put. Something about this feels… staged. Like he wants us to notice."

Donovan closed his eyes briefly. "He always did like control."

"And attention," Trevor added.

"Ycah," Donovan said softly. "That too."

Another pause. Then Trevor said, more quietly, "Take care of her."

Donovan's eyes opened. "I am."

"I know," Trevor replied. "Just… don't underestimate how far Luc will go to get to you. Both of you."

The communicator beeped once more, then went silent.

Donovan lowered his arm slowly, staring at nothing.

Aura shifted beside him. "The compound," she said carefully. "That's where you grew up."

He nodded. "Where we were altered. Where everything started."

She didn't press further. She could hear the edge in his voice, the tightly locked door behind those words.

"Luc being there…" she said after a moment. "It means he's not just running."

"No," Donovan agreed. "He's circling."

He turned back toward her then, drawing her close again, slower this time, as if grounding himself in her warmth.

"We'll deal with it," he said, more to himself than to her. "Whatever he's planning."

Some ghosts didn't stay buried.

And Luc was digging them up on purpose.

"We should sleep," he said quietly, his voice low and strained.

She didn't argue.

She turned into him, fitting against his chest as if she belonged there, her head resting beneath his chin. His warmth surrounded her, solid and steady, and the tension in her body eased despite everything she knew she should feel instead.

Warmth and danger tangled together.

She closed her eyes, letting herself stay there just for now.

This, she thought, could ruin her.

And she wanted it anyway.

CHAPTER 23

It took him a few sluggish seconds to understand what was wrong, that something felt off. The warmth beside him was gone. The sheets were cold.

Donovan rolled onto his stomach and lifted his head, scanning the room. Empty bed. Bathroom door open. No sign of her. Aura was gone.

He pushed himself upright, frowning. Her pack still sat where she'd left it, untouched. So, she hadn't left him. Not for good.

The clock read just past nine.

Breakfast, then, he reasoned. Or… something else.

He dressed quickly, irritation prickling beneath his ribs. He didn't like waking up alone when she was supposed to be there. Didn't like not knowing where she was. The feeling didn't ease until he was moving, heading down to the lobby, eyes already searching.

She wasn't in the restaurant.

"Damn it," he muttered.

Someone cleared their throat behind him.

Donovan turned to find the hotel manager standing stiffly at attention. "Your wife left a message for you, sir."

His brow lifted. *Wife.*

"She said she was visiting her family," the man continued carefully, "and that you were welcome to join her. Otherwise, she suggested meeting for lunch."

Donovan grinned despite himself. Aura hadn't said it like that. Not a chance.

"My thanks," he said. "I'll join her."

The manager nodded and retreated, posture rigid as ever.

Donovan stepped out onto the street and groaned.

Her family meant the brothel.

He exhaled slowly, squaring his shoulders. *You survived it once. You can do it again.* They were just women. Forward women. Aggressively forward women.

He entered cautiously, eyes sweeping the room.

There she was.

Standing in the entertaining room, laughing with several people, relaxed, open in a way he rarely saw. Relief washed through him just before panic hit.

The women noticed him.

The squeals started.

"Oh hell—"

He lunged.

Grabbing Aura around the middle, he yanked her back against him, lifting her clean off the floor. She yelped, twisting in his arms.

"Donovan! What the hell—"

"Shield," he hissed. "You're a shield."

The women froze, mid-advance, laughter bubbling.

"You scared the hell out of me!" Aura snapped.

"You're scared?" He shot the women a glare. "You keep them away from me. If they touch me again, we're leaving."

"They're not going to hurt you!"

"They absolutely are. I see it in their eyes."

Several women giggled.

"For God's sake, put me down!"

Maggie's voice cut through the noise. "What is going on here?"

She took in the scene—Donovan clutching Aura like a lifeline—and sighed. "Honestly. I've never seen a man so terrified of women."

"I'm not terrified," he growled. "I just don't want to be mauled."

Aura squirmed. "Put. Me. Down."

Instead, Donovan carried her to a couch and sat, settling her firmly in his lap, arms locked around her hips.

Her glare promised violence.

"You are the most stubborn, paranoid—"

"I believe you had business," he interrupted, nodding toward Maggie.

Maggie handed Aura the packet of papers.

The room shifted.

For the next three hours, the mood sobered. The investigation was combed through piece by piece. Sylvia's last night. The guards who were killed. Angie's tears as she described finding the body.

Donovan stayed quiet. Aura asked the questions. The right ones.

In the end, there was nothing new.

Luc had come and gone like smoke.

But Donovan noticed something else.

Aura was lighter here. Softer. She smiled more. Laughed easily. The women responded to her warmth, not fear.

This is who she could have been.

She relaxed against him as conversation drifted to safer ground. When she laughed, the sound curled straight through him.

Before he could stop himself, his hand rose, turning her face toward his.

He kissed her.

Soft. Intentional.

She started, then melted, hands coming up around his neck.

Clearing throats. Knowing giggles.

He pulled back with a grin. "I'm not apologizing."

"I wasn't going to ask you to."

Maggie's voice cut in brightly. "Would you like the office?"

Aura smiled. "We're finished. For now."

Donovan liked the sound of that.

***

Lunch passed easily. Shopping. Repairs. Ordinary moments that felt dangerously close to *normal*.

Then Aura changed.

She stepped out of the bathroom dressed for the memorial and Donovan froze.

She was beautiful. Lethally so.

"You're going to cause a riot."

"I can handle it."

"You're going to get hit on."

"I always do."

She buckled on her gun belt.

Donovan swore.

The moment they stepped through the brothel doors, Donovan realized he had made a terrible miscalculation.

Sound hit him first.

Laughter, loud and unrestrained. Music spilling from the piano near the stage. Catcalls layered over conversation, boots thudding against the wooden floor as girls crossed the room with trays of drinks balanced on their hips. The air was thick with smoke, perfume, sweat, and spilled alcohol.

This was not solemn.

This was not quiet.

This was not *mourning* in any way he recognized.

Cheers erupted when Aura entered, a ripple of recognition spreading fast. Heads turned. Smiles bloomed. A few men whistled appreciatively, and Donovan felt something ugly coil low in his gut.

Maggie appeared at their side, voice raised to be heard. “Some party, huh?”

“I thought this was supposed to be a memorial,” Donovan shouted back, incredulous.

“It is,” Maggie said brightly. “In Sylvia’s honor, all drinks are on the house tonight.”

That explained it.

Aura didn’t get a chance to respond before Maggie looped an arm through hers and began pulling her into the room.

“Come on, my dear. Time to make the rounds.”

The crowd closed around them immediately, bodies shifting, voices rising, hands lifting glasses in greeting. Donovan started forward, instinctively reaching for Aura, but the press of people swallowed her whole.

“Dammit,” he muttered.

Rather than try to bulldoze through, he claimed a spot at the bar where he could see most of the room. He leaned back against the polished wood, arms crossed, eyes never leaving her.

Aura moved through the crowd like she’d never left.

Her posture changed subtly, shoulders back, chin lifted, a looseness to her step that wasn’t quite flirtation but invited attention all the same. She smiled easily, laughed when spoken to, laid a hand on a wrist or forearm just long enough to feel intentional before withdrawing again.

She didn’t let anyone touch her.

But she let them *want*.

Donovan's jaw tightened.

He could tell the instant she slipped into what he privately labeled *working mode*. Her eyes half-lidded, her movements economical, her voice pitched just low enough to draw men in. She wasn't selling herself, but she was controlling the room.

Men leaned closer. Women watched with fond familiarity. Drinks appeared in her hands without her asking.

Donovan hated how natural it looked.

By the time Maggie climbed onto the stage and clapped her hands for attention, his temper was frayed thin.

"Settle down! Settle down now!"

The room gradually quieted, the piano falling silent, laughter tapering off into expectant murmurs.

"You're all aware we're here tonight in memory of our dear Sylvia," Maggie said, her voice warm but firm. "Taken from us far too soon."

"To Sylvia!" a drunken voice shouted from the back, glass raised high.

Cheers followed.

Maggie waited them out before continuing. "And we're also welcoming home one of our own. Miss Aura hasn't been back in over five years."

The reaction was louder this time, whistles, applause, delighted shouts.

"Yes, yes, I know," Maggie said with a grin. "But tonight, Aura has agreed to sing for Sylvia."

Donovan froze.

Sing?

Aura stepped onto the stage, her face composed but pale, hands briefly clasped in front of her as she took a breath.

When she opened her mouth, the room changed.

Her voice was clear and unadorned, no theatrics, no embellishment. Just grief and memory laid bare. The song was slow, aching, full of longing and regret, and it wrapped itself around Donovan's chest like a tightening fist.

The room fell silent.

No piano. No movement. Just her.

Halfway through, something inside Donovan shifted. He spotted the guitar resting beside the piano and moved without thinking, lifting it gently, letting his fingers find the strings.

He joined her softly.

Aura's eyes snapped to his.

For a heartbeat, they held each other there, sound, grief, recognition braided tight.

They finished together.

Silence followed, thick and reverent.

Maggie climbed onto the stage and hugged Aura fiercely, tears shining.

"That was beautiful," she whispered. "Just beautiful."

Then she turned to the room.

"Godspeed, Sylvia. Now, let's honor her properly."

The music surged back to life. Cheers erupted. The brothel roared.

Aura stepped down into the crowd, stopping in front of Donovan. He set the guitar aside, cupping her face.

"I didn't know you could sing," he murmured.

"I didn't know you could play."

"It was the most beautiful thing I've ever heard."

He kissed her.

It wasn't careful. It wasn't shy. It was instinctive, his hands firm at her waist, her fingers catching briefly in the collar of his shirt as if to steady herself before melting into it. The kiss was short but unmistakably claiming, a quiet statement made in the loudest room imaginable.

The room exploded in approval.

Whistles cut through the air. Someone clapped. A few men cheered outright, laughter rolling across the tables like a wave. A woman near the bar shouted something Donovan couldn't quite make out over the noise, but the tone was approving, amused, indulgent.

Then someone called out, too loud, too crude. "You gonna spread those kisses around, honey?"

Donovan felt it like a hook under his ribs.

His body went rigid, muscles coiling, already preparing to step forward, to put himself between Aura and the voice that had crossed a line he hadn't even fully identified yet. His hand tightened at her hip, possessive reflex flaring hot and fast.

But Aura was already turning.

She slipped from his grasp with infuriating ease, pivoting toward the offender with a smile that wasn't warm at all. It was sharp. Bright. Dangerous in the way a blade gleamed before it cut.

"Well now," she said lightly, planting one hand on her hip as she looked the man over. "That's a shame."

The man—half drunk, full of confidence—grinned wider. "Just sayin' what we're all thinkin', sweetheart."

A murmur rippled through the nearby tables. Interest sharpened. This was familiar territory to them. They leaned in, waiting.

Aura took two slow steps closer.

Close enough that the man's grin faltered just a touch.

"You know," she continued pleasantly, "you used to be smarter than that. Back when you still had all your teeth."

Laughter burst from somewhere behind Donovan.

The man blinked. "Now hold on—"

Aura moved.

Not fast enough to startle, not slow enough to invite interruption. She placed her boot squarely on the edge of his chair, forcing him to lean back. When he rocked unsteadily, she leaned down, forearm braced casually on her raised knee, her face inches from his.

Her voice dropped low, intimate, unmistakably serious.

"You will apologize," she said softly, "or you will spend the rest of the night explaining to your wife why you need help walking."

The room went silent for a heartbeat.

Then the man laughed, short, nervous, and raised both hands. "Alright, alright. My mistake. No offense meant."

Aura held his gaze another second, then smiled again. This one was genuine. Almost fond.

"Good," she said, straightening. "We all have lapses in judgment now and then."

She tipped his chair and sent him crashing to the ground.

The room roared with laughter and applause, tension snapping like a rope cut clean through. Someone slapped the table. A woman near the stage raised her glass in salute.

Order restored.

Aura turned back toward Donovan as if nothing out of the ordinary had happened.

He was staring at her. Shaken.

She didn't ask why. She just stepped back into his space, close enough that her shoulder brushed his chest, her warmth unmistakable even through layers of fabric. Her mouth curved, knowing, unapologetic.

"You look like you're reconsidering something," she said lightly.

"I am," he admitted hoarsely.

She belonged here.

Not because of the men. Not because of the noise or the chaos or the reputation that clung to the walls of the place.

She belonged because she *commanded* it.

And somehow—terrifyingly—she also belonged with him.

The thought didn't comfort him.

It rooted itself deep and refused to let go.

CHAPTER 24

They never made it back to the hotel that night, the revelry continuing until nearly dawn. Several of the girls eventually managed to talk Donovan into drinking, insisting he couldn't very well refuse a toast to Sylvia's memory. Lightweight that he was, four shots of whiskey later he had passed out on one of the plush couches.

He woke several hours later missing his shirt and belt and glared suspiciously around the room, as if he might catch the culprit sneaking off with them. He didn't, of course.

Donovan sat up slowly, running a hand through his tousled hair, wincing faintly as his head protested. His gaze swept the room until he spotted Aura on the far side, seated on a couch with Maggie, the two of them speaking quietly.

As he approached, Aura glanced up. "Oh, good. You're up. I was just going to—" Her eyes flicked over him. "What happened to your shirt?"

He ignored her look of surprise and shot Maggie a glare. She grinned unabashedly back at him.

"I have no idea," he said stiffly. "My belt's gone missing too."

Aura bit her lip, clearly fighting laughter. "Well, that's tragic. But we only have about two hours before we need to catch the train. Just enough time to change—in your case, get dressed—gather our things, and grab breakfast."

He scowled at her tone but nodded. They bid Maggie goodbye, returned to the hotel to pack, and managed a quick breakfast before heading for the station.

The trip to Brookstone would take four days. Donovan had already sent word ahead to an old friend, asking him to secure a place for them to stay. William Hartly was well-connected, respected, and exactly the sort of ally one wanted in a city as large as Brookstone.

Donovan found himself smiling as he watched Aura sleep across from him. She had stretched out along the bench, hat tipped low over her face, one arm tucked beneath her head. Her chest rose and fell steadily. She'd admitted to getting no sleep at all, spending the night circulating through the brothel, drinking, laughing, reconnecting with people she hadn't seen in years.

She'd also consumed nearly a bottle and a half of whiskey. An impressive feat considering Donovan was nursing a mild headache from just four shots. She, on the other hand, seemed entirely unaffected.

An older woman shared the car with them, friendly and talkative, explaining she was traveling east for the funeral of an uncle she barely remembered. Donovan entertained her easily, charming and attentive. When she asked his reason for traveling, he extended the lie begun in Townsend, explaining that he and his wife were visiting an old family friend and doing some shopping.

The woman offered shop recommendations and eventually excused herself for the dining car, making Donovan promise to introduce her to his wife when she woke.

The door had barely closed when a voice said lazily, "So. I'm to be your wife again?"

Donovan blinked. Aura hadn't moved, her hat still covering her face.

"How long have you been awake?"

"About an hour," she said, sitting up and adjusting the brim. "Turns out you hear a lot when people assume you're asleep."

"So, you were eavesdropping."

She shrugged. "Seems it was wise. You didn't bother to mention we were keeping up the married act."

"I wasn't planning on it," he said cautiously. "Didn't want to offend her."

"Ah. Yes. The lady," Aura said dryly. "She seems quite taken with you."

"Oh, for God's sake. She's old enough to be my mother."

"You learn early in my business that age has nothing to do with it."

Donovan grinned suddenly. "Aura, you're incredibly entertaining when you're jealous."

"Jealous?!" she snapped, yanking her hat off her face. "I don't care what you do with other women."

He crossed to her bench, bracing his hands on either side of her, leaning close.

"Sweetheart, I haven't noticed another woman since the moment I met you."

"You noticed the girls."

"I noticed danger," he said dryly. "And fled."

Her expression tightened.

"Because they're whores?"

"Partly," he said, just to provoke her. Then, softer, "Mostly because I want you so badly no one else matters. I don't want their hands on me. I want yours."

Fire lit in her eyes.

"So," he murmured, "are you going to behave? No more jealous displays?"

She swung at him. He dodged easily, laughing as he retreated.

"Temper," he teased.

"Go to hell."

"Oh, honey," he said quietly, leaning forward again, "I've been there ever since I met you."

Her defenses snapped up instantly. "Pretty words. But all you need is money. Whores don't need wooing."

That did it.

He surged to his feet. "You hide behind that word every time someone gets close," he snapped. "You use it to disgust, to drive people away. It won't work on me."

"The hell it won't."

"If you try it again," he growled, "I'll turn you over my knee."

"I'll shoot you first."

"Try."

The tension between them was taut enough to snap, both of them breathing hard, eyes locked, neither willing to yield.

"Oh my," came a gentle, amused voice. "Fighting already?"

Donovan and Aura turned at the same time.

The older woman stood a few paces away, hands folded neatly at her waist, her expression one of polite interest, as if she'd stumbled upon a mildly entertaining tableau rather than a near-explosion. Her sharp eyes flicked between them, lingering just a moment too long on Aura's clenched fists and Donovan's rigid posture.

Donovan felt heat rush to his face. Damn it all.

"You should be doing everything in your power to please your wife, young man," she said lightly, though there was a knowing glint in her eyes. "Not provoking her temper so early in the day."

Aura opened her mouth, fury already rising.

Donovan didn't give her the chance. "You're absolutely right, ma'am."

He stepped in, one arm snapping around her waist, lifting her cleanly off her feet before she could react. Her protest died instantly as his mouth claimed hers, hard, thorough, unapologetic. It wasn't gentle. It wasn't tentative. It was possessive and decisive, meant as much for their audience as for her.

Aura stiffened for half a heartbeat—

Then melted.

Her hands slid into his coat, fingers fisting tight as she kissed him back just as fiercely, anger bleeding seamlessly into heat. The kiss deepened, slowed, became unmistakably intimate.

The woman chuckled softly.

"Ah," she said with satisfaction. "Newlyweds."

Donovan broke the kiss reluctantly, keeping Aura tucked firmly against his side, one arm still locked around her hips as if daring anyone—Aura included—to challenge the claim. He cleared his throat.

"Ma'am," he said, regaining composure by sheer force of will. "This is my wife, Aura."

He liked entirely too much how that sounded.

Aura shot him a sideways look that promised retribution.

The woman took Aura's hand warmly. "A pleasure, my dear. You're quite lovely."

"Thank you," Aura said tightly.

"And spirited," she added, eyes dancing. "I can tell already."

"Oh, I'm sure you can," Aura replied, her smile sharpening into something dangerous. "Spirited tends to get noticed. Usually right before things get… messy."

Donovan felt the shift instantly. Oh no.

The woman laughed politely. “Marriage will smooth that edge.”

Aura’s smile widened, just enough.

“Hasn’t yet,” she said pleasantly. “Though my husband does try. Usually after I’ve finished cleaning blood off the floor.”

The woman blinked.

Aura continued, undeterred. “You’d be amazed how many men underestimate a woman’s patience. Or her aim.”

Donovan hissed, “Aura—”

“I’m teasing,” she said sweetly, patting his chest. “Mostly.”

The woman’s smile stiffened, laughter turning faintly brittle.

“Well,” she said after a moment, “you certainly keep life interesting.”

“We try,” Donovan said quickly.

“Yes. I can see that.” She inclined her head. “Do enjoy your travels.”

With that, she retreated down the aisle, dignity intact, curiosity firmly extinguished.

Aura slipped out from under Donovan’s arm the second the woman was gone.

Without a word, she stalked toward the exit.

Donovan watched her go, equal parts exasperated and stunned.

CHAPTER 25

Donovan rapped sharply on the townhouse door. It opened almost at once, the butler already poised, as though he'd been waiting just out of sight.

"Hello, George," Donovan said easily. "How are things?"

"Very well, sir," George replied with impeccable stiffness. "If you would care to wait in the parlor, I'll inform Mr. Hartly you've arrived."

Aura stepped inside behind Donovan and immediately felt it. The quiet authority of wealth. The house didn't glitter or shout. It didn't need to. Everything was solid, deliberate, restrained. The sort of place where nothing was accidental and nothing was cheap.

Donovan gestured toward the seating, but Aura shook her head and remained standing, arms crossed loosely over her chest. Donovan leaned back against the mantle, perfectly at ease.

She noticed that.

"Donovan, my boy!" William called as he crossed the room and pulled him into a firm embrace. "Good of you to come visit. A shame you don't do so more often." He pulled back and fixed Donovan with a mildly reproachful look.

"Nice to see you too, William," Donovan replied with a grin, clapping him on the back. "I was planning on coming by a couple of months ago, but… things came up."

"Oh?" William said, his gaze shifting at once to Aura. His expression softened into polite curiosity. "And who is the young lady?"

Donovan stepped slightly aside. "This is Aura Black."

"I'm the things that came up," Aura said stiffly.

Donovan rolled his eyes. William chuckled, clearly amused.

He moved closer to her and took her hand, lifting it to brush his lips across her knuckles. "A pleasure, Miss Black."

"Just call me Aura, Mr. Hartly."

"Only if you call me William," he replied warmly.

He stepped back, studying her face with a thoughtful tilt of his head. "You remind me of my daughters," he said after a moment. "Something in your expression, I think."

"Thinking of adopting again, William?" Donovan teased.

William turned back to him with a grin. "There's always room for more."

"Adopting?" Aura asked, glancing between them.

Donovan sighed theatrically. "William more or less adopted me after I saved his life."

Aura's brow rose a fraction.

William laughed outright. "She doesn't believe you."

"It's not disbelief," Aura said. "It's common sense. I've heard too many heroic stories about him to accept them all."

"I assure you, this one is quite true," Willims said as he waved her to a seat, his humor fading.

Aura took the offered spot on the couch, brows creased in curiosity as she glanced between the two men.

William settled back into the opposite couch with a quiet sigh, folding his hands together as if bracing himself.

"I have two daughters," he began, his voice steady but softened by memory. "Celeste and Serenity. Both very different, both very dear to me. Celeste was my eldest. Stubborn, brilliant, and far too much like me for our own good." A faint smile touched his lips, then faded. "We argued. Over something that seems very small now. I raised my voice. Said things I should never have said to my child."

Aura watched him closely. She recognized that tone. The one people used when the moment replayed endlessly in their minds.

"She left that night," William continued. "Just… gone. No note. No word. I spent years searching for her. Hired detectives. Followed every rumor, every whisper. I was convinced that if I just tried hard enough, I could fix it."

Donovan remained silent, eyes forward. He'd heard parts of this before, but never all at once.

"A few years ago, I received word that she'd gone west," William said. "It wasn't much—barely more than a suggestion—but it was enough. I went myself. Foolish, perhaps, but I couldn't sit here any longer wondering."

Aura leaned forward slightly. "Did you find her?"

William shook his head slowly. "No. The trail vanished again. I don't know if she moved on… or if I was already too late."

The words hung heavy between them.

"I was preparing to return home," he went on. "The town I was in had no rail line, so I booked passage on a stagecoach to the nearest station. There were four other passengers. Ordinary folk. None of us expecting trouble."

His fingers tightened together.

"We were ambushed halfway there. Bandits. Efficient. Ruthless. They shot the driver first. Two of the passengers tried to run." His voice lowered. "They didn't make it."

Aura's jaw clenched.

"They took everything from us," William said. "Money, watches, rings. Then they lined us up. One by one." He swallowed. "When they ordered me to my knees, I knew I was about to die."

He paused, drawing a slow breath.

"I remember thinking, this is it. I've lost my daughter, and now I won't even live long enough to find out what became of her."

Aura felt something twist in her chest.

"I heard the gun go off," William said quietly. "But I wasn't the one who fell."

Aura's eyes flicked to Donovan.

"When I opened my eyes," William continued, "the man holding the gun was screaming. His weapon was gone. His hand… ruined." A faint, incredulous smile crossed his face. "And there stood Donovan. Calm as you please. Moving faster than I could follow."

Donovan shifted, uncomfortable with the attention.

"He disarmed every one of them," William said. "Didn't kill a single man. Had them bound and helpless in minutes. Then he took the reins of the stage and drove us himself to the next town. Stayed until authorities arrived. Made sure the other survivor and I were safe."

Aura stared at Donovan now, seeing him differently.

"I asked him why he did it," William said. "Why he risked himself for strangers."

Donovan exhaled through his nose. "You were in trouble."

William smiled at him fondly. "Exactly."

He turned back to Aura. "I insisted on repaying him. He refused. So, I bought him that motorcycle instead." His eyes twinkled. "I decided that if my daughter ever came home, I wanted to be able to tell her that at least one good thing had come out of my search."

Silence settled over the room.

Aura finally said, softly, "You never stopped looking for her."

"No," William replied. "And I never will."

He paused a moment.

"And that," William said, glancing back at Donovan, "is how this infuriating young man became family."

Aura looked at Donovan, really looked at him. The man who stepped into violence without hesitation. Who carried guilt that wasn't his. Who stayed when others ran.

"Five men," she murmured. "You could have been killed."

Donovan shrugged. "Seemed worth the risk."

Aura leaned back slowly, crossing her arms, eyes distant.

William and Donovan exchanged a quiet, knowing smile.

"She listens better to you than she does to me," Donovan muttered.

William chuckled. "Some people only hear truth when it isn't spoken about themselves."

"So," Donovan said at last, clearing his throat and rolling his shoulders back as if bracing himself, "when is Angela going to appear and tell me I'm unwelcome in her house?"

As if summoned, a cool, composed voice said from the doorway, "I hear my name being used recklessly again."

Angela Hartly stood framed in the doorway, tall and elegant, her posture impeccable. She moved with the ease of a woman accustomed to being obeyed without raising her voice. Her pale hair was swept up in an immaculate style, every pin in place, her gown understated but undeniably expensive. She surveyed the room in a single, practiced glance before her eyes landed squarely on Donovan.

"You," she said flatly.

"Angel," Donovan replied, unabashed, a grin spreading across his face as if he'd just been handed a gift instead of a reprimand.

Her mouth tightened then betrayed her. She crossed the room with deliberate steps, leaned in, and kissed his cheek despite herself.

Donovan took that as permission.

In the next instant, he had her swept up into a crushing embrace, lifting her clean off the floor. Angela let out an indignant yelp that dissolved into laughter.

"Put me down this instant!" she protested, smacking his shoulder with far less force than her tone suggested.

"Only if you promise to leave William and run away with me," Donovan said cheerfully, waggling his brows.

"Oh, you are impossible," she declared, though she was still laughing when he finally set her back on her feet.

Aura, watching the exchange, rolled her eyes heavenward. Families, she decided, were exhausting.

Once everyone had settled again—Angela beside William, Aura beside Donovan—William's expression shifted. The warmth didn't leave his eyes, but his posture straightened, his hands folding together.

"As much as we'd hoped your visit was purely social," he said calmly, "your letter suggested urgency."

Donovan nodded, the humor draining from his face. "We're looking for my uncle. His trail led here."

Angela's brows knit at once. "Your uncle?" she repeated. "Why not involve the authorities?"

"Because," Donovan replied evenly, "they wouldn't survive him."

The bluntness of it left a brief silence in its wake.

William's gaze slid to Aura, sharpening slightly, not suspicious, but assessing. "And you, my dear?"

"He murdered my mother," Aura said.

The words landed clean and final.

Angela was on her feet before anyone could stop her. She crossed the space and gathered Aura into her arms with a soft gasp, one hand smoothing Aura's hair instinctively.

"Oh, you poor child," she murmured. "How unspeakably cruel."

Aura went utterly still.

Not in fear. Not in resistance.

In confusion.

She had no reflex for this, no instinctive defense, no script for comfort freely given without expectation. Her hands hovered uselessly at her sides.

"How long ago was this?" Angela asked, brows knitting in maternal concern.

"I was a child," she said quietly.

Angela made a small, wounded sound, her grip tightening.

William rose quickly. "Angel," he said gently but firmly, placing a hand on his wife's arm. "Let her breathe."

Reluctantly, Angela stepped back, still looking stricken. Aura exhaled slowly and shot Donovan a glare sharp enough to cut glass.

He only smiled at her, unrepentant and entirely unhelpful.

Hospitality was offered. Declined politely. Overruled immediately.

"You'll stay here," William said, his tone leaving no room for argument.

"And you'll attend the ball at the end of the week," Angela added, her distress already transmuting into brisk enthusiasm.

Donovan's eyes lit up. "Aura doesn't own any dresses."

"No," Aura said instantly. "That is not happening."

Angela smiled, the serene, confident smile of a woman who had won battles long before they were declared. "We'll see."

Donovan's grin turned dangerous.

Moments later, he rose and steered William toward the doorway, one arm draped companionably over the older man's shoulders. Aura watched him lean in and whisper something that made William bark out a laugh.

Her eyes narrowed.

CHAPTER 26

Torture. That was the only word for it. Plain and simple.

The yanking, the pulling, the pinching, the stretching. She might as well have been strapped into a medieval rack. Aura was fairly certain she was moments away from confessing to crimes she hadn't committed if it didn't stop. And she'd thought being shot hurt.

She stood in the center of Angela Hartly's dressing room while Angela and her long-suffering maid, Lizzy, subjected her to the ordeal of becoming *presentable*. Angela had been up at dawn preparing herself for the ball; the remainder of the day had been set aside exclusively for Aura. She claimed she didn't trust anyone — including Lizzy, who had served her faithfully for over thirty years — to do Aura justice without supervision.

Aura suspected it was simply an excuse to oversee every detail personally.

They bathed her, layered her into garments she'd never known existed, tugged and fastened until she could barely breathe, then turned their attention to her hair and face. The makeup was minimal, just enough to accent what was already there. The emerald silk gown had been chosen to match the velvet choker Aura refused to remove. Emerald drops adorned her ears, catching the light when she moved.

The gown required only minor alterations: the hem shortened to fit Aura's height, the bodice let out to accommodate her generous curves. Otherwise, it fit as though it had been made for her, the narrow waist flaring into full skirts, sleeves slipping just off her shoulders, the neckline dipping low enough to be indecent without crossing the line.

Green satin slippers and long white gloves completed the transformation.

"Lovely," Angela breathed when they finally stepped back. "Just lovely. I'm so glad we worked around the cameo. It suits you beautifully. It reminds me of one I gave Celeste when she was a girl."

Aura flushed harder.

"Oh, do stop blushing, dear," Angela laughed. "You have such a beautiful complexion."

Aura barely recognized the woman staring back at her from the mirror. She had always known she was attractive — that had never been in question — but this was something else entirely. If not for the scar on her cheek, she might have believed she was looking at a stranger.

"I think Donovan will be quite pleased," Angela added smugly.

Aura snorted. "More likely he'll insist I stay here so he doesn't have to kill every man in attendance."

Angela's smile faltered. "Is he truly that jealous?"

"I wouldn't call it jealousy," Aura said. "More like a deeply ingrained urge to protect people whether they want it or not. It's only gotten worse since I was shot."

Angela stiffened. "Shot?"

"By his uncle," Aura said simply. "Donovan took care of me while I recovered." She paused, then scowled. "Correction. He bossed me around while I recovered."

Angela laughed softly. "Yes. That does sound like Donovan."

Angela studied her for a long moment. "May I ask, what is your relationship with him?"

Aura's jaw tightened. "We're hunting the same man."

"And that's all?"

Color crept into Aura's cheeks again. She looked away. "I don't know what it is."

Angela squeezed her hand gently. "That's alright, dear. Some feelings take time to sort."

A maid appeared in the doorway. "Madam, the gentlemen are waiting in the parlor."

Angela straightened. "Come along, my dear."

They descended the stairs together and as they reached the bottom step, Donovan appeared in the parlor doorway alongside William.

Donovan stopped dead.

For a long moment, he simply stared.

"Good God," he breathed. "You're beautiful."

Aura gave him a crooked smile. Behind her, Angela looked smug.

He looked damned good himself, Aura admitted. Black formalwear emphasized the breadth of his shoulders, the cut of the jacket clean and elegant over his powerful frame. His white shirt was crisp, his bolo tie understated. His hair had been brushed back, though already rebelling at his temples, and his Stetson sat in his hand like an extension of him.

He shook his head slowly. "I don't know how you keep surprising me when I already know how beautiful you are," he said softly. "But you just did."

"Didn't I tell you?" Angela murmured.

"Well, hell," Donovan muttered. "I'm taking my gun. You're going to get mobbed."

Aura laughed outright at Angela's horrified expression. "Is this where I say I told you so?"

"No," Angela said primly. "You said he wouldn't let you leave the house."

Donovan grinned. "Now there's an idea."

William cleared his throat pointedly. "We cannot very well waste all this effort. Let's go."

Donovan took Aura's hand, lifting it to his lips. "You'll save me a dance."

She sighed theatrically. "If I must."

His smile softened. "You take my breath away when you smile."

"I'm having trouble breathing myself," she shot back, eyeing him deliberately.

He leaned close. "Keep that up and we're not going anywhere."

***

Aura had not expected to enjoy herself.

That realization struck her somewhere between her second dance and her fourth near altercation between overly eager gentlemen. She had entered the ballroom braced for scrutiny, contempt, or worse, recognition. Instead, she found herself laughing. Moving. Breathing easier than she had in days.

The music swept her along, lively and elegant, the kind that carried a body whether it wished to go or not. Her partners were competent enough, some better than others, and she quickly learned which smiles were harmless and which needed careful management.

What unsettled her most was how *easy* it was.

No bargaining.

No calculation.

No careful guarding of tone or posture to avoid provoking the wrong kind of interest.

They looked at her as if she were a prize. As if she were untouched by anything ugly.

And that… that terrified her.

She caught Donovan watching her from across the room more than once. Every time their eyes met, something in her chest tightened with a dangerous warmth she didn't trust. His expression never quite settled. Pride, hunger, irritation, something darker beneath it all. He stayed close, circling like a tether she hadn't agreed to but didn't entirely resent.

When he cut in to rescue her from her admirers, she should have been annoyed.

Instead, relief slid through her like a guilty pleasure.

"You're enjoying yourself?" he asked casually as they turned through thc steps.

"Yes," she admitted before she could stop herself. Then, because she couldn't ever leave a truth unqualified, she added, "At least until I remember how differently they'd look at me if they knew."

She watched his jaw tighten.

There it is, she thought. *The moment the illusion cracks.*

But he only sighed. "You're not doing this tonight."

"I wasn't planning on it." She wasn't lying. Not entirely. But the thought lingered anyway, coiling tight behind her ribs. How easily admiration could sour. How fast kindness turned once truth entered the room.

He smiled then, brighter, pulling her closer as if proximity alone could banish the idea. His hand was warm at her back, steady. Confident.

Too confident.

Dancing with him felt different from dancing with anyone else. Not because he was better — though he was — but because he didn't look at her like she was something to be *won*. He looked at her like she was something already claimed.

That should have angered her.

Instead, it made her pulse stutter.

Careful, she warned herself. *This is how you forget who you are.*

***

By the time the third man proposed, Aura barely blinked.

Marriage. Always marriage. As if possession were the natural conclusion to attraction. As if a ring could erase everything she carried beneath her skin.

She smiled politely. Declined gently. She was practiced at this.

Still, each offer left a faint bruise, not because she wanted them, but because some small, traitorous part of her wondered what it would feel like to say yes without consequence. To be chosen without calculation. To be wanted without debt.

"You must let me call on you," her current partner nearly begged. "Tea, dinner, anything."

That was when Donovan appeared behind her, voice cutting sharp through the noise.

"She's otherwise occupied."

Her first instinct was irritation.

Her second, shamefully, was relief.

Without another word, he took her hand in his and led her away.

He didn't slow, didn't glance back to see if she was following willingly. He simply took her wrist and led her through the tall glass doors, out onto the patio and into the cool night air beyond.

The music dulled behind them, replaced by the soft hush of the garden. Lantern light glimmered against stone paths and low hedges. The scent of flowers hung heavy in the air.

He stopped abruptly near the railing.

Aura stumbled a half step closer before catching herself. He was still holding her wrist. Too tight.

She had the distinct impression he'd forgotten he was doing it.

"You know," she said lightly, because anger would only escalate him, "if he finds us again, he might call for pistols or some such foolish thing. Considering he probably thinks I didn't come with you willingly."

Donovan made a strangled sound that was half laugh, half groan.

"And if he does," she continued, eyes flicking to his face, "we both know you'll shoot him first, and then I'll have to do something truly ridiculous. Like marry him out of sympathy."

That got his attention.

He finally turned to face her and released her wrist. Aura rubbed it absently, more out of principle than pain.

"And all of that," she finished calmly, "could have been avoided if you'd just let me tell him no myself."

"Would you have?" he asked.

He hadn't moved closer, but his voice had dropped. Careful. Controlled. Dangerous.

Aura snorted. "That's a stupid question."

He turned fully now, frowning down at her. "I thought it was rather pertinent. You did seem to be enjoying his company."

"And I was," she said without apology. "That doesn't mean I intended to accept his proposal."

His brow snapped upward. "Proposal?"

She blinked at him. "He asked me to marry him."

Silence.

Then — "I'm going to kill him."

Donovan spun back toward the doors.

Aura caught his arm and hauled him to a stop. "The hell you are! Are you out of your mind?"

She planted herself in front of him, blocking his path. "Are you going to kill the others who proposed too?"

His gaze shot back down to her. "Others?"

"Yes. Others." She folded her arms. "Three of them, Donovan. And I didn't take a single one seriously."

His jaw tightened. His hands flexed at his sides.

"That wouldn't stop a persistent man from trying to change your mind."

She rolled her eyes. "You've been around me all this time and you still haven't figured out that if a man presses too hard, he gets my gun shoved in his gut?"

He turned away again but this time toward the railing instead of the ballroom. His hands gripped the iron, knuckles whitening.

"I'm not deluding myself," she said more quietly, "into thinking I can have anything to do with these people past tonight. You may like to conveniently forget what I am, but I don't have that luxury."

"You don't understand," Donovan said, his voice lower now, strained. "It doesn't matter what *you* think. They'll pursue you anyway."

She scoffed softly. "If it comes to that, I'll tell them the truth. That will put an end to it."

He turned sharply. "It won't matter! Half the men in there would want you anyway."

She laughed, genuinely laughed this time. She couldn't help it. The sound surprised even her.

Donovan stared at her like she'd lost her mind.

"I hate to break it to you, Donovan," she said once her laughter had died down, "but most people don't think the way you do. And I *know* it bothers you, too. You just like to ignore that fact."

"What *bothers* me," he said tightly, "is that you use it to belittle yourself."

"I'm being honest."

"No," he snapped. "You're guessing. And you're wrong more often than you think."

She shook her head slowly. "It doesn't matter. Even if I wanted something different, I wouldn't allow it to go any further."

"But you *would* like it to."

The words were quiet. Almost reluctant.

She met his gaze.

"I can wish all I want that things had been different," she said softly. "That doesn't change what is and I'm fine with what I have."

"And what do you have, then?" he demanded. "Besides your revenge?"

Her smile was sad but steady.

"A couple of trinkets from my parents. My horse. A few good memories." She shrugged. "It might not be much, but it's mine."

Donovan stepped toward her then, hands lifting to cup her face. His touch was gentle, reverent.

"But you're not alone," he said. "You have family. With those women. And with me."

He kissed her, tender, possessive, restrained.

"I—"

"Donovan! There you are, my boy!"

They broke apart instantly as William stepped through the doors, cheerful as ever.

Donovan had been summoned to play for the guests.

Aura watched him cross the room, hat tilted low, confidence rolling off him, and for the first time, she wondered what it would mean to belong somewhere like this.

And what it would cost her.

CHAPTER 27

Donovan sat at the piano, flexed his fingers for effect—though he didn't actually need to—and smiled at the room. The hostess had stopped the music to introduce their newest entertainment, and the attention of every guest had settled on him.

He took a breath and began pounding out a lively tune, something more suited to a saloon than a ballroom. It was simple at first, easy, the sort of piece anyone with a little skill could manage. But as he played, the rhythm shifted. The melody grew more complex, the tempo quickening, the notes layering until his fingers were flying over the keys.

The audience clapped along, cheers rising as his hands blurred. Then, gradually, the tempo slowed. The tune transformed into something softer, more classical. The shift was seamless. The melody grew wistful, almost sad, and Donovan closed his eyes as he played.

The room fell silent.

It was his favorite piece despite the fact that his mother had taught it to him.

After the surgery that had replaced his hands, piano had been used as physical therapy. It had taught him how to move again. How to *think* again. Cybernetic fingers could move far faster than human ones but retraining his mind to control them had taken time. Their parents had done the same with Janice, though she'd gravitated toward the violin instead.

Donovan had kept the piano—and the guitar—long after their deaths, simply for the love of music. All three siblings were accomplished musicians. Trevor had focused on guitar alone, knowing he lacked the same dexterity and preferring not to compete with the piano or violin.

And when the three of them played together—

Nothing in the world compared to it.

The final chord rang out. Applause exploded through the room.

Grinning, Donovan stood and threw his arms wide in an exaggerated bow. Laughter and cheers followed. When he straightened, his eyes lifted automatically, searching for Aura.

Instead, they locked onto someone else.

The grin vanished.

Luc stood near the patio doors at the back of the room, clapping slowly. He wore a broad smile, though there was nothing pleasant about it.

A low growl tore from Donovan's chest.

He vaulted off the stage and shoved through the crowd, barely catching sight of Luc slipping through the doors before the bodies closed in again. Donovan burst onto the patio just in time to see Luc descend the stairs into the garden.

He followed.

Luc stood in the glow of an upper window, arms crossed, waiting. He grinned, expecting Donovan to follow.

Donovan stopped several paces away, fists clenched, rage burning through him. He wanted to beat Luc bloody. To kill him for what he'd done to Aura.

But there were too many questions.

And dead men didn't answer them.

"What are you doing here, Luc?" Donovan demanded tightly.

"Recruiting," Luc said mildly, shrugging. "And now that I'm finished, I'll be heading back west."

"Recruiting who?"

Luc only grinned. "How's the pretty little bird? Didn't ruffle her feathers too badly, did I?"

"If you mean Aura, she's inside," Donovan snarled. "Would you like me to get her? I'm sure she'd *love* to see you."

Luc chuckled. "No. Let's keep this conversation between family."

"Then tell me why you're doing this."

Luc clicked his tongue. "You haven't figured it out yet? I left you so many clues." He tilted his head, studying Donovan. "I do like to see who notices. It tells me what I'm working with. Such a shame you didn't inherit your father's intelligence. He was nearly as smart as me."

The words caught, wrong in a way Donovan couldn't place.

He shoved it aside. "Don't talk about my father."

Luc ignored him, studying Donovan's face. "You look like him. Your mother's eyes, though."

"I don't care what I look like. They're dead and I'm glad."

Luc smiled faintly. "Expected."

"Stop evading."

"You don't really think I'm going to explain myself, do you?" Luc laughed. "That would make things easy. No, boy, you'll just have to wait."

"What the hell are you talking about, old man?"

Luc's brows lifted. "No need for insults."

Donovan flushed. It was a cheap shot but being called "boy" was irritating him.

"I suppose you told your siblings about me?"

"You think I wouldn't?"

"Were they surprised?"

"To say the least."

"And little Trevor?" Luc mused. "He was such a quiet child."

"He wants you dead."

Luc chuckled. "And Janice? As pretty as your mother?"

"Why do you care?"

"You're family," Luc shrugged. "Curiosity, that's all."

Then his smile sharpened.

"And the little whore? Is she as good as she looks?"

Donovan growled.

"I remember her mother," Luc continued. "Pretty thing. Unsatisfying. Had to kill her before I finished."

"Stop it."

"Glad I didn't kill the girl. She's better. Fighters always are."

"Luc—"

"Maybe I'll go find her." Luc's smile turned vicious. "I like it when they fight."

That was it.

Donovan lunged, driving his fist hard into Luc's ribs—and hit metal. The impact rang up his arm, wrong and jarring, something in his hand giving with a sharp, unnatural crack that stopped him cold.

That wasn't supposed to happen.

Luc smiled. “Oh,” he said lightly. “You didn’t know? You *are* behind.”

Then he moved.

The backhand came fast—too fast—and Donovan barely registered the motion before it connected, the force snapping his head to the side as the world exploded into white.

***

Aura had been stunned by Donovan’s playing.

She’d known he was good with a guitar—she’d heard that much already—but this was something else entirely. The room faded away as his fingers flew over the keys, the music shifting beneath his hands from lively to mournful, playful to devastating. It wrapped around her chest and squeezed, pulling at something she hadn’t realized was still raw.

She hadn’t looked away once.

So, she didn’t miss it when he straightened from his bow and went unnaturally still.

The grin vanished from his face like it had been cut away.

Her stomach dropped.

Her gaze followed his, straight to the back of the room.

Luc.

He looked… *natural*. Dressed like everyone else. Blended in. Smiling as if he belonged there.

The thought chilled her.

When Donovan vaulted off the stage and shoved through the crowd, panic hit hard enough to steal her breath.

“What’s the matter, dear?” Angela asked, concern sharpening her voice.

Aura barely heard her. “I need air,” she said hoarsely, already moving.

She shoved through bodies that suddenly felt too slow, too solid, every second stretching thin and brittle with urgency. By the time she reached the patio doors, Donovan was already gone—and so was Luc.

Her hands were shaking as she slipped out of sight of the ballroom, fingers flying to her skirt. She didn’t hesitate. She hiked the fabric up, drew the revolver strapped to her thigh, and barely registered the relief that she hadn't left it behind before she was moving again, taking the stairs two at a time.

Donovan shouted.

The sound ripped through the garden, sharp and furious—and cut off too abruptly. Aura's heart slammed into her throat as the silence that followed rushed in to fill the space, her mind supplying the worst possibilities without hesitation. Blood. A fall. Donovan already down before she'd even made it outside.

She ran.

Rounding the hedge, she saw Luc first—standing there calm, impossibly calm, his gun angled downward as if the moment belonged entirely to him. Then her gaze snapped past him and found Donovan on the ground, motionless, wrong in a way that hollowed everything out of her chest.

Her vision tunneled as she fired. The recoil jolted up her arm, snapping through bone and muscle as Luc's gun flew from his hand. Relief surged hot and sharp—

until he turned.

Smiling.

"Pretty girl," he crooned, voice slick and intimate. "Just like your mother."

The words barely registered. Her finger tightened again without thought, the second shot cracking through the air and striking his temple.

Metal rang.

The sound didn't belong.

Her mind rejected it instantly, stumbling over the wrongness of it. No. That wasn't right. That wasn't how this ended.

Luc's head jerked slightly—nothing more—and then he laughed, the hollow sound stripping the air from her lungs.

"What… what are you?" she whispered, horror threading cold and sharp beneath the rage.

"Stupid girl," Luc said lightly, as if she were an inconvenience rather than a threat. "You'll have to choose."

The word hit like a detonation.

He pointed, casual, almost bored, toward Donovan's unmoving body, and for one sickening moment Aura couldn't tell if he was breathing, couldn't tell if she was already too late.

Luc bent, vanishing briefly behind the hedge.

Aura lurched forward instinctively, heart hammering—

and then he rose again, Donovan's hat in his hand.

Mocking.

"Me," he said pleasantly. "Or him."

Then he ran.

Aura took two steps after him before instinct snapped hard in the other direction, her focus tearing free and locking back onto Donovan. He hadn't moved. Hadn't made a sound.

"Oh God."

She dropped beside him, hands shaking as she grabbed his shoulder and shoved. He was heavy—too heavy—and panic clawed up her throat as she tried again, harder, forcing him to respond.

He groaned.

Relief hit so hard it nearly folded her in half. When he rolled onto his back, she scanned him in quick, ruthless sweeps—no blood, bruising already blooming, dirt smeared across his face.

Alive.

The relief curdled almost instantly into anger.

Then she saw his hand—the split synthetic skin, the damage beneath—and something hot and vicious snapped into place.

"What did you do?" she demanded, her voice sharpening with it.

He spat blood and squinted at her. "Got punched."

She surged to her feet, pacing hard enough to bleed the excess out of her system. "You scared the hell out of me."

"I noticed," he muttered.

"You went after him alone."

"He was baiting me."

"And you took it," she snapped, spinning back on him. "He made me choose, Donovan. He made me choose."

He watched her, something shifting in his expression—something quieter, more dangerous in its certainty.

"You cared," he said softly.

Her temper exploded.

She shouted. Paced. Threw accusations she didn't fully believe—

because believing them hurt less than the truth.

When he laughed at the gun strapped to her thigh, she nearly shot him out of pure spite.

When she produced the snub-nose from her bodice, his laughter broke loose completely.

She stormed away, shaking with fury and relief and something terrifyingly close to loss.

Luc was gone.

Again.

And she hated—*hated*—that the choice he'd forced had come so easily.

Because she'd choose Donovan.

Every time.

CHAPTER 28

"He's a mod."

"What?" Trevor's voice cracked over the line, overlapping with Janice's sharp, "What the hell?" as both of them spoke at once.

"A mod," Donovan repeated grimly, flexing his damaged hand once before letting it hang.

"How do you know?" Trevor demanded.

Donovan let out a short breath. "I punched him. Broke my hand. Aura shot him in the head and he didn't die. And before he knocked me out, he confirmed it. That enough proof for you?"

The silence that followed wasn't disbelief—it was recalibration.

"How much of him?" Janice asked at last, her tone quieter now, focused.

"Enough," Donovan said flatly. "At least half his head, one hand, most of his side. Possibly more."

"Well, damn," Trevor muttered.

"That changes nothing," Janice cut in immediately. "We're still killing him."

Donovan huffed a breath. "That's exactly what Aura said."

There was a beat—then Janice's voice snapped back to full volume. "You mean I agree with that whore?"

"The whore agrees with you, bitch," Aura said from beside him, her tone low and lethal.

Janice barked out a laugh, clearly delighted by that, and despite himself, Donovan felt the corner of his mouth lift. It didn't last. Not with the way Aura had gone cold again the second she'd spoken.

"We're leaving today," he said, dragging the conversation back on track. "Luc told me he's finished here and heading west."

"You believe him?" Trevor asked.

"He wants us following him," Donovan replied. "He's never tried to hide. No reason to start now."

"Is it just me," Janice said, irritation creeping back in, "or does our uncle make absolutely no sense?"

"Insanity rarely does," Trevor answered dryly.

"At least I got my gun back," Donovan muttered. "He doesn't get to use it on anyone else."

"He doesn't need a gun to hurt people," Aura said quietly.

Donovan glanced at her. "No," he agreed. "But it felt damn personal when he used mine." His hand rose absently to where his hat should have been, then stilled. "Figures he'd steal my hat and leave me alive."

The memory sat wrong.

They'd left the ball early. Aura had handled the Hartly's with practiced ease while Donovan stayed out of sight, the bruise already darkening across his face. William had promised to smooth things over, and this morning he'd gone ahead to the station to secure their tickets.

"Did you find anything else at the compound?" Donovan asked.

Trevor exhaled slowly. "I pulled some of Dad's files. Didn't read them there. Something about that place made my skin crawl."

"Bring them to Tony's," Donovan said. "If there's anything on Luc, it'll be in there."

"I didn't even know they were experimenting on him," Trevor admitted. "I didn't know about any of it until it was my turn."

"They kept it from us until they couldn't," Donovan said quietly.

"I knew," Janice added. "I was younger, but not stupid."

The line sat silent but pregnant.

"Be careful," Donovan said finally. "Luc isn't done."

The line went dead.

Donovan lowered his hand slowly and turned toward Aura. "You've been quiet."

"Nothing worth saying."

He didn't buy that for a second. He could feel it in the tension running through her—tight, controlled, waiting to snap.

"What did he say to you?" he asked.

"Drop it."

She turned away.

He moved before he thought about it, catching her arm just as she reached the stairs. "What's wrong?"

"Nothing."

"That's a lie."

Her eyes flashed. "Leave it alone."

"No." His voice hardened. "I won't let you shut down again."

"What am I to you?" she snapped, jerking against his grip. "A project? Something to fix?"

"That's not—"

"I never asked for your help!"

"But you needed it."

The words landed wrong the second they left his mouth.

Her laugh was sharp, cutting. "You force yourself into people's lives because they wouldn't come to you otherwise." She stepped in close, voice dropping, deliberate. "You and I are more alike than you want to admit."

Then she struck where it would hurt most.

"They wouldn't want anything to do with you either," she said coldly, "if they knew what you really were."

The words hit like a physical blow.

Donovan didn't move. Didn't speak. He just stood there, the words settling in, reshaping something he hadn't realized was still fragile.

Aura turned and walked away, leaving him with it.

His fist met the wall before he realized he'd moved, the impact cracking through plaster and sending the portraits rattling against their hooks. Dust sifted down in a soft, steady fall as Donovan dragged in a breath and looked at the damage—

then froze.

The portrait beside the hole pulled at him, insistent enough that he stepped closer without thinking.

Celeste. William's lost daughter.

He'd seen the painting before. Never really looked.

Now he did.

Pale blonde hair. Green eyes. The soft curve of her mouth, the fullness of her figure—and there, resting at her throat, the cameo.

His stomach dropped.

Luc's voice echoed in his mind.

Remember her mother.

Donovan stared, the pieces shifting into place with a slow, sickening certainty. The resemblance wasn't exact—the lines didn't match perfectly—but it didn't need to. The eyes. The bone structure. Close enough to haunt.

Aura's mother had come from the east.

Aura wore that cameo every day.

My God.

If he was wrong, he would shatter people who didn't deserve it.

If he was right—

Aura wasn't alone.

She never had been.

And she might never forgive him for telling her.

Donovan stepped back slowly, forcing distance between himself and the painting, between himself and the conclusion pressing in on him.

Not now. Not with Luc still breathing.

He turned and descended the stairs in silence.

Aura waited in the entry, distant and guarded, her expression already closed off again. Neither of them spoke as they stepped out into the street, the space between them heavier than before.

And the truth followed him.

A weight he wasn't ready to carry out loud.

CHAPTER 29

Aura sat in silence as the train rattled along the tracks, staring out the window at the passing scenery though she didn't really see any of it. Her foot was propped on the seat, her elbow resting on her raised knee, fingers pressed absently to her lips as she brooded. Donovan sat across from her, just as silent.

She knew he was staring at her, though she didn't look to confirm it. She could feel his eyes on her. His silence made her feel even more guilty than she already did.

Her comment in Brookstone had been cruel. She knew it. She'd wanted to hurt him in that moment and she'd succeeded. The knowledge sat heavy in her chest.

But he had pushed her when she wasn't ready. She'd been too raw, too tangled in the aftermath of the garden. Angry that Luc had escaped. Angry that he had tricked her into thinking Donovan was gravely injured. Angry that Donovan had gone after him alone. Angry that he hadn't come for her first.

But worse than all of that.

She had been terrified.

Terrified when she thought Donovan was hurt. Terrified enough that she'd hesitated. Terrified enough that Luc had slipped away again.

She wasn't supposed to care. She was supposed to use Donovan to get to Luc, then leave without a backward glance. Instead, she was drowning in guilt because she'd hurt him and she'd seen it land. The shock. The pain. She'd hit something tender.

He was too perceptive. He knew she wasn't truly furious about losing Luc. And that realization infuriated her all over again.

Why *wasn't* she more upset?

She'd shot Luc in the head and he'd walked away. That should have consumed her. Instead, her thoughts had been filled with Donovan, his body on the ground, the relief when he moved, the rage that he'd put himself in danger.

There hadn't been room for Luc after that.

She'd lashed out to make him stop pressing her for answers she didn't have. She wasn't ready to admit—to herself or anyone else—that her fear had a name.

She'd barely admitted to herself that she cared. She certainly wasn't going to tell him. Distance was necessary. Distance was survival. When this was over, she planned to disappear somewhere quiet and forgettable, where she couldn't poison anyone else with what she was.

Some might call that noble.

She knew better. It was cowardice.

And in that, she and Donovan were painfully alike.

People turned away when they knew the truth. Every time it happened, it hurt. So, she built walls. Brick by brick. Careless cruelty was faster than honesty.

And Donovan kept tearing the wall down anyway.

God, if only he didn't feel like home.

They didn't speak for two days.

Aura's guilt grew heavier with every mile. She wasn't used to letting things sit this long—usually she snapped, then fixed it. Knowing she'd chosen cruelty and walked away instead made it worse.

By the third morning, her distress was written plainly on her face. Donovan didn't comment, but she knew he noticed. He always did.

She missed him. His teasing. His way of lightening the air. Some ridiculous remark that would make her laugh despite herself.

But she'd wounded him. So, if this silence was to end, she would have to be the one to break it.

Her throat tight, eyes burning, she finally spoke.

"Donovan?"

"Hm?"

Relief fluttered through her at the sound of his voice.

She turned to look at him. He was staring out the window.

"I'm really sorry," she said quietly.

"About what?"

Her brows knit. “About what I said. Back in Brookstone. I didn’t mean it.”

“Yes,” he said softly. “You did.”

“No. I didn’t. I said it because—because I didn’t want to talk about what was really bothering me.” She swallowed. “But it wasn’t true.”

He turned then, and she saw the guarded edge in his eyes.

“No,” he said evenly. “You were right. I’ve thought the same thing myself.”

Her chest tightened. “That’s not true. You’re loved. You’ve built families everywhere you go. People adore you, Donovan. Anyone who would turn away from you because of what your parents did isn’t worth your time.”

She looked away, missing the faint curve of his smile.

“Then tell me why you said it.”

“Because you wouldn’t let it go,” she said honestly. “And I still don’t want to talk about it.”

“Not good enough.”

She sighed. “I’m not ready. But I *am* sorry. And if you don’t forgive me, I might actually cry.”

That startled him.

“You’re that upset?”

She nodded.

He exhaled. “God. I forgave you days ago.”

She blinked. “Then why the silence?”

“I thought *you* needed space.”

They stared at each other, realization dawning.

“You could have said something,” she muttered.

“And you hadn’t apologized yet,” he countered gently. “It was a cruel remark, but I knew you were cornered.”

“So… I’m forgiven?”

He considered her, then smiled slowly. “That depends.”

Her eyes narrowed. “On what?”

“Well,” he said lightly, “you haven’t finished the apology.”

Understanding sparked and heat followed.

She rose, crossed the narrow space between them, and climbed into his lap. His breath caught as she straddled him, hands braced beside his head.

“Promise you’ll forgive me,” she whispered.

"I'll promise you anything you want," he said hoarsely.

Her lips brushed his, retreating just enough to torture him.

"Say it."

"I forgive you."

She smiled, brilliant, devastating, and then she kissed him.

He wrapped his arms around her instantly, pulling her close. Her body pressed against his, her breath hitching as desire surged. She rocked against him without thinking, her moan loud enough to make him groan in return.

Reality intruded a moment later, the car swaying as it rounded a curve.

They broke apart, breathless.

"One hell of an apology," he murmured.

She grinned. "As long as I'm forgiven."

"Completely. Though next time, maybe pick a better location."

She slid off his lap, but he caught her wrist and pulled her close again, arm settling around her shoulders possessively.

"When this is over," he said quietly, "we're having a serious conversation."

She snorted. "You? Serious?"

He chuckled. "For you, I'll try."

She leaned into him despite herself.

"And Donovan?" she added softly.

"Yes?"

"…Thank you."

He kissed her temple.

The train rattled on.

CHAPTER 30

"Welcome home, honey!" Tony called just before sweeping Aura up in a tight hug.

He released her almost immediately when Donovan growled low in his throat. Tony shot him an incredulous look. "Still? Honey, you need to sleep with him already. He's not gonna be agreeable until you do."

Donovan's cheeks flushed and Aura shook her head, momentarily too startled to respond to anything else.

"Home?" she asked instead.

"Of course," Tony said easily, grinning at her. "Donovan told me you don't have one, so I decided— which makes it official —that this is your home. Means you're as welcome here as they are." He nodded toward Donovan, then Trevor.

The word settled strangely in her chest.

Home.

She smiled, though something tight twisted beneath it. A home to return to. Not that she would ever take him up on it once Luc was dealt with. She wouldn't be staying.

Still… the thought lingered.

Trevor smiled at her. "Welcome back, angel. None the worse for wear, I trust?"

"For the most part," Aura said, returning the smile. "Donovan can't say the same."

"How bad's the damage?" Tony asked eagerly.

Donovan lifted his hand for inspection. "Not as bad as I thought. A couple fragile components shattered, some dents, a few misaligned knuckles. Still functional, just awkward."

Tony hummed approvingly. "That's my favorite kind of problem. Let's get you in the back."

They moved deeper into the garage. Aura would have hung back, but Trevor's hand at the small of her back guided her along before she could object.

Donovan settled sideways into the old dental chair Tony used for maintenance, resting his damaged hand on the table beside it. Aura winced when Tony peeled the synthetic skin back without ceremony.

Donovan noticed her reaction and glanced up, surprised to see her still there. He smiled reassuringly and reached out, catching her hand and pulling her down beside him. His grip tightened just enough to keep her from pulling away.

"Moral support," he said lightly.

Tony snorted. "Moral support, my ass. You just don't want her out of your sight."

"Damn right," Donovan said. "And Tony, I don't care if you're my best friend. touch her again and I'll rearrange your face."

Aura's brow shot up. Tony only chuckled.

"Relax," Trevor said dryly. "Tony's not stealing your girl."

"Shows how much you know," Tony replied cheerfully.

"You wouldn't steal your best friend's girl," Trevor said.

"That depends," Tony shrugged. "She hasn't declared herself yet. Just 'cause Donny says she's his doesn't mean she agrees."

"She damn well agrees," Donovan growled.

"The hell I do," Aura snapped.

"There you go," Tony said brightly. "Still fair game."

"The hell she is!" Donovan shouted.

"At this rate," Trevor emphasized mildly, "she's going to turn both of you down."

Aura glared at Donovan, tugging again at her hand. He didn't release her.

"We've been getting along fine the last few days," he said quietly. "Do you really want to go back to arguing?"

She didn't. But she also wasn't going to let him speak for her.

"Next time," she said tightly, "ask what I think instead of answering for me."

He studied her a moment, then nodded stiffly and turned back to Tony.

Tony hadn't stopped working. "Almost done."

A thin line of blood slipped down Donovan's hand. Aura stiffened.

"It doesn't hurt?" she asked.

"No," he said softly, squeezing her hand. "I'm good."

He looked to Trevor. "Any new trails?"

"Nothing," Trevor said. "He's gone quiet."

"And the files?"

"Some are corrupted. Haven't gone through them all yet."

Tony finished sealing the synthetic skin. Donovan flexed his fingers, relief evident. "Perfect. As always."

They regrouped at the terminal. Aura stood behind Trevor, watching the screen. Tony took the other chair, leaning aside to keep Donovan's view clear.

Most of the files were useless. A few schematics matched the siblings' known modifications.

One set did not.

Luc.

The scope of it stunned them.

"Jesus," Tony muttered.

An audio file flickered on the screen. Trevor hesitated, then played it.

Donovan went rigid instantly.

"Our father," he said flatly when Aura leaned in.

The voice crackled through static.

"…Subject 01 progressing… alignment issues corrected… Subject 02 recovering… physical therapy once arms—"

Static.

"…begun plans for 03… hesitant about extent… months to complete… not as extensive as Subject Zero…"

Aura's breath caught.

"…one year until she… material accepted… problems with 02's joints resolved in 03… weaponization rejected…"

The recording dissolved into noise.

Donovan's fist slammed into the terminal.

The screen shattered.

"Hey!" Tony barked. "I just fixed that!"

"I'll buy you a new one," Donovan said without turning.

"I meant your hand!"

Donovan was already halfway up the stairs.

Trevor swore softly. Aura stared after him.

"I should've listened first," Trevor said.

"Would it have mattered?" Aura asked.

"I wouldn't have let him hear it," Trevor admitted. "He always took it hardest."

"Why?" she asked quietly.

"He thinks it makes him less than human," Trevor said. "What they did to us."

Aura's gaze lingered on the stairs.

"I thought he was getting past that," Trevor added. "Hearing how clinical they were… This is going to hurt him all over again."

Aura didn't answer.

But something cold and resolute settled in her chest.

CHAPTER 31

This was going to hurt him all over again.

Aura was moving before she consciously decided to. The thought of Donovan in pain—physical or otherwise—hit her hard and fast, sharp enough to steal her breath, followed by that same instinct she still didn't fully trust: the need to fix it, to steady him, to make it stop.

She didn't hesitate.

She took the stairs quickly, not quite running until the crash came—sharp, violent—somewhere ahead of her. Glass shattered. She flinched, then broke into a full run, rounding the corner and stopping hard in Donovan's doorway, fingers gripping the frame.

He was hunched over the dresser, elbows braced, head in his hands. A shattered vase lay behind him, water streaking down the wall.

"Donovan," she said softly.

A rough, strangled sound left him, but he didn't turn.

She closed the door behind her and crossed the room, slower now. Careful. When she touched his shoulder, he jerked upright, and she caught the look on his face before he could hide it.

Pain. Raw. Unguarded.

"Are you alright?"

"I already thought the worst of them," he said, voice tight. "I didn't need it confirmed."

He dragged a hand over his face—and she saw it.

The torn synthetic skin across his knuckles. Blood, still wet along his fingers.

"Your hand—" She reached for the cloth on the dresser and gently pulled his hand down, dabbing at it. The cuts had already stopped bleeding, but the sight of it made something twist deep in her chest.

"It doesn't matter," he muttered. "It's not real."

Her eyes snapped up to his.

That hurt him more than the injury did. She could see it—feel it.

"Donovan." She pressed his palm flat against her chest, right over her heart. "Can you feel that?"

His breath hitched. His fingers spread instinctively, pressing in.

"Yes," he whispered.

"Then it's real enough."

His eyes lifted to hers.

The pain was still there—but something else was rising beneath it now. Something sharper. Warmer. Urgent in a different way.

She cupped his face, thumbs brushing his cheeks. His hand stayed where she'd placed it, her heartbeat quickening beneath his palm.

He exhaled roughly and leaned down.

Aura met him halfway.

The kiss was soft at first—tentative, almost careful, as if neither of them wanted to push too far, too fast. Comfort. That's what it was supposed to be.

It didn't stay that way.

Her lips parted as his tongue pressed in, and the shift was immediate. The restraint snapped. His arms came around her, lifting her clean off the floor, pulling her hard against him.

She didn't think.

Her legs wrapped around his waist as his hands slid down, gripping her, pressing her against him. The heat of him, the pressure—it tore a sound from her she couldn't stop, and he answered it with one of his own.

He broke from her mouth only to find her throat, his lips dragging over her skin, his breath hot, uneven. Aura tipped her head back, fingers tightening in his hair as sensation chased down her spine.

"If anyone interrupts us this time," he muttered against her skin, voice rough, "I'm shooting first."

She let out a breathless, almost-laugh. "They'll get two bullets."

He smiled against her throat—and then his mouth was on hers again, harder now, any pretense of restraint gone.

Clothing became an afterthought.

Her blouse was gone before she registered the loss of it, his shirt following just as quickly. When his mouth closed over her, she arched into him, a sharp gasp leaving her as her hands tightened in his hair.

He didn't linger—couldn't. His hands were everywhere, moving, learning, as if he couldn't get enough of her fast enough.

They barely made it to the bed.

He tossed her down and followed, his weight settling over her, his gaze dragging over her in a way that made her breath catch again—hunger, yes, but something softer threaded through it.

She felt it.

And it undid her faster than anything else.

His hands moved over her—arms, waist, hips, down her legs and back again—slow enough to feel, fast enough to leave her restless beneath him, her body reacting before she could think, chasing every touch.

She didn't have words anymore.

Only need.

When he finally pressed between her thighs, the contact alone made her inhale sharply, her body already anticipating, already reaching for him. The first slow movement drew a broken sound from her, her hands tightening against his back as sensation flared bright and immediate.

He stilled for just a fraction of a second.

Then moved again.

Deeper.

Steady.

The rhythm built quickly—too quickly for anything else to exist. Her body answered without thought, rising to meet him, matching him, the friction, the pressure, the overwhelming closeness pulling her under faster than she could hold onto anything else.

Her breath broke. So did his.

The world narrowed to that single point—heat, motion, the relentless build of something she couldn't slow even if she'd wanted to.

She didn't.

Neither of them did.

When it broke, it shattered through her completely, leaving her breathless, shaking, clinging to him as everything else fell away.

For a while, neither of them moved.

Then Donovan shifted slightly, his lips brushing her cheek, her temple, the corner of her mouth—softer now, grounding, as if he needed to reassure himself she was still there.

Aura smiled faintly, her fingers tracing along his jaw, her chest still rising and falling too fast.

"Aura," he murmured. "That was—"

"Wonderful?" she offered quietly.

He let out a breath that was almost a laugh. "That doesn't even come close."

She pulled him down against her, holding him there, surprised at how right it felt—how much she didn't want to move.

"I know you've... done this more than I have," he said carefully. "But have you ever—"

"Never," she said immediately, lifting her head to meet his eyes. "Never like that."

His expression shifted—something warmer, brighter.

"That was perfect."

His smile came slow. "I like the sound of that."

She huffed a quiet breath. "I think you're fishing for compliments."

"I think once isn't going to be enough," he murmured.

She felt the shift before she fully registered it—his body already responding again—and her breath caught, a soft laugh escaping her.

"I think," she said, breathless, "you're right."

CHAPTER 32

Aura woke by slow degrees, squinting against the brightness flooding the room. It was well past midmorning, hardly surprising, considering they hadn't slept until nearly dawn. She rolled onto her back and stretched languidly, muscles pleasantly sore.

A glance to the side told her she was alone in the bed. Another, that she was alone in the room as well.

That, she supposed, was to be expected.

She didn't usually sleep this late. But she'd been… energetic the night before.

They'd spent the entire night tangled together, Donovan seemingly incapable of keeping his hands off her, and she hadn't tried very hard to stop him. She'd taken her time exploring every hard plane and familiar curve of his body, memorizing him by touch until she was certain she could find him blindfolded.

They'd only been interrupted once. Tony had banged on the door to ask whether they planned on coming up for dinner…or air. Donovan had shouted at him to get lost. They hadn't been disturbed again.

Aura pushed herself upright and ran her fingers through the tangled mass of her hair. She needed a shower. She needed food. They'd skipped both lunch and dinner yesterday, and her stomach was now making its objections known with enthusiasm.

Still, she wasn't quite ready to leave the bed where she'd experienced the most incredible pleasure of her life.

She closed her eyes, smiling faintly as the memory rose unbidden, heat, laughter, breathless whispers in the dark. She'd known sex with Donovan would be electric.

She hadn't known it would be explosive.

It hadn't just been the intensity. Something had shifted between them—quiet, undeniable—and she wasn't entirely sure what to do with it yet.

The door opened.

Her eyes slid open lazily and fixed on Donovan as he stepped inside, balancing two plates with practiced care. Her smile shifted, slow, sultry.

"I come bearing waffles," he announced, nudging the door shut with his foot.

"Waffles sound wonderful," Aura said, swinging her legs over the side of the bed and rising in one smooth, unselfconscious motion.

Completely naked.

Donovan sucked in a sharp breath and froze.

Aura crossed the room without hesitation, pressing herself lightly against him, one hand splayed over his bare chest. With the other, she dragged a finger through a pool of syrup on one of the plates, then lifted it to his mouth.

He didn't break eye contact as he closed his lips around her finger, drawing the syrup away. Aura rose onto her toes and kissed him, tasting sweetness and heat.

Donovan groaned softly into her mouth.

"God," he muttered. "You keep that up and we won't eat at all today."

Aura stepped back with a grin, plucked one plate from his hands, and turned away.

"Say that again," she tossed over her shoulder, "after I've already eaten."

She dropped onto the bed, settling the plate on her lap.

Donovan didn't move right away.

Aura noticed it absently at first, the way he stood there a little too still, the plate forgotten in his hand, his chest rising more deliberately as if he were bracing himself. His gaze followed her with open hunger, not subtle in the slightest.

The look made warmth curl low in her belly.

Good.

She bit into the waffle with deliberate enthusiasm, savoring both the taste and the effect she was having on him. If he was struggling, that was his problem. She'd had enough years of pretending not to notice desire. Her own or anyone else's.

When he finally moved, sitting at the foot of the bed, she caught the faint shake of his head, as if he were reining himself in. The knowledge pleased her more than it probably should have.

"These are really good," Aura said between bites. "Did Tony make them?"

"No," Donovan replied. "I did."

She looked up at him, genuinely surprised. "Really?"

"You find that hard to believe?" he asked, one corner of his mouth lifting.

"No. It's just, Tony's been doing all the cooking since I got here."

"That's because I didn't leave your side long enough to cook," Donovan said easily. "I can handle a few things. Tony's the better cook overall but he burns waffles every time. And I wanted waffles."

Aura laughed softly. "Then I'm very glad you did. These are delicious."

"Thank you."

Donovan watched her a moment longer than necessary, like he still wasn't entirely sure what to do with her now.

***

It was several hours more before they made their way downstairs. Tony was buried amidst the piles of junk in the garage, working on a project for one of the town's residents when he heard their laughter floating down the stairs ahead of them. He put down his tools, standing to lean against the bare frame of some forgotten project, and smiled lazily at them when they came into view.

"Well, it's about time," he called to them.

"That we came downstairs?" Aura asked him, brow raised.

"No. That you two slept together," he grinned. Donovan groaned behind her and Aura burst out laughing.

"Don't be jealous, Tony," Aura teased as they reached him. "Donovan found me first."

"Jealous? I couldn't be happier for you two!" Tony said, throwing an arm across her shoulders to hug her to him. "Just tell me when the wedding is and I'll start sending out invitations."

Aura scowled at him now and Donovan sighed heavily. "Tony, you can be such an ass."

"You mean you haven't asked her to marry you yet?" Tony asked, eyes wide in feigned surprise. "Then I guess there's still a chance for me!" Without warning, he scooped Aura up in his arms, giving her a loud kiss on the cheek. Aura shrieked in alarm.

"Put her down!" Donovan growled, taking a menacing step towards him.

"If you're not going to ask her, I'm going to keep her," Tony grinned at him, though he took a step back.

"Put me down, Tony!" Aura yelled at him. "He isn't going to ask me, and I wouldn't say yes even if he did." She tried to shove against his chest, but he had a firm hold on her and wasn't letting her go. He may have been slimmer than Donovan, but he was more than capable of holding on to her slight weight.

Tony ignored her comment as Donovan took another step towards them, fists clenched. He chuckled, """Careful, Donny—this seems like a bad idea for everyone involved. Is pummeling me worth it?"

Donovan stopped, lowering his fists, though they remained clenched at his sides. "I love you like a brother, Tony, but don't make me kill you."

Tony grinned again. "You know how to solve that, don't you." He took another step back and slowly released Aura's legs to set her back on her feet, keeping his eyes locked on Donovan. His hands rising to cup her cheeks, his eyes found her confused ones and he whispered, "This is for your own good."

His head dipped, but he stopped with a grin before his lips touched hers.

Donovan's fist still snapped his head back and sent him falling backwards. Donovan grabbed Aura about the middle before she could go down with him, and he pulled her tightly to his side. Tony was sitting on the ground laughing, completely ignoring his bloody nose.

Aura stared at him incredulously. "Are you insane?! He could have killed you!" She was shoving at the iron band about her waist, but Donovan wasn't releasing her any more than Tony had.

"Feel better?" Tony asked Donovan with a grin.

"Not until you convince me you're not going to try that again," Donovan said stiffly.

"I was just making a point, which you proved quite splendidly."

"And what point was that?" Donovan asked, ignoring Aura's attempts to free herself.

"That you can't stand the thought of anyone else touching her and that you're insecure in *her* affections. Which is why you need to marry her, so that you know where her affections lie."

"Would you two stop talking about me like I'm not here!" Aura ordered angrily. "I swear! I've never been manhandled this much in my life. Let go of me, Donovan!"

He looked down at her, his expression still angry, but finally he nodded and released her. Aura spun around and swung her closed fist at his face. It cracked against his cheek and Donovan cried out in surprise.

"What the hell was that for?" he demanded, his hand rising to his throbbing cheek.

Aura stood, arms akimbo, her dark eyes flashing angrily at him. "That was to remind you that you can't manhandle me," she growled at him, "and that I can take care of myself. I've had years of practice fending off unwanted attention. You didn't have to break his nose over me. For God's sake, he's your *best friend*!" She stalked past him and quickly mounted the stairs.

Donovan watched her leave, the surprise at her attack still on his face.

"Well, damn!" Tony chuckled from the floor. "Did she just defend me?"

Donovan tuned to scowl at Tony, though he reached out a hand to help his friend up. "I'm not sure if she's mad at me for manhandling *her*, or for hitting *you*. Is it really broken?" He indicated Tony's nose. The bleeding had stopped and Tony had wiped away the blood at some point during Aura's tirade. But Donovan could see that there was going to be bruising beneath both eyes, and he felt a bit guilty now.

"Damn near feels like it," Tony grumbled, lightly touching his nose with a wince.

"Sorry."

"Sorry I provoked you to it."

"Well, you sure as hell know how to ruin a morning," Donovan growled at him.

Tony grinned back. “Don’t let her pout too long or she’ll forget she’s supposed to be feeling pleased at your perfect display of jealousy.”

“Pleased? Why the hell would she be pleased?”

Tony shrugged. “It’s a female thing. They seem to think it means you feel more for them than just lust. Give a woman a reason to think you’re jealous and she’ll be crawling all over you to prove her affections are right where they belong. At least, it’s always worked that way for me.” He grinned again and Donovan rolled his eyes.

“You’re such a cad, Tony.”

“And the ladies just love it,” Tony said, wiggling his brows.

Donovan laughed. “I think you missed your calling, Tony. You should be in one of the big cities, seducing all the young society misses.”

“I’ve thought about it,” Tony admitted with a wicked grin, “but as much as I love the ladies, they take a back seat to family. You need me more.”

Donovan put an arm around Tony’s shoulders, giving him a quick squeeze. “I’m sure I speak for my siblings as well when I say, we’re glad you stuck around.”

“Well, hell!” Tony exclaimed, shoving Donovan off him. “Don’t get all mushy on me.” But he grinned at him. “Go get your lady out of her sulk so you can resume your pleasant day. I promise I’ll be on my best behavior from now on… Unless I feel you need another nudge.” Tony winked and Donovan rolled his eyes again, but he quickly bounded up the stairs.

Donovan was only slightly annoyed when he didn’t find Aura in his room. He opened the door to hers a second later and found her sitting cross-legged in the middle of the bed, staring pensively down at the blanket.

She spared him only a glance before saying stiffly, “I’m not ready to talk to you yet, Donovan.”

“That’s fine,” he said with a shrug. “I wasn’t planning on saying anything anyway.” He strode the few feet to the bed and quickly picked her up, ignoring her startled protests.

Aura’s temper flared instantly.

“Put me down, Donovan!” she yelled as he carried her from the room. “Didn’t we *just* talk about this?”

"I heard you," he said, not slowing.

"That doesn't mean you get to ignore it!"

He crossed the hall and entered his own room, depositing her on the bed.

She shoved away from him the second she touched the mattress.

He leaned over her, giving her a stern look. "Pout all you like, Aura, but you'll do it in *my* room."

"I am not pouting," she snapped at him.

"Call it whatever you like," he said, straightening and folding his arms. "But I'm done sleeping on that cot. Anything you have to do in a room, you'll do in mine. Sleep, dress, argue—I don't care."

He hesitated, just briefly.

"I've finally got you here," he added, quieter, "and I'm not letting you go."

Aura's eyes narrowed. "You don't get to decide that."

The words landed clean.

He felt it.

Not as a blow—but as resistance. Real resistance. Not the kind he could override with a hand on her wrist or a shift of his weight.

Something in him tightened.

"I don't," he admitted after a beat. "But I'm not pretending I don't want to."

She held his gaze, searching, measuring.

"If I didn't need the company at night," she muttered, "I'd tell you exactly what you could do with your room."

That pulled a grin from him, automatic. "As long as you're in it with me, sweetheart, I could put up with anything."

She snorted and looked away, arms crossing again.

Donovan dropped onto the foot of the bed, watching her—really watching her this time. The tension in her shoulders. The way she held herself tight, controlled. Not embarrassed.

Angry.

And not entirely wrong.

That part sat poorly with him.

He'd acted without thinking. Again. The same way he always did—decide, move, deal with the fallout later.

Except this time the fallout mattered more.

He leaned forward, reaching out to take her chin gently between his fingers. She resisted for half a second before letting him turn her face back toward him.

"Tony's sorry for causing trouble," he said quietly. "He promises to behave himself."

A flicker of amusement touched her expression, gone almost immediately.

"And I'm sorry I upset you."

She didn't answer.

His thumb brushed lightly along her jaw, slower this time. Careful.

"You don't get to pick me up every time I disagree with you," she said finally.

"I know."

"Do you?"

He exhaled. "I'm working on it."

That earned him a longer look.

He helped her off the bed, but this time he didn't pull—just offered his hand. When she took it, he didn't tighten his grip.

Just held it.

When she finally looked up at him, irritation still flickering in her eyes, he dipped his head and kissed her—quick, soft, restrained.

Not claiming. Asking.

He pulled back first. "Let's not do that again," he said quietly.

Her brow lifted. "Which part?"

He huffed a breath. "All of it."

She studied him for a moment longer. Then nodded.

Reluctantly.

They had barely reached the garage when Trevor came in through the front entrance, took one look at the three of them, and stopped short.

"Good God," Trevor said flatly. "Was it really necessary for you two to pummel each other?"

Donovan frowned, sliding an arm loosely over Aura's shoulders. "Why would you assume it was me?"

Trevor gestured between them. "When you're both wearing bruises to prove it, what else am I supposed to assume?"

"Both?" Donovan echoed. His hand came up to his cheek, and he winced when his fingers brushed the tender skin. "Damn. You've got a mean right," he added, glancing down at Aura.

"She hit you?" Trevor asked incredulously.

"For hitting Tony," Donovan said dryly. "I think. Why did you hit me, sweetheart?"

Aura shot him a glare sharp enough to cut glass. He grinned back, like her anger was something to be entertained. "We're not starting again. You'll notice nobody else is really upset."

"He is," she snapped, pointing at Trevor.

"He's just mad because he thought Tony and I were fighting."

"Weren't you?" Trevor demanded.

"Not exactly," Tony said cheerfully.

Trevor pinched the bridge of his nose. "I'm not going to get a straight answer out of any of you, am I?"

Aura opened her mouth.

Donovan clamped his hand over it—

—and immediately knew that was the wrong move.

She twisted, furious, and he gave her a sheepish smile but didn't remove it. Instead, he looked at Trevor. "It's not important. The issue's already resolved. No need for you to involve yourself, big brother."

Trevor's brow rose as his gaze slid pointedly between the three of them, lingering on Aura, who was still glaring murderously behind Donovan's hand.

Finally, he sighed. "Don't let it happen again."

"I don't think that'll be a problem," Tony said quickly. "Once was enough." He gingerly touched his nose and winced.

"Quite right," Donovan agreed, finally releasing Aura.

She immediately rounded on him. "Manhandle me again," she growled, "and I'll give your right eye a bruise to match."

Donovan laughed. "But then you'd have to look at them. Do you really want to be staring at my bruised face in bed?" His grin turned wicked. "Or was that just to keep other women from staring at me? I'm sure I don't look very handsome like this."

Aura snorted despite herself.

Trevor crossed his arms. "It isn't enough that you have a mortal enemy in our uncle? You have to go for each other's throats as well?"

"I don't mind going for throats," Donovan said easily, tugging Aura back against him and nuzzling the side of her neck.

She gasped and shoved at him. "Donovan!"

"Knock that off," Trevor snapped.

Donovan released her just enough to keep peace, though his hands stayed on her waist. He could see the stubborn anger trying to hold on and watched it finally crumble when he wiggled his eyebrows at her.

She rolled her eyes and gave up.

"I know you're inordinately pleased with yourself," Trevor said flatly, "but we have more pressing issues."

Donovan cleared his throat, straightened, and adopted his most solemn expression. "Quite right."

Aura snorted. Trevor rolled his eyes. Tony burst out laughing.

"Well," Donovan said with a grin, "don't say I didn't try."

Trevor sighed. "Fine. What's next with Luc?"

Donovan sobered. "Until we know where he is or what he's doing, all we can do is wait."

He loosened his hold just enough to let Aura turn, then immediately wrapped his arms back around her shoulders, pulling her against him. He couldn't help it. Even now, he wanted contact, needed it. She didn't pull away.

"He said he was 'recruiting,'" Donovan continued. "No idea who."

"And the terminal's down," Trevor said. "So, no tracking."

"Sorry," Donovan muttered.

"Don't worry," Tony said. "I'll get a replacement screen. I'll be gone a few days."

"I'll head out too," Trevor said. "There's a bounty nearby. I'll stay close."

"Thanks," Donovan said sincerely.

"I'll call Janice," Trevor added. "Something's coming. I can feel it."

When they finally dispersed, Donovan leaned closer to Aura, smiling softly.

"Looks like it's just you and me for a bit, sweetheart."

The heat that leapt into her eyes tightened his chest.

God help him, having her to himself sounded perfect.

CHAPTER 33

For a week, Aura and Donovan barely left their room as they explored the new facets of their relationship. They marveled at the things they learned about each other. What pleased them, what pushed them to the edge of madness. Their passion didn't diminish no matter how many times they spent it. Between bouts of desire, they talked. And sometimes, they found they were just as content holding each other in silence.

It took her longer than she expected to notice the difference in him, but once she did, she couldn't ignore it.

Donovan, for all his instincts, learned quickly where she would not bend, and, more importantly, when to let her come to him instead.

Once Tony returned, they emerged and settled into a comfortable routine. The days passed quickly. While Tony repaired the network terminal and worked through the backlog of projects for his customers, Donovan went around town picking up odd jobs, partly to help out, partly to keep himself occupied. Aura, discovering she had no patience for idleness, begged Donovan to find her something useful to do.

He eventually convinced one of the saloon owners to hire her on as a bartender and Donovan stressed that *bartender* was all she was to be there. The position kept her busy several afternoons a week and, just as importantly, allowed her to listen to the gossip of travelers passing through town. If Luc left a whisper behind, she intended to hear it.

Every day, Aura spent two hours riding Aries. She took him out past the edge of town into the desert and let him have his head. The rides cleared her mind and gave her the solitude she still needed. She enjoyed Donovan's and Tony's company, but after years spent alone, the constancy of companionship sometimes pressed too close. A third hour each day was devoted to shooting practice. She had no intention of letting her edge dull.

They gathered for dinner every evening, the conversation easy and familiar, and afterward Donovan and Aura would retreat to his room. Once the door closed, it took them only seconds to lose themselves in each other again.

Three months passed.

Pleasant months, but not peaceful ones.

Waiting had never suited her. Not like this. Not when he was still out there, moving when he chose, deciding the terms of the hunt.

They watched. Listened. Waited for a sign that never came.

Aura's patience wore thin long before she admitted it.

For five years, she had chased him without rest.

Now she was standing still.

And she hated it.

***

Trevor tethered his horse outside the saloon, lit a cigarette, and shoved his hands into his pockets as he strode down the boardwalk. The jail was several buildings down, and he intended to ask about any outstanding bounties in the area.

Bounty hunting suited him. It gave him reason to roam, and it let him feel useful. After failing spectacularly to protect his younger siblings from what their parents had done to them, hunting criminals gave him the illusion that he was protecting someone now.

His rifle hung slung across his back. His brown trench coat flapped around his legs in the rising wind, and his hat was tipped forward, shadowing his eyes. Trevor was always alert. His parents had made sure of that.

One brown eye saw the world as most people did. The other—carefully matched, artificial—registered far more than the human brain should comfortably process. Distance. Angle. Speed. Trajectory. Nothing small escaped its notice. It was why he was such a good shot. Hard to miss when your eye told you exactly where the bullet would land.

He flicked the cigarette into the dirt before entering the sheriff's office.

Sheriff Whelmsly looked up from his scarred desk and broke into a broad smile. Nearing fifty, with a thick mustache and a belly that testified to a fondness for beer, he didn't look especially intimidating. What most people missed was that he was an excellent shot and had little patience for paperwork.

"Well, good God, MacHaven!" Whelmsly boomed, standing to clasp Trevor's hand. "What're you doing in town? You're usually down south this time of year."

Trevor dropped into the chair across from him, kicking his heels up on the desk. "Good to see you too, Sheriff."

"Yes, yes," Whelmsly waved it off. "I wasn't expecting you till spring."

"Normally you'd be right," Trevor said. "But I'm sticking close to home for a bit. Thought I'd see if you had anything local."

Whelmsly's brow lifted. "And what's got you hovering?"

"Anticipating trouble," Trevor replied. "Wanted to be nearby."

"Women?" Whelmsly grinned.

Trevor laughed. "If only it were that simple. My brother's had that problem covered for months now. No, this is worse."

Whelmsly leaned forward eagerly. "You need a posse?"

"Not this time."

"Pity," Whelmsly sighed.

They talked a while. When Trevor stepped back outside, he carried two new bounties and a handful of posters stuffed into his coat. He tipped his hat back and studied the sky. Heavy clouds rolled in fast. Rain was coming.

The wind snapped at his coat as he turned back toward his horse.

The first bullet struck wood less than a foot from Trevor's head.

He didn't hear the shot. Only the ugly *thud* of impact, the vibration shivering through the wall beside him. His body reacted before his mind caught up. Muscles coiled. Breath cut short. Instinct screamed **move**.

Two more bullets followed, chewing splinters from the wall.

Sniper.

Trevor lunged forward, shoulders hunched as he ran. His artificial eye was already feeding him data—angle, elevation, trajectory—overlaying the street with invisible lines. High angle. Rooftop. Distance closing fast.

He risked a glance.

There.

A figure prone on the grocer's roof, rifle braced, body tucked into shadow. No scope.

The sun peeked out of the clouds and for just a moment highlighted long brown hair.

Trevor's stomach tightened.

No scope?

That meant confidence. Or something worse.

He ducked hard into the alley, boots skidding on packed dirt. Another shot cracked past him, close enough that he felt heat brush his cheek. Too close. Too precise.

She's not missing.

That realization landed cold and heavy.

Trevor pressed himself flat against the wall, breathing slow, controlled. His heart pounded, but his hands were steady. They had to be. Panic got you killed faster than bullets.

A shadow moved overhead.

He edged backward and froze as the figure skidded to a stop at the far end of the alley, rifle already rising.

The world narrowed.

He *saw* the bullet this time.

Time stretched thin as glass. Trevor twisted, stepping back and turning his head just enough.

The shot clipped the cigarette clean from his mouth.

His lips burned. The cigarette spun away, glowing briefly before vanishing into the dirt.

Trevor didn't wait to see if she'd fire again.

He ran.

The warehouse loomed ahead, squat and ugly, its doors half-rusted but unlocked. He threw himself inside and slammed the door shut behind him, chest heaving.

The lights were still on.

Too bright.

Too exposed.

His gaze flicked across the interior, rows of crates, scattered machinery, and barrels.

Oil.

His mind snapped into motion.

Trevor kicked the first barrel hard. It tipped, rolled, burst open. Oil sloshed across the floor in a widening pool. He knocked over another, then another, boots slipping as the stink of it filled the air.

The door slid open behind him.

He didn't look back.

Trevor sprinted for the breaker box and flipped the switches.

Darkness swallowed the warehouse whole.

The sudden absence of light was suffocating. Even his artificial eye was blind now, no contrast, no input. Just black.

Good.

He moved carefully, silently, edging away from the breaker, placing each foot with deliberate care. Oil slicked under his boots. He memorized its position, committed it to instinct.

Come closer, he thought. *Just a little closer.*

"I can see you," a calm voice said.

Trevor's breath hitched despite himself.

She was inside.

Too far in.

That wasn't confidence. That was certainty.

"See me?" he asked slowly, forcing his voice steady.

"Yes."

His gut twisted.

The accuracy, the lack of scope, the deliberate misses.

Mod.

"Night vision?" he asked, angling his body slightly, trying to triangulate her position by sound.

"Among other things," she replied.

Closer now.

"What other things?" he asked, buying time, shifting weight carefully.

"Targeting. Heat sensors. Zoom."

Luc, Trevor thought bitterly. *Of course.*

"So, you're not a bad shot," he said. "You're just enjoying yourself."

"I'm a master marksman," she snapped.

Anger. Good. Anger made people careless.

"Then why miss?"

"I wanted to play with you," she said lightly. "I was told I could. As long as I killed you in the end."

Trevor swallowed.

"Luc," he said.

"Yes."

Oil squelched softly beneath his boot.

He stilled.

Perfect.

"So, this is it?" he asked. "No chance to fight back?"

"That's the idea."

She was close now. Too close.

"Mind if I make a last request?"

She paused.

"If it's reasonable."

Trevor reached slowly into his coat, fingers brushing the familiar shape of his cigarette pack.

"One last cigarette."

Another pause.

"That's reasonable."

He brought the cigarette to his lips and fumbled deliberately for the lighter, heart pounding as he listened to her breathing somewhere in the dark.

Fifteen feet.

He flicked the lighter.

The lighter flared—

and she hissed, sharp and immediate.

Trevor smiled grimly.

"Funny thing about night vision," he said calmly. It amplifies light. Even the smallest spark."

Her rifle came up.

"Time to die, cowboy."

Trevor whispered, "*Let there be light*."

The lighter hit the oil.

The explosion was immediate.

Fire roared through the warehouse. She screamed—high, piercing, raw—as the light overloaded her systems.

Trevor moved.

He lunged through the heat, slammed a fist into her stomach, and felt the air leave her in a choking gasp. She collapsed forward and he caught her, hoisting her over his shoulder as flames licked up the walls.

He didn't hesitate.

He carried her out.

Outside, rain began to fall as the warehouse burned behind him, fire hissing and crackling under the darkening sky.

Trevor stood there a moment, chest heaving, watching the flames.

She'd tried to kill him.

Luc had sent her.

And still he hadn't been able to let her die.

Damn you, Luc.

He looked down at the unconscious woman.

What did you do to her, he wondered, *that made this seem worth it?*

One thing was certain.

This wasn't over.

Not by a long shot.

CHAPTER 34

Janice tipped the bottle of tequila back and drank, her sharp eyes scanning the street even as the liquor burned down her throat. She'd swiped the bottle straight from the bartender's hand and taken it outside without a word, planting herself against one of the wooden posts holding up the boardwalk awning.

She was looking for something.

A fight.

A man.

Maybe both.

She hadn't decided yet.

The bottle was already half empty, and she didn't feel a damn thing. That annoyed her. It meant she'd need another soon, but she had no interest in drinking it inside the saloon. She'd taken one look at the men in there—too soft, too slow, too boring—and dismissed them all. If she was going to bother with company, it needed to be worth her time.

The sky was thick with clouds, the sun sinking somewhere behind them. It would rain soon. She hoped it would. Janice loved storms. The way the air went electric, the way thunder vibrated through bone and muscle alike. There was nothing quite like being outside when the sky split open.

And nothing like a man pressed against you while it happened.

She grinned faintly at the thought.

God, her brothers would lose their minds if they knew how many men she'd shared a night, or a few hours with over the last couple of years. Not that she planned on telling them. She loved them, but they were suffocatingly protective, especially Donovan. Trevor tried to hide it better, but he was just as bad.

They'd lock her in a room if they knew how often she *chose* danger.

Janice lived for it.

She didn't blink at walking into a group of armed outlaws with her weapon still holstered. She didn't hesitate when odds tilted against her. Eight men once, all convinced they were about to teach her a lesson. She'd taught them instead.

Her fingers brushed the grip of the revolver at her hip affectionately. That hadn't even been a challenge.

Nothing ever was.

She could outdrink, outfight, and outshoot anyone she crossed paths with. Even her brothers, though she'd never test that seriously. They were her family. That was different.

Unlike them, Janice didn't wrestle with morality. Donovan tried not to kill. Trevor did when he had to. Janice didn't see the point in hesitation.

If someone was going to end up with a noose around their neck anyway, why waste the effort? She was efficient. Cleaner. Faster. The law didn't have to bother with paperwork when she was done.

Tonight, though, she leaned more toward finding a man than a body. Fights were only satisfying in bulk, and this town didn't look promising in either regard.

She drained the bottle, frowned when it came up empty, and pushed off the post. Her body uncoiled smoothly, compact and balanced. At just over five and a half feet, she was easy to underestimate. Slim, modest curves, young-looking enough that people routinely mistook her for harmless.

She let them.

Men especially struggled with the idea that a woman could be better than them at the things they prided themselves on most. Janice found that weakness endlessly useful.

She descended the steps to the street, barely sparing a glance for the old man shambling down the center of it.

"Hey, girlie!"

She stopped.

Slowly, she turned her head just enough to look at him over her shoulder and took another drink, out of habit more than anything. The bottle was empty, but she didn't lower it yet.

"You Janice?" the man called, still coming toward her. "I been lookin' fer ya."

She didn't answer. Didn't move.

"Yer Janice, right? Yer uncle sent me."

That got her attention.

She turned fully this time, her expression flat, bored. The man was ancient, near sixty at least. Gray hair hung in matted ropes, his beard thick and unkempt. His skin was darkened and cracked from a lifetime under a brutal sun.

"Yer uncle sent me to kill ya," he continued cheerfully, grinning wide. "Gave me this new body. Strong. So, I could do the job proper."

Ah.

Janice glanced past him, momentarily distracted by a noise further up the street, then looked back.

"This new body made me strong ag'in. Nothin' kin stop me now. Gonna make a name fer myself."

He laughed, high and unhinged.

"Don't ya wanna know the name of the man who's gonna kill ya, girlie?"

Janice tipped the bottle back again, then scowled when nothing came out. She turned it upside down, annoyed.

"Well," the man said, clearly enjoying himself, "I'm gonna tell ya anyway. Won't matter none. My name's—"

The shot cracked through the air.

The man fell backward, dead before he hit the ground, a neat hole centered between his eyes.

Janice holstered her gun without a second glance.

"Damn," she muttered, already turning back toward the saloon. "Knew I was gonna need another bottle."

She stepped over the body as if it weren't there, deciding absently that this town had officially run out of entertainment.

Time to move on.

CHAPTER 35

Donovan stood at the bank of windows in Tony's living room, arms crossed, watching the storm gather on the horizon. Lightning flashed in the distance, followed several seconds later by a low, rolling rumble. The air felt heavy, charged in that unmistakable way that came just before a downpour.

He hoped Aura and Tony were back before it broke.

Tony had ridden out to check on a client just beyond town, and Aura had taken Aries out for a run. Something about the horse needing it, though Donovan suspected she needed it just as much. Both should have been home by now. He glanced at the clock, irritation pricking beneath his concern.

Dinner was already underway. Chicken baked in the oven, the scent filling the house, rice warming on the stove. All that remained was to throw together a salad once they returned. It was simple. Domestic. Almost normal.

The thought sat uneasily in his chest.

He exhaled slowly and, despite himself, let his mind drift back to Aura.

Three months.

He hadn't stayed in one place this long since childhood, yet he'd felt no urge to move on. Not with her here. Being with Aura was easy in ways that still surprised him. The shared silences that didn't demand filling, the sharp bursts of laughter, the way she fit against him at night as if she belonged there. He had never known this kind of contentment.

And that, more than anything, unsettled him.

Because she could also drive him to the edge of his patience like no one else.

She challenged him. Fought him. Forced him to feel everything more sharply than he ever had. Frustration, desire, fear, something dangerously close to tenderness. She stirred it all, whether he wanted her to or not.

He had never been so alive.

And that made her dangerous.

Donovan already knew he would do nearly anything to keep her. Permanently. But he felt her hesitation like a constant pressure beneath the surface. She still didn't believe he could want her the way he did. Every time he edged closer to saying it outright, she retreated behind that wall of hers. And every time, he let her.

Coward.

He had had moments—quiet ones—where she might have listened, where she might have let him speak. Moments where it had been on the tip of his tongue to tell her everything, to push past that barrier between them. And every time, he had chosen silence, unwilling to risk the fragile peace they had built.

Now peace wasn't enough.

He straightened slightly, jaw tightening as the decision settled.

He was going to have to risk the argument.

Slender arms wrapped suddenly around his waist, gripping him tight.

Donovan started, breath catching, then relaxed with a smile that came too easily.

Aura.

Of course she would come up behind him like that. She moved quietly when she wanted to.

Before he could turn, a voice murmured against his back, low, intimate, too familiar.

"Did you miss me?"

Donovan's stomach dropped.

For half a heartbeat, his mind refused to place it. The tone was wrong. The cadence was too soft, too practiced. Aura didn't speak like that. Aura didn't—

Recognition hit.

Cold. Immediate.

His body reacted before the thought fully formed, shoulders tightening, breath locking in his chest as the past surged forward unbidden. Blood on the floor, her hands shaking, the sound of her breaking apart in his arms.

No.

Not here.

Not again.

The smile vanished. Slowly, deliberately, he reached for the arms around him, already pulling away.

They tightened instead.

Possessive.

Familiar.

A grip he remembered far too well.

"Let go of me, Alice," he said flatly.

"But I like it right here," she said, soft and certain. As if everything between them had always been this simple.

Donovan wrenched free and stepped away, turning to face her fully.

She stood there like she belonged.

Like she had never left.

"What are you doing here?" he demanded.

She stepped closer as if nothing had passed between them, as if the months, the rejection, the blood on the floor had simply… dissolved.

"I came to see you," she said lightly. "Obviously."

"I told you not to," Donovan snapped, the edge in his voice sharper now. "I told you I didn't want to see you again."

She sighed, faintly exasperated, like he was the one being difficult. "You really should stop pretending this isn't inevitable."

"It is not inevitable," he said, each word clipped, controlled.

Her brows lifted, genuine surprise flickering across her face as if the idea had never occurred to her. "Of course it is. You just haven't realized it yet."

That certainty tightened something in his chest.

This wasn't just persistence.

It was conviction.

And he had seen where that led.

"I was clear from the beginning," Donovan said, forcing himself to slow down, to keep his voice level. "I was never interested in anything serious with you. Why do you keep doing this to yourself?"

Her expression shifted, the calm cracking just enough to reveal something sharper beneath. "Because I love you."

"What you feel isn't love," he said coldly. "It's obsession."

She moved suddenly, closing the distance between them and clutching at his chest, fingers twisting in his shirt like she could anchor him there.

"I need you, Donovan," she said, her voice rising, urgency bleeding through the softness. "We're supposed to be together. He made me like you so we could be."

Donovan stilled.

"What did you just say?"

She hesitated, just for a fraction of a second.

Too late.

His hands closed around her arms, firm, unyielding. "Who is 'he,' Alice?"

Her gaze darted away.

"Where did you go?" he demanded, tightening his grip. "What did you do?"

"I went with him," she said quickly, words tumbling now, eager, almost proud. "He said he could make me like you. That if I was like you, you'd finally want me."

The blood drained from Donovan's face.

Like you.

The words echoed, wrong in a way he couldn't immediately name. And then the meaning hit, slamming into place with brutal clarity.

"No," he said under his breath.

She smiled.

Bright.

Pleased.

"I fixed the problem."

She slipped one glove free. Then the other.

Donovan didn't move.

Couldn't.

Metal gleamed where skin should have been.

Not hidden. Not disguised. No attempt to soften it or make it pass for flesh. Just exposed structure, articulated joints, segmented fingers moving with quiet, mechanical precision. The faint whir of internal components carried in the silence between them.

His stomach turned.

Dear God.

For a moment, all he could see was his own hands.

Not as they were now but as they had been. Torn open. Rebuilt. Forced into something that looked human only because someone had decided it should.

Violation.

That was the word.

It had always been the word.

And she had chosen it.

His communicator chirped.

"Donovan," Trevor's voice came through, tight with urgency. "We've got trouble."

"I know," Donovan said hollowly, unable to take his eyes off her hands.

"You alright?"

"Call me back in twenty minutes."

He lowered his hand slowly.

"Alice…" His voice came out rough, scraped thin. "Why?"

"I did it for you," she said, flexing her fingers again, admiring them. "Now we're the same."

Something inside him recoiled violently.

"Why would you think I'd want this for you?" Donovan demanded, the control in his voice beginning to fracture. "This was done to me. It was a violation. Why would I ever wish it on someone else?"

He caught her wrist and yanked her hand up between them. The metal gleamed under the light, exposed and unapologetic, the articulated joints moving with quiet precision.

"This is inhuman."

"But I love you!" she cried, her composure breaking, desperation pushing through the certainty. "Aren't you pleased?"

"Pleased?" The word tore out of him, raw and disbelieving. "I would have been pleased if you'd stayed away from me. If you'd left this alone. But this—" His grip tightened without thought. "This is madness. How could you do this to yourself? How could you let him do this to you?"

"For you!" she screamed. "Everything I do is for you!"

She reached for his face.

Instinct snapped through him, sharp and immediate. Donovan recoiled, revulsion flashing hot under his skin as he knocked her hand away, his jaw tightening hard enough to ache.

"You don't have me," he said, each word precise, final. "You never did. And you never will."

Something in her expression broke, splintered into something jagged and dangerous.

"It's her," Alice hissed, her voice dropping into something colder, more focused. "That little blonde whore. I'll kill her. I'll watch her die."

The shift was immediate, and Donovan felt it as clearly as if the room itself had tilted. Her attention was no longer on him. It had already moved past him, toward the door, toward the world beyond this room.

Toward Aura.

He moved without hesitation.

His hands closed around her wrists before she could take a step, grip locking down hard enough to halt her completely. She struggled at once, laughing under her breath, the sound unsteady and wrong, but he didn't release her.

"You're not going to use these to hurt anyone," he said, his voice low, stripped of anything but intent.

She twisted against his hold, trying to wrench free, her movements turning sharper, more frantic as resistance met resistance. The strength in her arms was real—enhanced, reinforced—but not enough.

For a fraction of a second, Donovan became acutely aware of what he was doing.

Not reacting. Choosing.

He could restrain her. Tie her. Lock her away and wait for help. There were other options, less final, less irreversible. He knew that.

But over that logic came her voice again, clear and certain:

I'll kill her.

And with it, the image of Aura unprotected, unaware, within reach of something this dangerous.

The hesitation burned out.

Donovan adjusted his grip, deliberate now, tightening his hold at the weakest points in the structure. He felt the resistance in the metal, the engineered precision of it, the way it tried to hold under pressure.

Then he squeezed.

The sound came sharp and unmistakable. A grinding snap as the first joint failed, followed by a cascade of smaller fractures as the internal mechanisms collapsed in on themselves. Alice's scream tore through the room, raw and immediate, her body buckling as she fought to pull away.

He didn't release her.

Not yet. Not while there was still any chance she could use them.

He tightened once more, ensuring the damage was complete, the structure beyond function, before finally letting go and shoving her away from him.

Alice crumpled to the floor, clutching her ruined hands to her chest as sobs overtook her, rocking forward with the force of them. The manic certainty was gone, stripped away as quickly as it had surfaced, leaving something hollow in its place.

Donovan stood over her, chest heaving, the taste of bile rising sharp in his throat. For a moment, he couldn't move, the reality of what he had just done settling in with a weight that pressed hard against his ribs.

God help me. What have I just done?

The answer came just as quickly, cold and steady.

What you had to.

He dragged a hand down his face and forced himself to breathe through it, to think instead of react. He knew how far he could take it if he let himself.

Not this time.

"Alice," he said tightly, the words measured despite the tension still coiled in him, "I didn't want this. But you leave me no choice."

She didn't look at him. Her head hung forward, hair falling around her face as the sobs quieted into something softer, emptier.

That frightened him more than the screaming had.

Donovan stood there a moment longer, forcing his breathing to steady before he moved. Reacting had gotten him through the last few minutes. It wouldn't get him through what came next.

He turned away from her and went to the garage, returning with a length of rope. When he knelt beside her, she didn't resist. Didn't look up. She moved when he directed her, pliant and unresponsive, as if whatever had been driving her had burned itself out completely.

That unsettled him more than the struggle had.

He bound her methodically, upper arms pinned tight against her torso, wrists secured despite the damage already done. He checked each knot twice, not trusting the stillness, not trusting her.

When he finished, he helped her to her feet. She swayed once, then steadied, head still bowed.

They left the house without a word.

The walk to the jail stretched longer than it should have. The first drops of rain began halfway there, a slow, steady drizzle that soaked through fabric and skin alike. Donovan didn't hurry. He let it fall, let the cold seep in, welcomed it in a distant way. It gave him something to focus on besides the churn in his gut.

Alice walked beside him without protest, silent, compliant.

It felt wrong.

Everything about this felt wrong.

The sheriff looked up when they entered and immediately went pale.

"Jesus Christ," he breathed, taking in the sight of her. "Is that—"

"Yes," Donovan said sharply, cutting him off before the name could fully form. "And you are not to contact her family. Anyone asks, she isn't here. Do you understand me?"

The sheriff swallowed and nodded, whatever questions he might have had dying behind his teeth. He'd known Donovan too long to push when his tone sounded like that.

They secured her in a cell at the back. Alice sat when directed, folding in on herself on the narrow bench, her hands cradled uselessly against her chest. She didn't look up as the door closed, didn't react to the sound of the lock sliding into place.

Donovan lingered a moment longer than he should have, his hand resting briefly against the cold metal of the bars.

"Alice," he said quietly, the edge gone from his voice, leaving something more tired in its place. "This is temporary. My brother will be here soon. We'll figure this out."

She didn't respond, didn't move, didn't even seem to hear him.

The silence that followed pressed in heavier than anything she could have said.

After a moment, he stepped back, turning away from the cell with his jaw set hard enough to ache.

The walk back blurred at the edges.

He registered the rain, the empty streets, the distant roll of thunder, but none of it held his attention for long. His mind kept circling the same words, over and over, refusing to settle.

Donovan slowed, then stopped in the middle of the street, the rain plastering his hair to his face as the words settled in with a weight he couldn't ignore.

The thought came automatically. Something to cut the tension, to make it manageable.

It didn't land.

Donovan let it go.

Luc hadn't just modified Alice. He had shaped her. Taken something unstable and made it useful. Taken obsession and refined it into something sharper, more focused, more dangerous. The same way he had tried to reshape Aura. The same way he treated everyone he touched, not as people but as material.

Donovan's stomach tightened as the pattern clarified.

This wasn't isolated. It wasn't accidental. It was deliberate.

Luc wasn't running anymore. He was building. Not soldiers, but something far more dangerous. Devotees. People desperate enough, broken enough, to accept what he offered and call it purpose. People willing to let him strip them down and rebuild them into something that reflected him. Something obedient, something loyal, something convinced they had chosen it.

Donovan's hands curled slowly into fists at his sides.

And he had helped make it possible.

The realization settled in with a cold, unforgiving weight. Every delay, every missed opportunity, every time he had chosen to wait instead of act. It had given Luc more time to refine whatever this was becoming.

His communicator beeped sharply, cutting through the rain and the spiral of his thoughts. He answered immediately this time, lifting it to his ear without breaking stride as he resumed walking.

"You still alive over there?" Trevor asked.

"For the time being," Donovan replied. His voice sounded distant even to himself, stripped down to function.

"How bad was it?"

"He modded Alice," Donovan said flatly, the words tasting bitter.

"Alice?!" Trevor swore. "God. And I thought the one I ran into was bad enough."

Donovan straightened slightly, the phrasing cutting through the haze. "What happened? Are you alright?"

"Fine enough now," Trevor said. "But it was dodgy for a while. You were damn near short a brother."

Donovan closed his eyes briefly, a sharp exhale leaving him. The list of things Luc had almost taken from him was growing longer by the day.

"We have to stop this," he said, the tension returning, coiling tight beneath his words. "He can't be allowed to keep doing this to people."

"I agree," Trevor said. "I'm more worried about Janice, though. That's two now. Do you think he'd send one after her too?"

"I wouldn't put it past him," Donovan replied. "You haven't heard from her?"

"No. I'm calling her as soon as we hang up. I'm on my way back now, and I'm bringing a… guest."

"A guest?" Donovan frowned slightly. "That makes two, then. I've got Alice secured in the jail."

"Between the two of them," Trevor said grimly, "we should be able to get something useful out of this."

"I'll see you tomorrow?"

"Provided nothing happens to prevent it."

"Be careful."

The line went dead just as Donovan stepped through the garage doors.

"Where the hell were you?" Aura demanded immediately.

He stopped short.

"The chicken is practically charcoal."

"Damn it," Donovan muttered, dragging a hand through his damp hair. "I forgot about the chicken. Was it salvageable?"

"Not even remotely," she said. "Tony's upstairs trying to air the place out and find something edible." Her gaze sharpened on him. "So you want to explain what happened?"

Donovan didn't answer right away. He just turned and started for the stairs, knowing she would follow.

On the third floor, he didn't bother easing into it.

"I'm sorry, Tony," he said. "We've got a serious problem."

"It better be worth nearly burning down my home," Tony muttered, waving a towel through the lingering smoke.

"Alice showed up here."

Tony grimaced. "Alright. That's borderline forgivable."

"Luc modded her."

Tony froze mid-motion, then slowly lowered the towel. "Good God. You're forgiven."

Aura's eyes narrowed. "Alice. The one who disappeared? The one who tried to kill herself here?"

Donovan nodded. "The same."

"And Luc made her like you and your siblings," she said, slower now, more deliberate.

"Yes." He exhaled, the tension still sitting too close beneath the surface. "Trevor ran into another one. He's bringing them here. We haven't heard from Janice yet, but I don't think Luc would overlook her in something this deliberate."

"Where is she?"

"In a cell. I didn't want her here overnight. Even restrained, I don't trust her."

Aura studied him for a moment, her gaze moving over his face, his posture, the way he held himself.

"Are you alright?"

"I'm not hurt."

"That's not what I asked."

He met her gaze and held it, aware that anything he said past this point would be for her, not the truth.

"I'm fine."

She didn't look convinced.

"Try again," she said.

A flicker of irritation rose, brief and sharp. Not at her, but at the fact that she was right to push. He ignored the question instead, dragging his hand through his damp hair. "She wasn't even pretending," he said. "There was no artificial skin. Just gloves. Like a costume."

Tony's expression tightened immediately. "That's sloppy. The skin protects the components. Leaving them exposed like that…" He shook his head once, visibly displeased.

"Wouldn't matter now," Donovan said.

Aura's attention snapped back to him. "What did you do?"

He didn't look away. "I crushed her hands."

Tony winced, a reflexive reaction to the damage. "That's a waste," he muttered, more irritated than sympathetic.

Aura held his gaze a moment longer, searching his face for something he wasn't offering. Whatever she saw there made her still, her expression tightening just slightly before she stepped closer.

Her hand came up, resting briefly against his chest, something solid to anchor him in place.

Her touch settled differently than words would have.

"When Trevor gets here tomorrow," Donovan said, shifting back toward something structured, controlled, "we'll decide what to do with both of them." He dragged a hand down his face, the movement sharper this time. "Right now, I just want to eat something and go to bed."

"That bad?" she asked.

He gave a short nod. "He's not improvising anymore. He's refining them. Each one better than the last."

Aura stayed where she was, her presence solid and unyielding at his side.

It didn't ease anything.

CHAPTER 36

Trevor strode through the garage doors late the next afternoon with his prisoner in tow.

Her hands were bound in front of her, the rope looped around her wrists and trailing back to Trevor's fist. Donovan and Tony emerged from behind the clutter at Trevor's call only to stop short when they saw who he'd brought with him.

"Yeah," Trevor said dryly, catching their expressions. "That was my reaction, too. Didn't have time to stand around and admire her, though."

Donovan's jaw tightened as his gaze swept over her. She was young. Pretty. Too composed for someone who had just been dragged halfway across town. A heart-shaped face, chestnut hair falling loose around her shoulders, light brown eyes bright with defiance.

"Another woman?" he said, sharp with surprise. "What's her modification?"

"Eyes," Trevor replied. "Like mine. Only hers are more advanced."

"That's odd," Donovan muttered. "Alice's mods were crude. Sloppy. Did Luc change tactics, or is he comparing outcomes?"

"Could be testing," Tony offered. "Seeing what works best."

They looked to the woman. She met their stares with clenched teeth and said nothing.

"Have you gotten anything out of her?" Donovan asked.

"Only her name. Regina St. John," Trevor said. "She stopped talking once I caught her."

Donovan's brow lifted in question.

"She was plenty conversational when she thought she was going to kill me."

Trevor recounted the ambush, brief, efficient, controlled, leaving out nothing that mattered. Donovan watched Regina closely as he spoke, noting the flicker of satisfaction that crossed her face when Trevor mentioned her *playing* with him.

When Trevor finished, Donovan stepped forward.

Regina tried to retreat, but the rope snapped taut. Fear flashed in her eyes, but her chin lifted in stubborn defiance.

"If you had succeeded in killing my brother," Donovan said coldly, "I would have hunted you down myself. Be grateful he's resourceful. Try it again, and I won't wait for you to finish the job."

She didn't cower. She surged forward instead.

Her bound fists cracked against his jaw.

"Goddammit!" Donovan roared, staggering back a step. "Why do you women always have to hit?"

Tony burst out laughing.

Trevor yanked the rope, hauling Regina back before she could swing again. He seized her face in one hand, forcing her to look at him.

"My brother is patient," Trevor said quietly. "But this situation has tested that patience. I wouldn't recommend testing it further."

He released her face, keeping her hands pinned.

Heavy footsteps thundered on the stairs.

Aura appeared at the edge of the garage, eyes already sharp. "What's going on?"

"Our guest is feeling bold," Tony said, still amused.

Aura took in the scene in a heartbeat, the rope, Donovan's hand at his jaw, Regina's defiant posture.

Then she moved.

Her fist slammed into Regina's face, snapping her head sideways and sending her crashing back into Trevor's arms.

Trevor went still, staring at her.

Donovan reacted instantly, grabbing Aura's arm before she could hit her again.

Tony laughed harder.

"Touch him again," Aura snarled, eyes blazing, "and I'll put a bullet in you."

Regina's bravado cracked. Her eyes went wide but she still found enough venom to spit back, "Protective bunch. Threatened by one brother, assaulted by a woman. Is he your brother too?"

"Oh, it's worse than that," Aura growled, struggling against Donovan's grip. "He's mine. So listen carefully, touch him again and I will end you."

Donovan drew her back against him. The word landed harder than he expected.

Mine. That mattered. More than she would ever admit.

"Easy," he murmured, turning her to face him, hands firm on her arms. "She's alive for a reason."

"I said I'd fill her full of holes," Aura snapped. "I didn't say I'd let her die from them."

Donovan's grip tightened slightly on her. "God, you're vicious when you're riled. But let's try talking first."

She nodded, reluctantly.

Regina barked a laugh. "I won't tell you anything. I promised him."

Aura's smile turned sharp. "Well, we tried polite. Now we do it my way."

"You're not shooting her," Trevor said.

"Oh, I don't need a gun," Aura said calmly. "Ten minutes alone with her. Untied if you want. She'll talk."

"Keep that crazy bitch away from me," Regina snapped, pulling back hard against the rope.

"You haven't seen crazy," Aura said softly. "Decide whether you want to talk before or after I rearrange your face."

She turned on her heel and mounted the stairs.

Donovan exhaled slowly.

"She's been simmering," he said. "The waiting's getting to her. She wanted Alice last night."

Tony winced. "I don't envy you the enemy you just made, darlin'."

Regina swallowed, suddenly less defiant.

"I wasn't here to make friends," she muttered.

"I suppose not," Tony said. "But courtesy goes a long way."

Donovan stepped closer. "One question. Why did you let him do it?"

"Because he promised me sight."

"You were blind?" Trevor asked quietly.

She nodded. "Blinded."

"An accident?" he pressed.

"They *called* it an accident."

Tony's voice was softer. "Why?"

Regina hesitated, stiffening.

"I was too good," she snapped, the words coming out sharper than she seemed to intend.

Trevor didn't react right away. He just watched her, steady, waiting.

"At what?" he asked after a moment.

Her mouth twisted, something bitter pulling at the corner of it. "Skeet shooting. Champion level."

Tony let out a low whistle, low and impressed despite himself.

"I was the only woman," she went on, her voice tightening again as the memory settled in. "They didn't like losing."

Donovan's gaze narrowed slightly. "So, they sabotaged your rifle."

She let out a short, humorless laugh. "It backfired." She paused. "And took my sight."

Trevor inhaled sharply. "Did they ever catch who did it?"

"No." She didn't look away.

"How long ago?"

"Four years."

"And Luc offered to fix you," Donovan said. "In exchange for my brother."

She didn't deny it.

"How many more are there like you?" Donovan pressed.

Her jaw set. "I've said enough."

"Your loyalty's misplaced," Donovan said. "He murdered Aura's mother. In front of her."

Regina flinched. "The woman just here?"

"She was five."

Regina's jaw tightened—then faltered. Just for a second.

When Trevor's arm came around her, she stiffened… but didn't pull away.

His grip lingered a fraction longer than necessary. "Donovan."

"He's raped and killed at least eight women. He doesn't deserve protection."

"That's enough," Trevor snapped as Regina paled and turned into him.

Donovan stepped back. "Aura isn't the only one done waiting."

He turned and followed her upstairs.

***

Donovan didn't seek Trevor out again until much later.

By then, his anger had cooled into something harder and more dangerous. Purpose.

Trevor was in his room, seated on the edge of the bed, watching Regina with a hunter's patience. She sat in a chair near the window, hands free now, posture rigid, gaze fixed stubbornly on the darkening sky outside.

Donovan leaned against the doorframe, arms crossing over his chest.

"So," he said mildly, "what are we planning to do with our captive birds?"

Trevor glanced at him, then back at Regina. "I assume you mean besides terrifying them into silence."

"I don't like Alice's parents discovering she's locked in a cell," Donovan said. "And I like even less the idea of her loose again. She's unstable. Dangerous. Even with her hands ruined, she'll go back to Luc if she gets the chance."

Trevor nodded. "You're lucky she didn't kill you."

"She could have," Donovan admitted, disgust curling in his stomach. "She had her arms around me before I even realized she was there. But she didn't come to kill me. She still thinks we're *meant* for each other."

Trevor grimaced. "We all regret the day you crossed paths with her."

"She's not going to stop," Donovan said quietly. "Eventually she'll snap. And next time, she won't hesitate."

"Permanent confinement?" Trevor asked.

Donovan scowled. "She doesn't belong in prison. She belongs in an asylum. But her parents won't believe me. She's fooled them for years."

"That limits our options."

"Yes." Donovan exhaled. "And before you say it, no. I won't kill her."

Trevor studied him. "You couldn't."

"No." Donovan's jaw tightened. "Even now."

A beat passed.

"What about yours?" Donovan asked, nodding toward Regina. "Your would-be assassin?"

"I could arrest her," Trevor said, his attention shifting briefly to her. Regina stiffened, her breath catching. "But if she can convince me she's not a threat, I may not need to."

Donovan smiled faintly. "Generous."

Trevor returned the look. "After Luc is dealt with."

"I don't think we should bring the two women together," Trevor continued. "That's an escape waiting to happen. I'll keep her here."

"I don't like you sleeping next to a loaded weapon," Donovan said flatly.

Trevor chuckled. "I'm still the older brother."

"Don't underestimate her," Donovan warned. "That mistake nearly got me killed."

Trevor sobered. "Noted."

He stood. "Now, shall we go talk to your caged bird before it gets too late?"

"By all means."

They went together.

Donovan and Trevor up front. Aura refusing to be left behind. Tony tagging along because, as he put it, *'before-dinner entertainment is rare around here.'*

They debated Alice's fate as they walked, and no solution satisfied anyone. Regina, they agreed—Aura grudgingly—was Trevor's responsibility.

The jail loomed ahead.

Donovan stepped inside first.

The world tilted.

"Son of a—" He turned away violently.

The sheriff lay slumped over his desk, a single bullet hole centered in his skull. Blood pooled across the scarred wood and dripped slowly to the floor.

Trevor brushed past him, checking the cells.

"Alice is gone."

Luc.

The name burned.

"He'll come for Regina next," Trevor said grimly.

"Damn it."

Donovan was already moving.

They reached the garage breathless and walked straight into six leveled guns.

Rough men. Mercenaries. Professionals.

Weapons were stripped from them quickly, efficiently. Even Aura's boot knife. Donovan caught her glare and shook his head once. *Not now.*

They were herded upstairs.

Why the third floor?

Why not kill us outright?

The answer waited.

Luc sat comfortably by the coffee table.

Alice sat beside him, her ruined hands resting uselessly in her lap.

Something in Donovan went cold.

"Well," Luc said pleasantly, "the family reunion can begin."

They were shoved onto the couches.

"What do you want?" Donovan asked tightly.

"Janice couldn't make it?" Luc sighed. "A shame. I was looking forward to meeting her."

Donovan's fists clenched. "We know you're not here to talk."

Luc gestured. Tea was served.

"I came for what's mine," Luc said calmly, indicating Alice. "But since our train doesn't depart yet, I thought I'd take the opportunity to observe."

"And Regina?" Trevor asked.

"I have no further use for the little doll." Luc shrugged. "Consider her a gift."

Aura laughed softly, dangerously. "You sent her to kill him."

Luc's gaze slid to Aura, lingering. "And she failed."

"Drop the pretense," Aura said. "You're not sentimental."

"Only amusing myself before my train departs," he said coolly.

"We could do without your amusements," Aura sneered.

Luc only smiled. "*We have been made a spectacle to the world…*"

CHAPTER 37

Luc sipped his tea as he regarded Aura with lazy interest.

"I'm starting to think I should have taken you with me that night," he mused. "Instead of letting your screaming startle me into leaving. I hadn't expected that after such a long silence from you."

"It's called shock," Aura growled.

Luc continued as if she hadn't spoken. "I'm disappointed I missed the chance to have you in my possession when you grew into such a little beauty."

"If you had," Aura said, a dark smile curling her lips, "I would have killed you long before now. So, I admit, it's my regret, too."

Luc chuckled softly. "I think I would have had trouble breaking you. You have a lot of spirit." His gaze drifted over her like a hand. "But I think by the time I was ready to take you, you would have been properly trained."

"Son of a bitch—" Aura shot forward.

Donovan caught her by the arm and yanked her back into the seat before she could clear the table.

Guns lifted immediately, six muzzles rising in perfect unison toward Aura.

Donovan's stomach went cold. He didn't move. Neither did Trevor.

"Enough, Luc!" he snapped, less at Luc than at the smug calm in him.

Luc didn't even glance at the mercenaries. He only lifted a hand, palm down, as if soothing dogs. "Put them away."

The guns lowered.

Donovan did not relax.

Luc's eyes flicked to Donovan with that same indulgent amusement. "I'm sure you've tasted that fire, boy. You must understand how I feel, then."

"I'm not like you," Donovan said, voice tight. "I don't have your sick perversions."

Luc smiled as if Donovan had said something charming. "We all have sick perversions, boy. I just act on them."

"And you'll die for them," Aura promised.

Luc acknowledged her, barely, by glancing in her direction, then checking his pocket watch like she was background noise.

He nodded once.

One of the mercenaries seized Alice by the arm and hauled her out of her chair.

Donovan's head snapped up. "Where are you taking her?"

Luc didn't look at him. "The baggage should be secured before I take my own seat."

The six men escorted Alice out, closing the door behind them.

For the first time since they'd been forced onto the couch, the room felt *smaller*. Not safer. Just… more intimate in the worst way.

Aura leaned forward again, muscles tight as wire.

Luc smiled wider. "By all means. If you think it will do you any good."

Donovan leaned in close to Aura's ear, voice low and fast. "Aura. Don't."

Her eyes cut toward him—hot, murderous—then snapped back to Luc.

Donovan kept his hand on her arm, not restraining so much as anchoring. "Remember his modifications. You can't do anything without a weapon." He swallowed, forcing himself to be blunt. "Think of Janice. He's built like her. Trevor and I couldn't take Janice if we ever had to. We couldn't take him either. If you jump him, we die trying to pull you off him and he still walks away."

Aura's nostrils flared.

Donovan felt the second stretch until it turned into a long, taut minute, Aura fighting herself in plain view, pride and rage wrestling her survival instincts.

Finally, she sat back with a low, furious sound and crossed her arms.

Donovan exhaled quietly, then flicked a glance at Trevor.

Trevor had been coiled and ready too. His jaw unclenched by a fraction.

Luc's grin widened, pleased by their restraint like it was his victory. "Smart children. But then, even a dog knows he's no match for a wolf."

Donovan's mouth curled. "Maybe not a wolf. But a rat wouldn't be any problem."

Luc laughed outright. "Your child's wit is adorable. Are you going to taunt me next? Throw rocks?"

Then his voice dropped, smooth as a knife sliding free.

"Will you cry?" Luc asked softly. "Your mother cried, you know."

Donovan's blood froze.

"What do you mean?" His voice came out rougher than he intended.

"When I killed her," Luc said, as if describing the weather. "I could hear her crying." He sipped his tea again. "But then, she thought you children would be caught in the same blast."

Trevor surged forward half a step without thinking. "You were the one who caused the explosion?"

Luc's eyes gleamed. "Of course it was me. They tried to have me killed. I couldn't let that go unanswered."

"He was your brother," Donovan said, something ugly rising in his throat. "Did that mean nothing to you?"

Luc considered that as though it were an interesting philosophical question.

"Should it?" he asked at last. "He served his purpose. Then he became a nuisance."

Aura's voice cut in, cold, steady, terrifyingly controlled. "Why are you surprised, Donovan? He's trying to kill his own niece and nephews."

Luc's eyes slid to Aura again, approving. "Yes. You understand me better than they do."

"I understand that you're a cancer," Aura said. "And cancers get cut out."

Luc smiled. "A poetic little thing."

He checked his watch again.

"I take it you're referring to yesterday," Luc continued, tone casual. "That was a test run. My toys needed to be tried before I move on to the next stage."

"What's the next stage?" Donovan demanded.

Luc shook his head. "Ever eager to ruin the surprise. You'll wait like everyone else."

He stood.

All three of them rose instinctively.

Luc's gun appeared so fast Donovan barely registered the movement before the barrel was trained on them.

"Now, now," Luc said mildly. "Don't do anything stupid." His smile sharpened. "Well… not any more stupid than usual."

His gaze shifted to Tony, who had been silent the entire time, too silent.

"By the way," Luc said conversationally, "Tony. Thank you for fixing my hand after the little whore shot it. It works perfectly now."

The color drained from Tony's face so quickly it was like someone had opened a valve.

Donovan felt the room tilt again. *Tony fixed his hand…?*

Tony's mouth opened, but nothing came out.

Luc backed toward the door, gun still steady. "It's been a pleasure, children. We'll have to do it again soon."

The door opened.

Janice stood there, eyes flicking across the room and landing on Luc with instant, sharp comprehension.

"Was that Alice I saw up the street?" she asked lightly, like she hadn't just walked into a knife fight. "I thought she'd left."

"Janice—" Donovan and Trevor barked together.

Luc turned toward her.

Janice's hand snapped out.

For one startling second—

Then Luc moved like something engineered for violence. He didn't fight for the gun. He used the momentary contact to shove Janice sideways hard, creating a gap, then slipped past her and into the hall.

"Janice—Go!" Donovan roared.

Janice's grin flashed bright and vicious.

And she was gone.

Janice hit the stairs like she'd been launched.

Donovan and Trevor thundered after her, Aura and Tony behind them, but Janice was already widening the distance with every step.

Outside, Luc was a shadow cutting through streets toward the station.

"Don't let him get on that train!" Donovan shouted.

Janice didn't bother answering.

She took the corner wide, accelerated, and spotted him again several blocks away.

The gap closed. She was faster, lighter, built for speed and endurance.

Luc cut into a side street.

Janice took a different one and burst out nearly parallel, so close she could taste it.

Fifty feet.

Thirty.

Twenty.

She launched herself at him.

Her body slammed into his back; her arms locked around his torso. Momentum carried both of them down. They hit hard, slid, scraped, and for a heartbeat Janice thought she'd gotten him.

Then Luc snarled, planted a foot, and wrenched.

He grabbed her arm and threw her away like she weighed nothing.

Janice twisted midair, landed on her feet, skidded, and came up grinning again.

The train whistle shrieked.

Luc was already moving. He had timed this.

Janice sprinted after him as the station platform came into view.

The train was pulling out slowly but gaining speed.

Luc grabbed for the railing, his grip impossibly strong. He hauled himself up with brutal efficiency, then climbed toward the roof like gravity had negotiated with him.

Janice didn't hesitate.

She leapt for a car farther down, slammed against the side hard enough that pain flared across her ribs, but her hands held. She climbed fast, ignoring the ache, and hauled herself onto the roof.

The wind whipped her hair back.

The vibration under her feet was a living thing, but her balance never wavered.

Janice ran across the roofs, jumping car to car in long, clean arcs.

Luc waited on a car ahead, feet braced, arms crossed like he was watching a show he'd paid for.

Janice's grin widened. *Finally.*

She landed on his car and used the impact to spring again, flipping feet-first toward his head.

Luc dodged.

Janice landed, corrected instantly—

—and Luc's fist cut through the air toward her face.

She danced back out of reach.

"So," Luc said with a chuckle. "You're Janice."

"In the flesh," Janice grinned.

"I wasn't sure you were still alive," he said. "Since you weren't with your brothers."

"Yeah." Janice shrugged. "Dragging my feet."

Luc's eyes flicked over her like he was assessing a weapon. "You're the one who killed my first toy."

"Old geezer?" Janice said with a careless wave. "He talked too much. I got tired of listening."

Luc's mouth tightened. "I admit he wasn't my best work. I was... impatient. I wanted to see my plans in motion."

"And you sent him after me?" Janice laughed. "You must've assumed he'd fail, then. What was his name anyway? I killed him before I found out."

Luc blinked, genuinely annoyed. "Some inane thing. Prospector Tom or whatever. I didn't bother remembering."

Janice laughed again, bright as glass breaking. "You should've. That's embarrassing."

She cocked her head. "So, what was the point? You making friends? Recruiting? Building yourself a little army because you can't handle my brothers and me directly?"

Luc's eyes sharpened. "It was a trial run."

"Well," Janice said sweetly, "it was pathetic. My brothers and I are simply superior to anything you could make."

Luc lunged.

Janice met him halfway.

Their fists collided.

Janice felt the metal in his hand give just a fraction under her strike.

Her grin went feral.

Luc cried out, more outraged than hurt.

"Far superior," Janice said smugly.

She gloated half a heartbeat too long.

Luc's boot drove into her belly.

The breath tore out of her lungs.

The world dropped away.

Janice clawed for the roof, missed—

—and went over the side.

The ground rushed up too fast to think.

She twisted on instinct, hit on hands and feet, skidded, sparks of pain ripping through her shoulder. She felt something in her arm snap—metal, not bone—felt synthetic skin tear away at her palms.

She came to a stop in a crouch, panting hard now, throat raw, eyes stinging with wind and rage.

The train roared away.

Janice stared after it, breath finally coming back in vicious gulps.

"Damn," she muttered hoarsely, taking stock of the damage. "Tony's going to yell."

And so were her brothers.

And that was the part that irritated her most, because when they yelled, it meant they'd been scared.

She pushed to her feet, flexed the damaged arm, hissed at the drag and grind inside it.

Then she looked down the tracks.

"...And now I get to walk."

CHAPTER 38

"Tony!"

Donovan's shout ripped through the garage as he stormed inside. Trevor brushed past him without a word, heading for the stairs, his expression tight and intent, already searching for Regina, unwilling to trust Luc's claim that she hadn't been taken.

Tony emerged from the back of the garage slowly, hands shoved deep into his pockets. His shoulders sagged, his face drawn and hollow, a man already braced for punishment.

Aura followed Donovan as he crossed the space between them. She had never seen him like this, this raw, this unrestrained. His body was rigid with barely leashed violence, his fists clenched as if it took conscious effort not to strike. Betrayal radiated off him in waves, layered with grief, rage, and something far more dangerous: loss.

Tony had been his anchor. His constant.

And now—

Donovan seized Tony by the front of his shirt and slammed him into the wall. Tools rattled. Metal clanged. Tony let out a sharp grunt of pain but didn't raise his hands, didn't resist, didn't even flinch afterward.

Aura noticed. She doubted Donovan did.

"How long," Donovan snarled, yanking him closer, "have you been working for Luc?"

"It's not like that," Tony said quietly.

Donovan slammed him back again. "Then explain it to me, because it sounded exactly like that."

"I only repaired him," Tony said, voice strained. "When he demanded it. I never upgraded him. Never gave him information about you. He doesn't even know I can do more than basic repairs."

Donovan laughed harshly. "Playing both sides? How industrious of you."

Tony's composure cracked. "He threatened my mother and sister!"

The words echoed in the garage.

Donovan froze, only for a second, then drove Tony into the wall again. "So that gave you the right to put *my* family in danger?"

"No!" Tony shouted back. "I moved them. Twice. He found them both times. Told me if I moved them again, he'd kill them."

"You could have told me," Donovan said hoarsely. "You're my best friend. You didn't think I'd help?"

"I knew you would. That's why he made me swear I wouldn't."

Donovan shoved away from him, pacing a step before spinning back, fury uncontained. "He shot Aura. He stole my weapons. He sent modified killers after my brother and sister. And all of it—*all of it*—could have been avoided if you'd trusted me!"

"I'm sorry—"

Donovan's fist slammed into the wall beside Tony's head, embedding deep into the plaster. Dust drifted down between them.

"Don't apologize to me," Donovan said, his voice low and lethal. "Apologize to the dead. And thank me for the fact that I still can't hit you, because if I could, you'd already be dead."

He turned away without another word.

Aura didn't look at him as he passed her. The roar of his bike tore through the night seconds later, fading fast.

Tony remained where he was, staring at the floor.

"I didn't want to do it," he said dully. "He left me no choice."

Aura studied him. The guilt had been there a long time, etched into the slump of his shoulders, the way he hadn't defended himself. He had expected Donovan to hit him. Had planned to take it.

That didn't absolve him.

She stepped closer.

"I am truly sorry," Tony said, lifting his eyes to hers. "For what I did to him. To you."

"Do you feel better now?" Aura asked flatly.

He shook his head. "No."

"Good."

Her fist connected with his face before he could react.

Tony staggered, catching himself against the wall, shock replacing resignation.

Aura turned away without a backward glance.

***

"You have to talk to him eventually. It's been over four hours and he's still standing down there where you left him."

"The hell I do."

Aura rolled her eyes and shifted, rolling on top of Donovan so she could rest her chin on his chest. The movement drew a low sound from him before he stilled again. Her fingers traced slow, absent paths over his bare skin, grounding more than seductive.

He'd ridden off after storming out of the garage, desperate for space that didn't feel like suffocation. Instead, he'd found Janice. She'd climbed onto the back of his bike without a word, listened to everything, and then, infuriatingly, grinned.

"A new twist," she'd called it. "Keeps the game interesting."

Three hours later, he'd brought her back, dropped her off, and gone straight to Aura.

He'd slammed the door behind him and pulled her into him with a ferocity that had nothing to do with desire and everything to do with survival. Aura hadn't resisted. She'd let him burn the edge off his fury in the only way he could right now.

It had helped, but the anger hadn't gone anywhere. It was just quieter now.

"You know why he did it," Aura said now, her voice steady. "Even if you hate him. Can you honestly say you wouldn't have done the same thing in his position?"

Donovan lifted his head slightly, one brow rising. "When did you become the voice of reason?"

"Sickening, isn't it?" she grinned.

He huffed a laugh despite himself, then sighed and let his head fall back to the pillow.

He *did* understand Tony's reasons. That was the problem. Understanding didn't make it hurt less.

What cut deepest wasn't even the betrayal, it was the realization that he hadn't *seen it*. Hadn't sensed that anything was wrong. Tony had always been his constant. His anchor. The man who thought the same way he did, half a step ahead or behind him at all times.

And Donovan had missed it.

That failure sat in his chest like a weight.

Aura shifted again, then leaned down and flicked her tongue briefly across his nipple.

Donovan sucked in a sharp breath, every thought scattering.

She grinned when she felt him tense. "So," she said lightly, "what are you going to do?"

"I'm going to make love to you again," he said promptly, sliding his hands over her hips and squeezing.

She gasped and smacked his chest. "Not that. About Tony!"

He winced more from surprise than pain. "I'm going to let him stew."

She hit him again, harder this time.

"Ow!"

Aura glared down at him. "You're going to go down there and tell him you understand."

Donovan rubbed a hand over his face. "Aura, if I see him right now, I'm going to hit him. And if I hit him like this," He exhaled sharply. "I'll kill him."

"You don't have to," she shot back. "Didn't I tell you? I already hit him for you."

Donovan burst out laughing, the sound rough but real. He pulled her down against him and held her there.

"What would I do without you?" he murmured.

"Live a long, happy, uneventful life," she shrugged.

He rolled them so he was above her, kissing her gently. "I'd rather have a short, miserable, eventful one with you."

"You don't mean that," she said softly, nibbling his jaw.

He pulled back, frowning. "Who says I don't?"

She deflected instantly. "So, are you going to put Tony out of his misery or not? Because right now he's probably debating whether offering you his head would help."

Donovan snorted. "He's doing no such thing."

"Fine," Aura conceded. "But he *does* feel awful."

"He should."

"And I'm not arguing that." Her tone softened. "But this isn't worth losing him over. I asked him why he chose them over you."

Donovan went still.

"He said you and your siblings could survive Luc. His mother and sister couldn't. He protected the ones who needed it most. He did it out of love."

Donovan stared at her for a long moment, then let his head drop to her chest. Her hands slid into his hair, slow and soothing.

"I know," he muttered. "I know why he did it. I just can't believe he didn't come to me. I need time to wrap my head around that."

"One hour," Aura said flatly.

He lifted his head again. "Excuse me?"

"One hour," she repeated. "Then you go downstairs. You tell him you get it. You don't have to forgive him—but you don't leave it like this."

Donovan traced her cheek with his fingers, studying her a long moment.

She met his gaze calmly, already certain of the outcome.

"I knew there was a reason I loved you."

Aura stiffened instantly.

"Don't do that."

"Do what?" he asked mildly.

"I think you should let me up now."

He rolled aside at once, cursing himself as she slipped off the bed and pulled on her clothes.

"I meant it," he said quietly.

"The hell you did," she snapped. "You love sleeping with me."

"Why do you keep insisting you're unlovable?" he demanded.

"Because I'm a—"

"If you say 'whore,'" he cut in sharply, "I swear I'll beat you."

She scoffed.

"What you *are* and who you *are* are not the same," he said fiercely. "And who you are is easy to love."

"I've known hundreds of men who'd disagree."

"And I'll bet you never showed them who you were, only what they wanted."

"There *is* no difference," she snapped, slamming out of the room.

"Goddammit."

***

Aura reclined against the arm of the couch, her spine curved just enough to ache, staring out the bank of windows as though the horizon might offer her absolution. It didn't. The glass in her hand caught the light as she swirled the amber liquid, watching it cling to the sides before sliding back down.

The first bottle hadn't dulled anything. The second wasn't doing much better.

I knew there was a reason I loved you.

The words hit her again, fresh and sharp, as if Donovan had just spoken them.

Her jaw tightened.

Damn him.

Damn him for saying it without hesitation. For saying it like it was *fact*, not a weapon. For dropping it into the space between them without warning, as if she had any idea how to catch something like that without bleeding.

She had *known* this was coming. She'd felt it building for weeks, months, even. The way he lingered longer. The way his touches had shifted from possession to something gentler, more reverent. She should have left then. Should have ended it before it grew roots.

She should never have touched him.

She was supposed to keep herself contained. Detached. Useful, but never wanted. Touch was meant to be transactional, not… intimate. She'd survived by drawing clean, brutal lines between herself and everyone else.

So why had Donovan crossed them so easily?

Her fingers tightened around the glass as a rush of warmth—traitorous, dizzying—spread through her chest at the memory of his voice. Not hunger. Not lust.

Something worse.

Something dangerously close to hope.

No.

She swallowed hard and took another drink, welcoming the burn.

She wasn't going to fall in love with him.

Love was a luxury for people who believed in tomorrows. For people who weren't living on borrowed time and borrowed bodies. For people who hadn't built their entire existence around a single inevitable ending.

She needed space. Distance. Control.

She'd move out of his room. Stop sleeping with him. Stop letting him touch her like she mattered. She would ignore the hollow, panicked ache that bloomed at the thought.

That was what was best. For both of them.

He shouldn't fall in love with a whore.

The thought came automatically, reflexive as a flinch. She'd spent years shaping herself into something disposable, something that could be used and discarded without consequence. She had *warned* him. Pushed him away. Given him every chance to leave.

But stubborn bastard that he was, he'd gone and done it anyway.

Fine.

She would change his mind. She always did.

After Luc was dead, she'd leave. No goodbyes. No explanations. She wouldn't give herself the chance to look back and wonder what might have been if she'd let herself want something more than vengeance.

Her eyes burned.

She hated that.

She finished the glass and refilled it with a sharp, angry splash.

She would *not* fall in love with him.

And if she repeated it enough, if she drowned herself in liquor and resolve, maybe she could silence the voice inside her that had wanted, so desperately, to say it back.

She drank again, then abandoned the glass entirely and lifted the bottle instead. The liquor scorched its way down her throat, fierce enough to almost feel like punishment.

Good.

Maybe a third bottle would finally quiet the questions.

Why she fought him so hard.

Why she couldn't let herself pretend the past didn't own her. Why she couldn't believe that someone might see her and still choose her.

Hope was dangerous.

Love was worse.

Voices drifted up the stairs. She barely reacted, only craning her neck when the door opened and Donovan and Trevor stepped inside.

"…Are you sure it's wise to trust her?" Donovan was asking.

Aura didn't move. Didn't turn. She listened with the practiced stillness of someone used to overhearing conversations she wasn't meant to be part of.

"She really didn't know about Luc," Trevor replied. "She's completely repulsed by his actions and is sorry for her part in them."

"That doesn't really answer my question," Donovan said. "She could just be a good actress, waiting for an opportunity to kill us."

Trevor shook his head. "I don't think she's faking. She's not a bad person. She's just had a lot of bad things happen to her. Luc was the first person to offer her something good in a long time."

Aura's fingers tightened around the bottle. *Good.* She almost laughed. As if anything Luc touched stayed that way.

"And he did do something good for her," Trevor continued. "He gave her back her sight."

"I suppose so," Donovan sighed. "I just don't want to see you get hurt."

Trevor chuckled. "I'm a big boy. I can take care of myself."

Only then did Donovan notice her.

"I've been looking for you," he said, sounding almost surprised.

"Then you didn't look very hard," Aura replied flatly, her head still tipped back over the arm of the couch. "I've been here since I left you."

He crossed the room, frowning when he took in the empty bottle on the table and the half-empty one in her hand. She saw the flicker of concern in his eyes and the restraint when he chose not to comment.

That restraint hurt more than judgment would have.

She straightened only when he sat across from her. "Was there a specific reason you were looking for me?"

"We wanted to discuss the situation with Luc," Donovan said, waiting for Trevor to join him.

"Go ahead," she shrugged, taking another drink. "Don't let my being here stop you."

"Aura," Donovan frowned, "we wanted to discuss it *with* you."

She let out a short laugh. "You usually discuss Luc around me. Why the sudden courtesy?"

"You are always included in the conversation."

Her jaw tightened. "You mean like when you told me to stay in that chair and shut up while you and your siblings decided my future for me?"

"That was different," he scowled.

"I beg to differ." She looked away and drank again.

"Aura," Donovan said carefully, "Trevor and I think we should put off going after Luc right now."

The bottle lowered slowly. Too slowly.

She swung her legs off the couch and sat up, fixing them both with a glare sharp enough to cut. "Tell me you're joking."

"I'm not. We think it's too dangerous to go after him now."

"But we know where he's going," she shot back. "It would be simple to go after him and end this."

"Not simple," Donovan shook his head. "We don't know what he has at the compound. We've seen his mods, the hired thugs. Who knows what else he's prepared."

"He's damaged," Aura snapped. "Alice is damaged. We should go after them *now*, before they can repair themselves."

"It's too dangerous," Donovan insisted. "If we wait, he'll come to us again and we won't be walking blind into his territory."

"Wait?" Aura laughed harshly. "I've been waiting for five damn years! I want him dead, Donovan."

"I know you do. That's why we wanted to talk to you."

"You don't want to talk to me," she growled. "You've already decided. You just want me to obey."

"That's not fair. We just want to get through this without anyone getting killed."

"Haven't you figured out yet," she demanded, standing abruptly, "that I don't care if I get killed as long as Luc goes with me? In fact, it would make things easier."

"Why are you so intent on destroying yourself?" Donovan shot back, rising to his feet.

"Because everything I have revolves around his death," she said, voice shaking despite her effort to steady it. "Once that happens, there's nothing left for me."

"My God, you never expected to survive," he said in sudden realization.

She swallowed. "No."

The word landed hard.

"If I didn't believe suicide was cowardly," she added, "I probably would have done it if I survived."

"Jesus, Aura!" Donovan exploded. "You won't even give me a chance to change your mind!"

"This was never about you!"

"Bullshit!" he snapped. "I offer you a life with me and you won't even consider it!"

"I have no life to offer back!" she screamed. "Every part of me was built around ending him!"

"If that were true," Donovan said, his voice breaking through the chaos, "I wouldn't have fallen in love with you."

The room tilted.

Don't.

Please don't.

"I didn't fall in love with your hunt," he continued. "I fell in love with *you*."

Something inside her shattered.

If she let herself believe him, she would have to let go of Luc. Let go of the one thing that had kept her alive when everything else had been taken.

She couldn't.

She wouldn't.

"I can't," she sobbed, hurling the bottle across the room before she turned and ran, tears blinding her as the glass shattered against the wall.

Damn him.

Damn him for making her want something she didn't know how to survive.

CHAPTER 39

Donovan dropped heavily back into his seat with a frustrated sigh and leaned his head back against the couch, closing his eyes. His hands were clenched tightly in his lap, his shoulders rigid with tension.

He'd handled that badly.

He knew he'd failed in explaining to Aura why waiting was safer than chasing Luc headlong. Worse than that, he'd failed the moment he'd asked her to give up her revenge, as if Luc were something she could simply set aside. He should have known better. The hunt was woven into her bones, bound up in the few emotions she allowed herself to feel.

But when she'd said she expected to die with Luc—

The memory sent a jolt of panic through him even now.

"That was an… interesting discussion," Trevor said dryly when Donovan didn't move.

"Shut up, Trevor," Donovan muttered.

"Aren't you supposed to get down on one knee when you propose?"

"Shut up, Trevor!"

"That was a proposal, wasn't it?"

Donovan opened his eyes and shot his brother a glare. "Yes. It was. And if you hadn't noticed, she turned me down."

"That was a rather distressing statement she made," Trevor said soberly. "I don't think any of us realized how deep her pain runs."

"I don't know how to fix this," Donovan admitted quietly.

"Maybe if you hadn't framed it like an ultimatum," Trevor said. "You or Luc."

"I didn't mean it that way," Donovan snapped, then scrubbed a hand over his face. "I'll take her any way she'll have me. But when she said she'd rather die than stay—" He broke off, jaw tightening. "I panicked."

Trevor studied him a moment. "Give her time. She's upset. When she calms down, maybe she'll understand what you were trying to say."

"As much as I'd like to think that, she's never given me any indication she would," Donovan said heavily.

"You proposed without knowing how she felt?" Trevor asked incredulously.

"The only time I think she feels anything is in bed," Donovan muttered.

"Well," Trevor said thoughtfully, "maybe that's the only way she knows how to show it."

Donovan snorted, but the comment lodged anyway.

Before he could respond, Tony appeared in the doorway.

"Hey," Tony said. "Where's Aura going?"

Donovan frowned. "What do you mean?"

"She just rode out. Packed. Wouldn't say where."

"Son of a bitch." Donovan was on his feet before the words finished. He ran for the stairs.

Trevor followed more slowly. "I believe our angel has deserted us."

"You mean for good?" Tony asked.

"If Donovan doesn't find her."

They moved back toward the windows just in time to see Donovan roar off down the street on his bike.

"I don't know if he'll catch her," Tony said.

"She doesn't want to be found," Trevor replied. "That gives her the advantage."

Tony crossed his arms. "Why'd she leave?"

"He proposed," Trevor said.

"Well damn," Tony said with a grin. "About time."

"He also asked her to give up Luc."

Tony winced. "Yeah… that'll do it."

"I don't think he expected her to run," Trevor said quietly. "I didn't either."

"Do you think she'll come back on her own?"

Trevor sighed. "I hope so. He'll be impossible until she does."

Tony nodded. "I think we've all gotten attached to her."

"It didn't take her long to worm her way into the family," Trevor said faintly. "*And now it is true that I am thy near kinsman.*"

"Where'd lover boy and the blonde bitch go?" Janice asked casually as she strode up behind them.

Trevor didn't bother turning. "Aura's running and Donovan went after her."

Janice raised a brow. "Ah. So, he finally said it."

Tony glanced at her. "You knew?"

"Please," Janice scoffed. "I could smell that coming a mile away."

Trevor turned back toward the window, watching the empty street.

Miles away now, Donovan rode hard, the wind tearing at his jacket, Aura's words still ringing in his ears. Underneath the panic and fear, another thought stirred, one he'd buried deep.

The portrait.

The woman's painted face at the Hartly estate. The resemblance he'd never spoken aloud. The implication he carried alone.

If Aura ever learned the truth—if there was truth to learn—it could shatter what little ground she stood on now.

Not now, he thought grimly. Not like this.

He leaned forward on the bike, pushing it faster.

He had to find her first.

CHAPTER 40

Aura sat at the bar, nimble fingers loosely circling a shot glass, eyes unfocused as she silently cursed herself for a fool.

Rule number one: never fall in love.

She'd broken it. Cleanly. Thoroughly. It had taken her barely an hour after riding out of town to admit it, and another hour to realize just how badly she missed the infuriating, earnest bastard. Damn Donovan. Damn him for smiling at her like she was something worth keeping. There had never been room in her plan for love, no space for it, no safety net.

Love was a liability.

Two weeks had passed since she'd stormed out of Tony's place. Two weeks spent chasing rumors of a compound that might not even exist, and fighting the urge, every damn night, to turn Aries around and ride straight back to Donovan.

Since leaving, the nightmares had sharpened.

Her eyes were rimmed dark with exhaustion, her nerves stretched thin as wire. Sleeping outdoors didn't help anymore. Nothing did. Night brought her mother's screams first, always first, then Donovan, dying in her place, Luc laughing as the world burned. She woke every time with her own voice tearing out of her, heart hammering, fingers clawing for a weapon that wasn't there.

She was unraveling. She knew it.

The only solution left was the one she'd always relied on.

Find Luc. Finish it.

After that… she'd do what she'd always planned if she survived. Disappear. Fade into nowhere.

She just hoped she found him before the nightmares finished the job.

With a weary groan, Aura let her forehead drop to the bar. The wood was cool against her skin. Solid. Real. The bartender appeared in front of her.

"Want a refill?"

She lifted the empty glass without raising her head. Whiskey splashed over her fingers as he poured.

"Are we playing guess the booze?" she heard behind her.

"Oh, for fuck's sake."

Her spine stiffened at the voice. She groaned louder.

"What the hell are you doing here, Janice?" she demanded, voice muffled by the bar.

"What do you think I'm doing?" Janice said brightly. "I'm here to drag your ass home so my whiny brother will shut the hell up about you."

Aura lifted her head and glared. Janice smirked.

"Jesus," Janice added. "You look like shit."

"Thanks," Aura said flatly, tossing back the shot. The burn barely registered. "Hadn't noticed."

She stood. Her legs were steady, too steady. Anger always burned cleaner than drink.

"You can go now. I'm not coming back."

"I suppose I shouldn't tell Donovan I found you?" Janice said mildly, folding her arms.

The name landed like a punch she hadn't braced for.

"I don't give a damn what you tell him," Aura said. "I won't be here when he gets here."

"You say that like I don't plan on dragging you back whether you want to go or not."

"Try it," Aura said as she brushed past her, "and we'll find out how many bullets it takes to put you down."

Janice doubled over laughing, clutching the bar.

"Oh, that's rich," she gasped. "You put *me* down."

Aura stopped and rolled her eyes. "If you're finished, you can leave."

"Oh, give it up, you silly bitch," Janice said, straightening. "You're family now. That means when someone runs, we drag them back."

"I didn't want a family," Aura snapped. The words came faster, sharper than she'd intended. "I didn't ask for one. Your devil of a brother forced me into it."

Janice snorted. "He didn't force you into shit. You wormed your own way in."

"I was there for information," Aura shot back. "He's the one who dragged me across the country and introduced me to everyone he's ever met."

"And because of that," Janice said bluntly, "you're still alive. Without what you learned, Luc would've broken you before killing you."

Aura slapped away a wandering hand at her backside, irritation flaring.

"That's not all he did," she said tightly. "He ruined me. He made me laugh. Made me see what it could be like to belong."

The words caught. She bit them back too late.

Janice tilted her head. "He made you love him."

Aura's jaw clenched. Love wasn't salvation. Love was a future she didn't know how to survive.

A heavy body pressed in behind her. Hands closed around her hips. Aura shoved them away.

"I can't go back," she said. "It's not—" She cut herself off. "It's not fair. I'm killing Luc, and then I'm gone."

"He's not letting you go," Janice replied. "He wants to keep you."

The hands at her hips tightened.

Aura's body went cold in that instant, not fear, not surprise, but the sharp, clarifying calm that always came before violence. Her weight shifted automatically, balance adjusting even as her mind catalogued threats.

Too close. Too bold. Too stupid.

"Oh, for fuck's sake," she snapped, slamming her elbow back into the man's midsection.

The impact landed solid, drawing a grunt from him, but when she spun and drove her fist into his jaw, she felt bone shift without the satisfying give she expected. His head snapped to the side, but he barely staggered.

Too big.

And her stomach sank as she registered the rest of them. Four more men nearby, spread loose and lazy, amused rather than alarmed. She cursed herself for not counting sooner. Drink had dulled her edge just enough to matter.

The big man touched his jaw, blinking at her like she'd offended him rather than struck him.

"Well, I'll be damned," he drawled, grinning wide and rotten. "Got some fire in you, don't ya?"

Aura exhaled slowly through her nose, centering herself. Her body loosened even as her mind sharpened.

"Care to step in?" she tossed back to Janice without looking away.

"Thought you could take care of yourself," Janice shot back, delighted.

"I can," Aura said quietly. "Just wasn't in the mood."

The man lunged.

She didn't have time to curse before the world tilted violently, his arm hooking around her waist, hauling her up and over his shoulder like a sack of grain. His grip was iron-hard, fingers digging into her thigh as laughter erupted around them.

Her pulse spiked. Adrenaline flooded her veins, hot and clean.

"You've got three seconds to put me down," she growled, voice low and lethal.

The laughter only grew louder.

Fine.

Aura twisted, using the momentum of his stride. She slid her weight forward, hooked her legs beneath his arms, and swung herself up until she was perched across his shoulders. Her thighs clamped tight around his head.

The sudden shift knocked him off balance.

Before he could react, she drove her fist down into his temple.

Once.

Twice.

Again.

He roared in pain, staggering sideways as his hands clawed for her. She caught his fingers mid-grab—one from each hand—and snapped them backward with brutal precision.

The scream that tore out of him was high and wet.

As his grip faltered, Aura slammed both palms hard against his ears.

She felt the pop more than heard it.

The man collapsed to his knees, hands flailing uselessly as he screamed, disoriented and bleeding from his ears.

Aura shoved off him and hit the floor running but the others were already moving.

A fist grazed her shoulder. Another whistled past her head close enough to stir her hair. She ducked, spun, drove her boot into one man's knee and felt it buckle sickeningly beneath the blow.

Someone grabbed her from behind, arms locked around her ribs, crushing the breath from her lungs.

Pain flared bright and sharp as another fist slammed into her cheek.

Stars exploded behind her eyes.

She bit down on a scream, tasting blood, and kicked backward with everything she had. Her heel connected with a shin. The hold loosened just enough.

Aura dropped her weight suddenly, throwing her head back hard into the man's face. He cursed, grip loosening further and she surged forward, planting a boot square into another man's chin.

He went down.

Her captor lost his balance, and they both hit the floor. Aura rolled instantly, barely missing a boot that crashed down where her head had been a heartbeat before.

She kicked sideways, felt cartilage give in a knee, heard another scream.

Then weight slammed into her.

Two bodies.

She hit the floor hard, breath punched from her lungs as fists rained down, shoulder, ribs, jaw. Pain flared everywhere at once, chaotic and overwhelming. She curled instinctively, arms up, trying to protect her head as boots scraped for leverage.

This was stupid, a distant part of her thought. *Reckless. Just like Donovan said.*

A snarl cut through the noise.

Suddenly the weight vanished.

Bodies flew.

Aura blinked, dragging air back into her lungs as the world swam into focus.

Janice stood over her like a demon unleashed, eyes bright and furious, stance loose and lethal.

"You fuck with my sister," Janice snarled, "you fuck with me."

One man rushed her.

Janice didn't even look strained as she caught his arms, twisted sharply, and snapped both with a wet crack before hurling him across the room like a rag doll.

That did it.

The remaining men broke.

Those who could still move ran for the door, tripping over chairs and each other in their panic. The bar erupted into chaos—shouting, scrambling, overturned stools—but no one moved to stop them.

The man with the shattered knee stayed where he was, curled on the floor and whimpering.

Janice turned back to Aura and offered her a hand.

Aura took it, letting herself be hauled to her feet. Her ribs screamed in protest; her cheek throbbed fiercely, swelling fast. She rolled her shoulder experimentally. Pain, but nothing broken.

She looked at Janice, brow raised.

"What?" Janice demanded.

"Thought we agreed I could take care of myself."

Janice scoffed, turning away. "Yeah. Well. You looked like you could use backup."

"And the sister thing?" Aura pressed.

Janice planted a hand on her hip and shot her a glare. "Family," she said bluntly. "We protect our own."

The words landed heavier than the punches.

Aura said nothing, but something in her chest twisted, sharp and unfamiliar.

***

Donovan sat at the back of the shop with his head in his hands, elbows braced on his knees, staring down at the floorboards as if they might offer absolution.

They never did.

His fingers were tangled in his hair, gripping hard enough to hurt, but he barely registered the pain. Compared to the hollow ache in his chest, it was nothing. Every breath dragged across something sharp, like his heart had been pierced with thousands of needles and his lungs insisted on rubbing against them anyway.

He replayed that day endlessly.

Every word. Every pause. Every moment he could have stopped himself and hadn't.

If he hadn't framed it like an ultimatum.

If he hadn't said Luc's name like a challenge.

If he hadn't let fear speak louder than love.

Her declaration haunted him most, not her anger, not even her leaving, but the quiet certainty in her voice when she admitted she'd never planned to survive Luc.

That knowledge sat in him like a poison.

He'd spent a week trying to track her down before finally admitting what he'd known from the start: Aura would never be found if she didn't want to be. And she clearly didn't.

At first, he'd clung to the hope that she would come back on her own, that she'd cool off, that she'd miss him the way he missed her. But that fragile glimmer dimmed a little more each day, worn thin by silence.

Janice was still out searching. The thought steadied him more than he liked to admit. Tony was working the repaired terminal relentlessly, calling in favors, leaning on contacts in every town within a week's ride.

Nothing.

No sightings. No rumors. No trace.

Every day she was gone, Donovan felt like something vital was being slowly carved out of him.

He hadn't realized—couldn't have imagined—how completely she had woven herself into his life. How much of his sense of *home* had quietly become *her*. Now the absence was everywhere. In the bed. In the silence. In the way his body still reached for her in the dark.

One thought, in particular, was driving him toward madness.

Luc finding her first.

Luc hurting her.

Luc killing her, and Donovan never knowing unless Luc decided to savor it.

His chest hitched. His body rocked forward as the images surged unbidden: Aura broken, bloody, screaming his name, or worse, not screaming at all.

Something in him gave way.

Donovan surged to his feet with a raw, shattered cry that tore from his throat and echoed through the shop. He kicked the chair away, sending it crashing into the far wall. His hands closed around whatever was nearest—tools, crates, scraps of metal—and flung them blindly, violently, as if he could tear the pain out of his body by force.

He barely registered the impact when a hard body tackled him from behind.

Sinewy arms locked around his chest, pinning his upper arms to his sides. He fought on instinct, a feral snarl ripping from him as he struggled but then Trevor stepped into his line of sight, gripping his head firmly, calling his name.

He hadn't even realized he was still crying out.

Gradually, Trevor's voice cut through the noise in his skull. Donovan's resistance faltered. Tony didn't release him immediately, holding him steady until the shaking subsided.

"Brother," Trevor said gently once Donovan had gone still. "You can't keep on like this."

"I need her," Donovan said hoarsely.

The words felt torn from somewhere deep and unguarded. His eyes burned, glassy and red, reflecting every ounce of his pain.

"I know," Trevor replied softly. "We'll find her."

"Before Luc does?"

The hesitation was brief but devastating. Donovan saw it. The flicker of fear Trevor couldn't quite hide.

Tony answered from behind him. "You can't keep torturing yourself, Donny. Aura's a tough girl. Smart. She'll be fine."

"You didn't hear her," Donovan said brokenly. "She has no intention of living. She's out there looking for Luc and he's going to find her."

"We'll find her first," Tony said firmly. "Janice and I are still looking. Maybe Janice has news. She said she'd be back this evening."

Hope sparked painfully.

"Do you think so?" he asked, voice cracking. "Do you think she found her?"

Tony released him then, stepping back so Donovan could turn to face him. "I hope so. She didn't say."

"God, I hope so," Donovan murmured, dragging a hand through his hair. "I'd give anything to have her back here. I don't even care if she never wants to marry me. I just need her here, with me. Safe. Even if she told me she never wanted me to touch her again—"

Tony snorted.

Donovan shot him a look.

"Well, okay," he amended, exhaling shakily. "That's pushing it. But you get my point."

Tony stepped forward and pulled Donovan into a tight hug. "You're my brother," he said quietly. "Doesn't matter that we were born to different parents."

He pulled back but kept his hands firm on Donovan's shoulders. "I hate seeing you like this. I know what I'm feeling, knowing she's gone—out there—with Luc. I can't even imagine what you're feeling. But you need to remember, we're here. We'll help. We'll do whatever it takes to find her and bring her back."

Then he grinned. "And you know I'll do whatever it takes to get her to marry you."

Donovan let out a breath that was almost a laugh and dropped his forehead to Tony's. "I don't know what I'd do without all of you."

He grabbed Trevor around the neck and pulled him in, forming a rough, ungraceful three-way hug. "Thank you. Both of you. I know I've been hard to be around."

"Ghastly," Trevor deadpanned.

"Just awful," Tony agreed.

Donovan managed a faint smirk. "Alright, alright. I won't give up just yet. I'm just going to cross my fingers that Janice found something."

He released them and finally looked around at the wreckage he'd made of the shop.

"…Uh. Sorry, Tony."

Tony laughed. "Oh, don't be sorry. You'll be cleaning it up."

***

As Donovan sat in despondency while Trevor and Tony tried, poorly, to distract him from his own thoughts, Janice strolled into the garage with none of the urgency he desperately wanted to see. She ignored both brothers completely and headed straight for the stairs.

Donovan was on his feet instantly.

"Did you find her?" he demanded, the edge in his voice sharp enough to cut.

"Do you see her?" Janice shot back without breaking stride.

To his credit, Donovan actually turned, eyes flying to the wide garage doors, his heart surging stupidly, irrationally, as if Aura might be standing there this very second.

She wasn't.

The hope collapsed just as fast.

His brow lowered and he bounded after Janice, taking the stairs two at a time. He caught her on the second floor just as she was entering her room.

"So, you didn't find her," he said flatly, disappointment dragging at every word.

"I didn't say that."

His eyes narrowed. "Dammit, Janice, did you find her or not?"

"Yes," she said casually, yanking a pack from beneath her bed and tossing it onto the mattress.

Relief hit him like a blow, followed immediately by frustration so sharp it made his teeth ache. He shoved a hand through his hair, barely resisting the urge to shake answers out of her.

"Which is it?" he demanded, stepping into the room as she began stuffing the pack with supplies, guns, ammunition, gear that made his stomach tighten.

"Yes, I found her," Janice said. "No, I can't tell you where she is."

The words landed hard.

Donovan froze.

She was alive. Found.

But not his.

"Is she alright?" The question came out rougher than he meant it to.

"As well as could be expected," Janice said, evasive as hell.

Panic stirred as he took in the pack more carefully. This wasn't a casual visit. This was preparation.

"Luc has her," he said urgently, stepping closer.

"No."

"Then she found the compound?"

"Of course not," Janice snorted. "No one can find that place."

The indifference in her tone nearly broke him.

Donovan grabbed her arm and spun her to face him, rage and fear crashing together in his chest. "Dammit, Janice, tell me where the hell she is!"

She looked up at him calmly. Infuriatingly calm.

"I can't."

He turned away, a raw sound tearing out of him.

"Why not?!"

"Because I promised her I wouldn't."

He stared at her in disbelief. "You promised her?" His voice rose despite himself. "I'm losing my damn mind here and you won't tell me because you *promised her*? Since when are you two such good friends?"

He knew he was yelling. Knew it wasn't helping. But fear had stripped him raw, and Janice—damn her—smirked like she was enjoying every second of it.

"Fine," he growled. "If you won't tell me, I'll just follow you to her."

"Who said I'm going back?" Janice said mildly.

"You're packing," he snapped, jabbing a finger at the bag. "And I'd bet my bike it has everything to do with Aura."

"That's because your head is filled with Aura," she laughed, crossing her arms.

"But you *are* going back to her," Donovan said. He was certain now.

"If I was, it wouldn't do you any good. She doesn't want to see you right now."

"I'll follow you."

"Won't help. If she sees you, she'll disappear again."

The sound he made then was ugly, raw pain dragged straight out of his chest.

Janice sighed, the humor finally fading. "She needs a reason to come back," she said seriously.

"I'm not enough for her?" The words tasted bitter.

"I'm sure you are," Janice replied. "But she's so tangled up in her own mess she can't admit it, even to herself. That woman is stubborn as a mule."

"So, you're going to fix it?" he asked warily.

"I'm going to make it easy for her."

"How?"

Janice shook her head, slinging the pack over her shoulder. "All part of what I can't tell you."

She brushed past him.

Donovan watched her go, arms crossing slowly over his chest. He knew she was done talking. Janice only ever explained herself when she felt like it.

But he wasn't blind.

Whatever she'd promised Aura, whatever she planned to do, he could see the shape of it forming already.

And this time, he wouldn't be caught off guard.

He'd involve Tony. Trevor. He'd let Janice leave first, no warnings, no interference. Aura *would* run again if she thought he was onto her.

But now he knew she was alive.

Safe.

For the moment.

And that was enough.

Donovan exhaled slowly, the tightness in his chest easing for the first time in weeks. A smile—low, dangerous, full of resolve—curved his mouth.

"I'll find you, sweetheart," he murmured. "And this time… I won't let you run from me."

CHAPTER 41

Despite telling herself repeatedly that she would stay away for at least a week—long enough that Donovan might give up looking—Aura found herself back in town two days ahead of schedule.

She told herself it was tactical. Information gathering. Making sure Janice hadn't decided to betray her to her brothers despite their plan to meet back here in a week.

Still, the guilt gnawed at her as she made a careful sweep of the town, watching rooftops, alleys, the saloon doors. No sign of the MacHavens. No ambush waiting to spring. Only after she was satisfied did she settle in to wait.

Janice arrived right on time.

Aura met her on the boardwalk and immediately took in the large sack slung over Janice's arm.

"Did you cut him up and put him in the sack?" Aura asked, one brow lifting.

"Nah. That would be too easy," Janice smirked. "But I did bring you provisions."

She set the bag down and opened it.

Aura leaned in and blinked.

Inside wasn't food. Or bedrolls.

It was an arsenal.

"Looks like you're ready to start a war," Aura said slowly.

"Damn. You guessed the plan," Janice said with a theatrical pout. "I wanted to surprise you."

Aura felt something tight in her chest finally loosen. Not relief. Anticipation.

"Please tell me we're taking that war to Luc," she said, hope creeping into her voice despite herself.

"Grabbing a few supplies and heading straight to the compound," Janice confirmed, slinging the bag back over her shoulder.

"Finally," Aura breathed, falling into step beside her.

Janice said it would take nearly a week to reach the compound.

Aura didn't question it. She was used to long rides, longer waits. They stocked up on supplies and rode out into the desert, the land opening wide and empty around them.

Aura hadn't expected to enjoy the trail with Janice.

She certainly hadn't expected to laugh.

Janice filled the days with stories—half brag, half absurdity—about jobs gone wrong, men who underestimated her, fights she probably should have lost but somehow hadn't. Some stories sounded impossible. All of them sounded *true*.

It was strange, being pulled out of her own head without effort.

On their second night out, as the fire crackled low and the desert wind cooled, Aura finally asked the question that had been needling her since the saloon.

"Why are you doing this?"

Janice didn't look up. "Doing what?"

"You know what," Aura said. "Taking me to the compound. Your family's been dead set against it. Against bringing the fight to Luc. Especially against taking me."

Janice poked at the fire with a stick. "Because you looked like you might change your mind about going back."

Aura frowned.

"And," Janice continued lightly, "because my brother doesn't get to tell you what to do. He tells *me* what to do, but… well. He's my brother."

Something twisted low in Aura's stomach.

"You didn't tell him what we're doing," she said.

"I did not tell him what we're doing," Janice replied, enunciating each word with care.

Aura stared at her.

Then swore softly. "He's going to be there, isn't he."

Janice shrugged. Smirked. "Probably."

Aura cursed again, leaning back and crossing her arms. Of course he would follow. Of course he wouldn't let her do this alone.

"Don't worry," Janice added. "Once you're there, he can't exactly stop you from going in."

"He'll try," Aura muttered, already running through contingencies. Distractions. Routes. Ways to disappear if she had to.

After a few minutes, she realized Janice was watching her closely.

Janice's serious expressions were rare enough to be unsettling.

"Can I ask you something?" Janice said.

Then, without waiting, "Why won't you marry my brother? And don't give me the revenge-is-my-life bullshit or the whore excuse. The real reason."

Aura didn't answer right away.

She watched the fire. Felt the weight of the desert pressing in. Long enough that Janice might have thought she wouldn't answer at all.

"Because he wants me," Aura said finally.

Janice blinked. "Well, that's just stupid. Of course he does. He wouldn't have bedded you if he didn't."

"No," Aura said quietly. "I mean, he wants *me*. Not the whore. Not the bitch. Me."

She swallowed.

"I don't even know who that is. What I am. But he sees something worth keeping. Something more than I've ever been allowed to be." Her voice tightened. "And that scares me."

Janice frowned. "Has he actually said that?"

"No. But I feel myself changing around him," Aura admitted, eyes closing. "He makes happiness look… easy. Like it's just there for the taking. And I don't know how to react to that."

She opened her eyes, staring into the fire.

"It's like standing outside a room where there's a party. Everyone inside is laughing, alive, happy. And you're afraid to step over the threshold because you're sure they'll see right through you and decide you don't belong." Her chest ached. "But you want to go in so badly it hurts. So, you just stand there. Frozen."

Janice snorted. "Then step into the damn room and fuck what everyone else thinks."

"It's not that simple."

Janice was quiet for a moment. Then, softer, "But if there's no hope for you two… what hope do I have?"

That startled Aura more than any of it.

She turned to look at Janice properly, really look at her, and realized how little she'd ever done that before.

Smart. Fierce. Loyal. Wild. Not built for polite boxes or easy futures.

Not so different from herself.

Aura felt something uncomfortable shift inside her.

In the end, she didn't have an answer.

So, she stayed silent, watching the fire burn low, knowing the road ahead would demand one soon enough.

CHAPTER 42

Four days later, they reached the compound.

It was a massive, one-story structure squatting low against the desert, its concrete exterior scarred by the unmistakable signs of a large explosion and fire damage. One entire side had partially collapsed inward. A barbed-wire fence circled the building, but most of it lay flattened or rusted through, long abandoned.

"This is it?" Aura asked quietly as they hunkered behind a large boulder overlooking the site.

"Welcome to the compound."

Janice's tone was uncharacteristically sober as she crouched and began sketching a crude map in the sand with her finger. "There's a second level below, but it's mostly old caverns and storage. He won't be down there."

Aura leaned in, eyes tracking Janice's movements.

"I don't know how much of the interior is still standing after the explosion," Janice continued, "but this is the main control room. Most likely place for him. Surgery bay's here." She drew a second square. "Problem is, we'd have to pass at least two dozen rooms to get to either."

Aura's jaw tightened.

"No idea who's inside," Janice finished, "or what they can do—"

"Which is why you shouldn't be going in there alone."

Aura and Janice both startled. Aura's hand went instantly to her gun.

Donovan's hand came down over hers just as fast, firm, unyielding. She sucked in a sharp breath and looked up at him, fury flashing in her eyes. His were just as hard.

"What do you two think you're doing?" he demanded.

"Killing Luc," Janice said brightly, glancing between Donovan, Trevor, and Tony as if this were all perfectly obvious. All three men were armed and ready. "Doesn't look like you guys came out here for a picnic."

"Well," Trevor said mildly as he flicked Janice's ear, "when you decided to leave ahead of schedule, we thought it might behoove us to follow. Armed."

Donovan hadn't moved. His hand was still over Aura's. Still holding her in place.

"You left me," he said quietly.

"I had to," she answered, equally low, refusing to look away.

"I know."

That startled her. Her breath caught, and some of the tension drained from her shoulders despite herself.

He released her and stepped back. "If we're doing this," he said, voice firm, "we do it together. As a family."

Trevor nodded solemnly. "*His eyes shall see his destruction, and he shall drink of the wrath of the Almighty*."

Aura shot him a look. "You pick the strangest moments for scripture."

"Trevor," Donovan said, refocusing. "You've been inside. What can we expect?"

As the men spoke, Aura studied Donovan's face. God, she'd missed him. The familiar lines. The steadiness. The way he seemed carved out of certainty while she felt like she was coming apart at the seams. Loving him had been the stupidest thing she'd ever done. And the most inevitable.

"The interior's a wreck," Trevor replied. "Collapsed ceilings. Blocked corridors. Locked doors. It's basically a maze. Getting to him quietly will be next to impossible."

"Then we don't try to be quiet," Donovan said. "Guns ready. Corners checked. Doors cleared before passing. No rushing."

They moved as one.

Past the fence. Past the debris. Past the charred remains of what had once been order.

Donovan took point at the left-side entrance, easing the door open with practiced care. The entryway was empty: broken seats lining one wall, a shattered desk on the other. Straight ahead, double doors led deeper into the compound.

White walls, once pristine, were now blackened with soot and scorch marks. No decoration. No warmth. Just sterile corridors turned into graves.

The hallway split.

"I only got the files from one terminal," Trevor murmured. "Didn't make it far."

"Surgery's left," Janice said. "Control room's right."

"We split," Aura said immediately.

Donovan nodded. "Trevor. Tony. Surgery bay. If it's clear, loop back. Janice, Aura, you're with me."

Tony hesitated, then met Donovan's eyes. "Be careful."

Donovan gave a short nod. No words. None were needed.

They separated.

Aura moved behind Donovan and Janice, every sense straining. The building creaked around them, shedding rubble like a dying animal. Each sound made her heart stutter.

This was it.

Five years of blood and hunger and fear, narrowing into these halls.

They weren't hunting anymore.

They were closing the trap.

A crunch echoed ahead.

They froze.

A man rounded the corner, one of Luc's mercenaries. Surprise flashed across his face as he reached for his weapon.

Donovan didn't hesitate.

The gunshot thundered down the corridor. The man dropped where he stood.

Aura flinched as the sound ricocheted and then the ceiling answered.

"Look out!"

The world exploded.

Concrete gave way above them, collapsing in a roar of dust and debris. Janice dove backward. Donovan wrapped an arm around Aura's waist and threw them sideways, rolling hard across the floor as the ceiling caved in where they'd stood seconds before.

They landed hard. Aura coughed violently, lungs burning as dust filled the air.

"Are you alright?" Donovan demanded, already scanning her for blood.

She nodded, unable to speak.

"Janice!" he shouted. "Answer me!"

"I'm good!" Janice yelled from the other side of the rubble, voice muffled. "Path's blocked. I'll find another way around. You two keep moving."

The debris between them was impassable.

Donovan hauled Aura to her feet. "That was too damn close."

"Whole place is ready to come down," Aura said hoarsely. "We breathe wrong and it might finish the job."

They moved down the hallway the dead man had come from.

One room stopped them cold.

Bodies.

Dozens of them. Some barely recognizable as human. Metal gleamed through torn flesh. Limbs half-attached. Faces frozen in agony.

Aura turned away, bile rising.

Alice lay on top of the pile, broken and incomplete.

"He's been busy," Donovan said tightly. "Trying to recreate my parents' work."

"Is he building an army?" Aura asked, voice hollow.

"If he sent the first three at us," Donovan replied grimly, "let's pray he didn't finish more."

Her stomach twisted. "There could still be people alive down here."

"I hope not," he said quietly. "No one deserves that."

Aura reached out and gripped his arm, not to comfort him, but to anchor herself. To remind them both they were still here. Still breathing.

He glanced down at her hand, then covered it briefly with his own before moving forward again.

***

Aura could feel the tension mounting the deeper they pushed into the compound.

It sat coiled beneath her skin, tight and restless, every muscle primed. She was so close now she could almost taste it, the sharp, metallic tang of vengeance coating the back of her tongue. Five years of pursuit had narrowed to this suffocating corridor. Her finger itched against the trigger of her gun, her breath measured and shallow, her thoughts pared down to one brutal truth:

This ends today.

Donovan broke the silence, his voice low but strained. "We've got to be close. I couldn't have been that far off the mark taking us down that other hallway. That bastard just better be here. If he escapes again—"

"Don't," Aura snapped, the word cutting him off hard. Panic flared in her chest, sharp and unwelcome. "Don't even think it."

She couldn't hear that. Couldn't allow the possibility. Not now. Not when she was finally this close.

"I'm sorry, sweetheart," Donovan said quickly. "I'm just frustrated." He hesitated, scanning ahead. "It's worrying me that we haven't come across more—"

The rest of the sentence died in his throat.

Four men stood in the hallway ahead, guns raised, bodies tense with anticipation. They'd been waiting.

A bullet ricocheted off the wall beside Donovan's head, spraying concrete dust. He reacted instantly, shoving Aura back from the corner as more shots followed, cracking against the stone.

"Damn it," he hissed. "We're stuck." Another round struck the wall. "We'll have to backtrack."

"The hell we will."

The fury that surged through her was immediate and incandescent. If these men were here, *Luc was here.* Protecting him. Buying him time. She would not—*would not*—let him slip away again.

She grabbed Donovan's sleeve and pulled him back from the corner, slipping past him to press herself flat against the wall.

"What the hell are you doing?" Donovan demanded in a harsh whisper.

"When I say, fire down the hall," she told him firmly. There was no room for argument in her tone. She dropped to the floor, rolling onto her side and keeping well back from the edge.

"Aura—"

"Now."

Donovan hesitated only a fraction of a second before thrusting his arm around the corner and firing blind. The gunshot cracked loud in the confined space.

It was all Aura needed.

While their attention snapped upward, she slid forward just enough to clear the wall and fired four precise shots from the ground, steady and lethal. Donovan grabbed her ankles instantly and yanked her back into cover.

"Are you insane?!" he nearly shouted, his heart pounding violently. Fear for her ripped through him far stronger than the firefight ever could.

"We can go now," Aura said calmly, pushing herself to her feet and brushing dust from her clothes.

"What? What are you talking about? What about—"

"See for yourself."

She stepped around the corner before he could stop her.

Donovan followed, breath catching hard as he took in the scene. All four men lay sprawled across the hallway, unmoving. Dead.

"Dammit, Aura," he snapped, spinning on her. "Don't ever scare me like that again."

She smirked, a flash of grim satisfaction lighting her eyes. "I don't practice with these guns just to put holes in cans. I told you I could shoot."

"Well," he muttered, "I can't argue with the evidence, but you scared the hell out of me."

His hand came up around her neck, thumb warm against her pulse as he pulled her gently toward him. His eyes searched her face, full of concern, relief, and something far deeper.

"Don't do it again," he murmured.

Then he kissed her.

It wasn't desperate. It wasn't rushed. It was soft and grounding, filled with everything he'd been holding back. Aura felt it ripple through her, straight to her bones. For a heartbeat, the compound vanished. Luc vanished. The years vanished.

There was only Donovan.

He pulled back first, because he always did when survival demanded it. But his voice betrayed him as he looked into her eyes.

“I love you, Aura. No matter what you think.” His breath was unsteady. “I love you, and I’ll take you any way I can get you. No ultimatums. No restrictions. Everything on your terms.” His forehead rested briefly against hers. “Just please… come out of this alive with me.”

Her chest tightened painfully.

She didn’t answer. She couldn’t. Not yet. Not with Luc still breathing somewhere ahead of them.

But she didn’t pull away either.

And for Donovan, that was enough. For now.

CHAPTER 43

They reached the control room and paused at either side of the doorway, guns raised as they peered inside.

Luc wasn't there.

Aura exhaled sharply, frustration tightening her chest. But the signs of him were unmistakable. A cup of coffee still steaming on the terminal panel, notes scattered beside it. The screens flickered with schematics she recognized instantly. Trevor's files. Their parents' work. Luc had been using the old designs as a foundation, trying to replicate and improve them.

He'd failed. Repeatedly.

The notes told the story in frantic scrawl, corrections layered over corrections, calculations scratched out and rewritten. Luc might have been brilliant, but he wasn't a scientist. He'd butchered the process more times than he'd succeeded.

Years, Aura thought grimly. He's been doing this for years.

The room itself was almost bare. One chair sat against the far wall, shelves built into the concrete left empty. Another door stood opposite the one they'd entered through.

And between them—

Aura's gaze snagged on the long, jagged crack running through the floor.

"Careful," she murmured.

Donovan nodded, already adjusting his steps as they moved around it. The concrete looked unstable, fractured beneath layers of old fire damage and neglect. Aura skirted the crack, every nerve humming.

Just as Donovan reached for the knob on the opposite door, it was yanked open from the other side.

His wrist was caught in a crushing grip.

Donovan didn't even have time to curse before he was hauled forward and thrown violently back into the room. He slammed into the lone piece of furniture, the impact driving the air from his lungs.

Luc stepped through the doorway, smiling.

"I'm glad you came to visit me at home, pretty thing," he said lightly, his gaze locking on Aura. "Unfortunately, I don't have time to play with you right now. There are rats I need to deal with."

Aura raised her gun, heart hammering. "I hope you burn in hell."

Luc's smile widened.

Instead of answering, he lifted his fully modded arm and brought it down hard against the floor.

The impact cracked the concrete like brittle glass.

Aura felt the ground shudder beneath her boots, then drop away.

She gasped as the floor collapsed, the crack tearing open into empty space. Her gun slipped from her fingers as she clawed for purchase, her body pitching forward. Luc's laughter echoed, distorted and wild, as the world fell out from under her.

She caught a ledge a few feet down, fingers screaming as they dug into rough stone. The cavern yawned below her, black and endless. Her boots scraped uselessly against the rock as she fought to brace herself.

"Aura!" Donovan's voice tore through the air.

He was at the edge now, flat on his stomach, arm stretched toward her. His fingers brushed empty air, close enough that she could see the strain in his face, the fear etched deep in his eyes.

"I've got you," he pleaded. "Hold on. Please, hold on."

She tried. God, she tried.

Her grip slipped another inch.

And then she saw Luc.

He stood behind Donovan, calm as ever, raising a gun. The muzzle lined up with the back of Donovan's head.

Time fractured.

Aura's breath caught painfully in her chest. The fear wasn't for herself. It was sharp and absolute, all for him. Donovan, who was still reaching for her, still trying to save her, completely unaware of the death behind him.

I should have married him.

The thought hit with devastating clarity. Not regret. Truth. A future she'd never allowed herself to imagine, slipping through her fingers just like the ledge beneath her hands.

Her grip failed another fraction.

Aura let go with one hand and drew the second gun from her left holster.

Her fingers were numb. Her arm shook.

She met Luc's gaze.

"I love you," she whispered to Donovan.

Then she fired.

The shot took Luc through the left eye.

Aura didn't see him fall.

She heard Donovan scream her name as her remaining grip finally gave way and the darkness surged up to meet her. Pain exploded through her body as she hit the cavern floor, and then there was nothing. No sound, no light, only black.

***

Donovan screamed Aura's name into the darkness, his voice tearing raw as it echoed back to him. He dropped to his knees at the edge of the pit, leaning so far forward he nearly lost his balance, desperate for any sign, any sound, that she was still alive.

He couldn't see her.

The pit yawned three stories down at least, too far to jump, too deep to climb without equipment. But he had heard the impact. The sound of her body striking stone still rang in his ears.

No.

He wouldn't think it. Not yet. Not until he knew.

"Aura!" he shouted again, his hands shaking as he gripped the fractured concrete. "Answer me! Please, Aura!"

Footsteps thundered behind him as the others burst through the doorway, skidding to a halt at the edge.

"Donovan! What happened?!" Trevor shouted over his brother's frantic yelling.

"She fell!" Donovan choked out, scrambling to his feet and pacing the edge, searching for any possible way down. "She won't answer me. Oh God, why won't she answer me? I need to get to her. I need to—"

Trevor moved quickly to his side, one hand gripping Donovan's shoulder to steady him, his eyes flicking to Luc's body sprawled lifelessly on the floor.

"She's down there?" Trevor said tightly. "We need to find the stairs."

"I'll go down," Janice said immediately.

Donovan spun on her, desperation blazing in his eyes. "Please, Janice. Please. Tell me she's okay. I need to know she's okay." His voice broke. "She said she loves me."

Janice nodded once, sober now, all humor gone. She didn't waste another second.

She jumped.

The landing was brutal. Her cybernetic knee shrieked in protest and blew out beneath her, sending her crashing hard onto the cavern floor.

"Damn it," she hissed, forcing herself upright despite the pain.

The light was poor, shadows swallowing the space, but she could make out Aura's body lying several feet away. Janice limped to her side and dropped to her knees, fingers already searching for a pulse.

Nothing.

Her breath caught as she leaned closer, pressing her ear to Aura's mouth.

No breath.

"Donovan…" Janice called up, dread tightening her chest. "She's not breathing."

"No!" Donovan's horrified shout echoed down. "Janice, do something! She can't die!" For one terrifying instant, the world narrowed to a single thought, not Luc, not vengeance, not even Aura herself, but everything she would lose if she didn't survive this.

The Hartly's.

She would never know what they'd taken from her. Never stand in that quiet hall again. Never see the truth in their faces when they finally understood who she was and what had been stolen from her.

Family, offered too late.

And worse, she would never get the chance to decide whether she wanted them.

The thought ripped through him harder than the fear of losing her body.

Please, he begged silently. *Not like this. Don't let her lose everything without ever knowing she had it.*

"Janice, do what you can," Trevor called urgently. "We're finding the stairs."

Their voices faded as they ran.

Janice looked back down at Aura, fear clawing up her spine. "Don't you dare die, you bitch," she growled, gripping Aura's shoulders and shaking her. "Donovan needs you. It'll destroy him if you don't come back."

She slapped Aura's cheek once. Then again. Harder.

Nothing.

"Breathe, damn you!" Janice shouted, panic spiking. She drew back and slammed her fist into Aura's chest.

Aura coughed violently, a harsh, wet sound tearing free.

Janice laughed and swore at the same time. "There you go. That's it."

Aura sucked in a ragged breath and groaned, pain rippling through her body.

"Don't move," Janice ordered quickly, gripping her hand. "I'm here. The guys are coming. Just—just don't move until we know how bad you're hurt."

"J-Janice…?" Aura rasped, eyes still closed. "Donovan…"

"He's alright," Janice said immediately, knowing the question before it was finished. "Luc's dead. Donovan's fine. We all are."

"I… love him…" Aura whispered.

"I know," Janice said softly, squeezing her hand. "And you'll get to tell him yourself."

Aura's grip slackened.

Janice's heart lurched as she leaned closer, watching Aura's chest. A shallow rise. Still breathing.

"Don't you scare me like that," Janice muttered, exhaling shakily.

Several agonizing minutes passed before footsteps echoed again. Donovan appeared first, sliding down to Aura's side and gathering her carefully into his arms.

"Careful," Janice warned. "She's breathing, but I don't know how bad the injuries are."

Donovan sobbed openly, relief shattering him as he cradled her. "Aura. Aura, my love. I'm here. I'm here," he murmured, kissing her hair.

Janice scooted back to give them space and immediately hissed as pain shot through her side. She couldn't stand.

Tony and Trevor knelt beside her, relief etched across their faces.

"She's alive?" Tony asked.

"She's breathing," Janice said. "That's all I know."

"Thank God," Trevor breathed, offering a quiet prayer.

Janice did too, though she'd never admit it.

"You alright?" Tony asked her.

"Blew out my knee," she said flatly. "I'll live. But I'm not walking anywhere."

"I've got you," Tony nodded.

Donovan brushed Aura's hair back gently. "Can you open your eyes for me, sweetheart?"

She managed a brief flutter before pain forced them shut again.

"That's okay," he said quickly. "We'll get you out of here. Can you move your feet? Can you feel them?"

One foot twitched faintly.

Donovan exhaled hard. "Good girl. That's my good girl."

"...love you," Aura whispered.

"I know, love. I know." His voice cracked. "We'll talk about everything later."

He lifted her carefully. She moaned and he winced, adjusting his grip.

Tony lifted Janice carefully, bracing her injured leg against his chest as if she weighed nothing at all. She hissed once under her breath but waved him off, already looking past her own pain. Trevor took the lead, weapon raised, eyes scanning every shadow as they retraced their path through the ruined compound.

The place felt different now.

Not empty exactly, just *quiet*, the wrong kind of quiet. The kind that settled after violence, when whatever hunger had lived there was finally dead. Donovan felt it in the way the air pressed close, in the echo of their footsteps that seemed too loud against the silence. He kept his arms tight around Aura, every muscle locked, afraid that if he loosened even slightly she might slip away from him again.

They moved slowly, carefully, stepping around rubble, past the collapsed hallway where Janice had been separated, past the room of bodies Donovan refused to look at again. He didn't want that image anywhere near her now. Not after everything.

When they finally reached the daylight spilling in through the broken entrance, Donovan drew a breath he hadn't realized he'd been holding.

Outside, he shifted Aura gently, adjusting his grip when she let out a faint sound of pain. His heart stuttered, then steadied when her breathing evened again.

He turned to Tony. "I'll take her horse. I can't put her on the bike."

"Of course," Tony said immediately, already moving to retrieve it without question.

"You three go ahead," Donovan continued. "Warn Doc we're coming."

Janice leaned slightly into Tony's hold and looked back at Donovan, her expression softer than he was used to seeing. "She's going to be alright now," she said, quiet but certain.

Donovan met her gaze. The words lodged in his chest, tangled with gratitude and a debt he knew he could never fully repay. "Thanks to you," he said. "I'll never forget it."

Janice snorted, the moment broken on purpose. "Come on, Tony. Before he turns into complete mush."

Tony chuckled as he adjusted his grip. "Anything for you, darlin'."

Donovan turned back to Aura, lifting her with infinite care and settling her into the saddle in front of him. He arranged her against his chest, one arm firm around her middle, the other steadying the reins. Her head rested against his shoulder, her breath warm through the fabric of his shirt, fragile and precious all at once.

You're still here, he told himself fiercely. *I've got you. I won't let go.*

"I'll see you soon," he said to the others, though the words were mostly for her.

They rode out, the compound shrinking behind them, its secrets buried in ash and silence, while Donovan focused on only one thing. The rise and fall of Aura's breath, and the promise he made without speaking it.

Come back to me. I'm right here.

CHAPTER 44

Donovan rode slowly, carefully, doing everything in his power not to jar her too badly. It was a long way back, and every uneven step of the horse felt like a small cruelty he couldn't prevent. He wished he knew more about medicine. At their current pace, it would take several days to reach Kinsville, and Aura would be in pain the entire way.

It was torture knowing he couldn't truly help her.

All he could do was get her home and pray it was enough.

Near dusk, Aura stirred with a soft, pained moan. Donovan reined the horse to a halt immediately.

"I know," he murmured softly. "I know you hurt, sweetheart. We're heading back to town, but it's going to take a while."

"I… I think my arm is broken," she groaned, her eyes squeezed tightly shut.

His chest tightened. "Alright," he said gently, forcing calm into his voice. "Let's get it splinted. I can do that much for you."

He slid from the saddle and carefully lifted her into his arms before setting her down on the ground. He moved quickly, searching for straight sticks sturdy enough to brace her arm. When he returned, he took the arm she indicated and straightened it as carefully as he could.

Her cry of pain tore through him.

"I'm sorry," he said immediately, his hands steady even as guilt twisted in his gut. "I know. I know it hurts."

He bound the makeshift splint in place with rope from her saddlebag, firm enough to hold but not so tight as to cut circulation.

"It's not perfect," he said quietly, "but it should keep it stable until Doc can look at it properly."

"Thank you," she murmured, exhaustion dragging at her words.

"Don't fall asleep yet," he said quickly, lifting her chin just enough that she cracked her eyes open. "I need you to drink some water first."

He helped her sip from the canteen, watching her closely. She looked too pale. Too sluggish. A cold dread settled in his stomach as he wondered if she'd struck her head in the fall. He didn't press her with questions—he couldn't bear to cause her more pain—but the worry stayed with him.

They rested only long enough to water and feed the horse before he lifted her back into the saddle and mounted behind her, one arm wrapped securely around her to keep her steady.

By the second day, her skin burned beneath his touch.

Aura had a fever.

Panic tightened in his chest, and he urged the horse onward, cutting their rests short and stealing only an hour or two of sleep at a time. He couldn't afford to be careless. Not now.

She loved him.

The thought anchored him even as fear threatened to drown him. She had said the words, and he knew—*knew*—she had meant them. Even if he never heard them again, he would carry that truth with him for the rest of his life.

He used precious water for cold compresses, pressing them gently to her forehead and neck, but the heat never seemed to fade. She needed a bed. A doctor. Not the relentless sway of a horse beneath her.

Aura mumbled in her delirium, her words tangled with pain and memory. He recognized the cadence of nightmares even when he couldn't make out the words. He spoke to her constantly, murmuring reassurances, reminding her that he was there. That she was safe. That she wasn't alone.

He didn't know if she heard him.

He prayed that she could.

They reached town on the fourth day.

Donovan barely remembered dismounting, only that the doctor was fetched in a rush and Aura was carried to their room. He stayed at her side through the examination, his presence a quiet, immovable thing.

A head wound, the doctor said. The cause of the fever. It should break in a day or two.

She had a broken arm, two broken fingers on the other hand, and bruises that mapped her body in shades of pain, but nothing that wouldn't heal with time.

Time. Rest. Care.

Donovan clung to those words as if they were promises.

Even after she was given medicine and allowed to sleep, he didn't leave her. Not once.

At night, he stayed with her, mindful of her fear of being left alone in the dark. If she woke and asked, he wanted to be able to tell her truthfully that he had never left her.

For two long days, he waited for the fever to break.

People came and went. Tony. Trevor. Janice.

Donovan barely noticed.

His entire world was the woman lying in his bed.

The woman who had carved her way into his heart and made him believe, against all reason, that he was worthy of love. He ached to hear her voice again, to see those emerald eyes open and focused, to feel her arms around him.

He hadn't known he could love someone this deeply. Not like this. Loving her felt like discovering a missing piece of himself he hadn't known was gone.

When she had fallen into that darkness, he hadn't thought of Luc. Or himself. Only her.

And when she'd looked at him from that ledge and spoken the words he had longed to hear, his heart had shattered with the certainty that he was about to lose her.

In that moment, a part of him had almost wished Luc had killed him too.

He could not imagine a life without Aura in it.

When Janice had said she wasn't breathing, something inside him had broken entirely.

Thank God for Janice.

She had saved Aura's life, Donovan was certain of it. And in doing so, she had very likely saved his as well.

CHAPTER 45

"You're being unreasonable, Donovan. You have to let me out of this bed sometime," Aura protested in her customary grouch. It had been a week since her fever had broken and, while her broken bones were still mending, she was more than ready to get up and move around. But Donovan was being his overprotective self, refusing to let her leave the bed even to stretch.

"You *died*, Aura. Do you realize that?" Donovan shot back at her. "You're not leaving that bed until your bruises are gone at least. You're lucky I'm not keeping you there until your arm is healed, too."

"I hate it when you boss me around," she growled. "I do know how to take care of myself, you know."

"I know, sweetheart," he said with a sigh, sitting on the side of the bed next to her and taking her hand. He brought the fingers to his lips, lightly brushing them across her knuckles. It was the most he had allowed himself, afraid to cause her any pain. "But I almost lost you and I'm so grateful to still have you, I don't want you to do anything that might jeopardize that."

"I know you're worried, Donovan, but I'm going crazy in this bed. Just let me walk around the room a little. You can even hold onto me if you want," she said in near desperation.

She watched closely as he mulled that offer over for several seconds, hope lighting up her eyes. In the end, he couldn't deny her and helped her out of the bed. She was unsteady at first but managed a short walk around the bed with his help. With a grateful smile to him, they paused by the window so she could look out to the street for a few minutes.

"Aura…" Donovan started slowly as he watched her. "I want you to know. I meant what I said at the compound." She turned her head to look at him curiously. "I want you to stay with me. No ultimatums and no restrictions. I just want you."

Her expression turned disgruntled as he spoke. Of course he had to bring that up again. She'd been expecting it sooner but figured they'd have to talk about it sometime. She had meant what she said to him. She loved him. She could admit it even to herself now. She wanted that happiness he gave her, that reason to smile. She'd even grown fond of his family, wanting more than anything to be a part of it.

"You don't have to marry me," he said quickly, seeing her expression and guessing she was about to protest yet again. "Just stay."

"I'll marry you," she mumbled under her breath so softly he didn't hear her.

"What did you say, sweetheart?"

"I said I'll marry you," she spat out gracelessly. Donovan's eyes flared wide at her admission and before he could stop himself, he pulled Aura to him in a tight hug of relief and joy. But her loud "ouch!" had him releasing her just as quickly.

"Sorry! Sorry!" he said as he steadied her, laughing. "But, Aura love, that is the sweetest thing I've ever heard." He took her face gently in his hands, eyes brimming with love for her. "I'm going to make it very hard for you to get rid of me."

"I know you will," she said, returning his smile. His joy filled her heart to bursting.

"I love you, Aura," he said just before he kissed her gently, carefully. She kissed him back, sliding her unbroken arm around his neck, ignoring the twinge of pain she felt. His touch, his kiss was more important than any pain. He thought he lost her? She thought she had lost him as well and was ashamed of how hard she had pushed him away.

He hadn't replaced anything.

He'd just made room for something new.

When the kiss broke, she said softly against his lips, "I love you, too, Donovan," then, more gruffly, "But a small ceremony. Just you, me and a judge."

Donovan burst out laughing. "Never change, sweetheart. I love your stubborn self just as you are." And he kissed her again.

Epilogue

It was six months after the wedding—Aura had finally healed by then—when Donovan suggested they visit the Hartly's again by way of a small honeymoon. His excuse was that the couple would be immensely happy for their union and he wanted to share it with them in person rather than sending a less personal letter. Knowing his affection for the older couple, Aura agreed. She even secretly hoped there would be another ball to attend, though she wasn't about to tell Donovan that.

The train ride was uneventful, and this time they took a hotel room, more concerned with privacy than inconveniencing their hosts since they knew they were more than welcome in the Hartly home. They were shown to the sitting room again to wait for William and Angela, who appeared with little delay.

There was a round of hugging and warm greetings, followed by joy at their announcement and then another round of hugs. Aura couldn't help but laugh at the jubilant reaction, and the Hartly's could see immediately how much she had changed.

All through dinner, Donovan held tight to his suspicions, letting the comfortable conversation stretch on longer than necessary. He watched Aura laugh with Angela, watched the easy affection she returned without realizing it, and felt the familiar tension coil in his chest. He was here for a reason, and he was nearly bursting to bring it to light, but he waited. This wasn't something to rush.

After dinner, while they enjoyed coffee in the sitting room, he waited for a lull in the conversation and decided to give Aura the chance to tell her story first.

"Aura, sweetheart," he began with a deceptively calm smile, "why don't you tell the Hartly's about how you ended up out west?"

Aura frowned slightly. "Why would they want to hear that?" she asked. "It'll only bring down the pleasant mood."

"I have a feeling it won't," he said gently. "Humor me?"

She sighed and set down her coffee cup. "My mother was from the east, like you," she began, nodding to the Hartly's. "She married a man her family disapproved of. A soldier who died in battle before I was born. Without a way to support us, my mother turned to whoring. After she died, the women at the brothel raised me."

"Oh my," Angela murmured, a hand rising to her chest. "How old were you when your mother died?"

"Five," Aura answered, her voice steady now in a way it had never been before.

William was watching her intently.

"What was your mother's name?" he asked carefully.

"Sarah Black," Aura said. "Though I once heard the others mention she changed it to protect her family."

William hesitated, then asked quietly, "May I see the cameo you're wearing?"

Aura blinked, confused, but unclasped the choker and handed it over. William examined it closely, then passed it to Angela. As soon as Angela's fingers closed around it, the color drained from her face.

"Where did you say this came from?" William asked, his voice no longer steady.

"It was my mother's," Aura said, unease creeping in. "It's the only thing I kept after she died."

"My God…" William whispered. "It can't be."

Donovan leaned forward, unable to contain himself any longer. "That's what I thought at first, too."

Aura's head snapped toward him. "What?"

"I believe," Donovan said carefully, squeezing her hand, "that your mother may have been their daughter. Celeste."

Aura's grip tightened on the arm of her chair. *It couldn't be.* The room felt suddenly too small.

"She looks just like her," Donovan said, turning to William. "I noticed it when we were here before, in the portrait, but I wasn't sure."

William nodded slowly. Angela had begun to cry in earnest now, pressing a handkerchief to her mouth.

“I never told you what the fight was about,” William said to Aura. “I wanted Celeste to marry well. She fell in love with a poor soldier instead. When I forbade it… she ran away.”

“And I gave her a cameo,” Angela sobbed. “My mother’s. I would know it anywhere.” She leaned forward, eyes shining through tears. “How did I not see it before? You have her eyes. Her cheekbones.”

Aura stared at them, her chest tight, her breath shallow. The realization hit with a force she wasn’t prepared for, and tears burned behind her eyes.

William exhaled shakily. “And I can finally stop searching.”

“Our girl…” Angel breathed shakily.

“I… I don’t know what to say,” Aura whispered.

“That’s alright,” Donovan murmured, bringing her knuckles to his lips. “You don’t have to say anything.”

Aura looked at him then, really looked at him, and felt the full weight of what he had helped her find. Not just love. Not just safety. But roots.

“Thank you,” she said softly. Then she leaned in and kissed him, quick but full of meaning. “I love you.”

Donovan smiled, heart full. And for the first time in her life, Aura didn’t feel thc nccd to run.

COMING SOON

She should have been turned over to the law.

Trevor MacHaven didn't do it. Now Regina St. James is still in his house, still under his control—and still a decision he hasn't corrected.

Turn her over and walk away clean. Keep her and answer for it himself.

Either way, something breaks.

Dead Reckoning

The MacHaven Legacy: Book 2

CHAPTER 1

What will it be? Jail? Or me?

He let the question sit between them.

He didn't soften it. He didn't step closer. If it sounded like an ultimatum, that was because it was. His voice stayed level, controlled the way it did when there were no good outcomes left. The restraints carried the rest.

She didn't answer.

The cuffs circled her wrists, iron darkened with age, the chain fixed to the bed frame at the headboard. Short enough to keep her where she was. Long enough to allow a margin of movement.

She sat upright against the pillows, back straight despite the narrow angle, shoulders squared, chin lifted. Her chestnut hair had lost its structure over the last two weeks, strands slipping loose where she hadn't bothered to bind it back. There was dried blood worked deep into the fabric of her sleeve, stubborn where it had soaked in and stayed.

Trevor MacHaven had learned not to read posture.

Two weeks had been enough to make that mistake expensive.

He stayed where he was, a few steps back. Close enough to reach her if he had to, far enough not to pretend this was a conversation.

The room was his. Plaster walls, painted clean and kept that way. A single window overlooked the street below the shop, the curtain drawn back for light. The lamp beside the bed had been shifted closer than he would have left it, adjusted without asking. The chair beside the bed was positioned for watching more than rest.

This wasn't a holding cell. It was his room, pressed into service because there had been nowhere else for her to go.

That wasn't true anymore.

A folded sheet of paper rested on the dresser, its seal already broken. He didn't look at it again. He didn't need to. The territory had a sheriff again. A name. A badge. Someone to hand problems off to.

The reason she was still here was no longer necessity.

Regina St. James watched him with steady eyes.

Both of them were wrong in different ways—too precise, too bright in the low light. Trevor knew the tell in himself; he saw it more clearly in her. The modifications sat clean in her face, seamless enough to miss if you didn't know what to look for.

He knew.

He couldn't look at her without knowing.

She didn't blink as often as most people. Didn't need to. When she looked at him, it was with the same focus she'd worn when she pulled the trigger.

He read calculation there.

Nothing else.

He'd replayed it often enough to know it hadn't been luck that day. The spacing of the shots. The discipline in them. The proof built into their restraint. She hadn't been missing. She'd been choosing, right up until she was ready to end it.

"Those are the options," he said when the silence stretched thin. "You decide."

He already knew what jail would look like. A handover. A cell with a door he didn't control. Consequences that belonged to someone else. Clean, in the way distance always was.

The responsibility of the other option stayed with him.

He was already the reason she was breathing instead of bleeding out on the warehouse floor. The reason there were cuffs instead of a grave.

A mistake, by any reasonable measure.

One he hadn't corrected.

Trevor waited.

Regina's gaze slid past him, brief and deliberate, to the dresser. To the folded paper resting there. She didn't test the cuffs. She didn't need to. The movement alone told him she understood the timing as well as he did.

"If I say jail," she asked, "you take me in today?"

Her voice was roughened by disuse, low and even, as if they were negotiating terms already decided.

"Yes."

He said it plainly. No room for interpretation. If he crossed this line, it would be without deception.

She nodded once, small and contained, like she was confirming a calculation already finished. Then her eyes came back to him.

"You already chose by offering yourself," she said. "You just waited until you had permission to ask."

The words landed cleanly.

Trevor didn't respond.

He stood very still. The room felt smaller than it had a second ago, as if the walls had shifted while he wasn't looking. He'd told himself the return of the law would simplify things. That it would restore order.

Instead, it stripped away the last excuse.

She was right.

He'd known it before she said it.

Offering himself instead of a cell wasn't hesitation.

It was intent.

He crossed the room and took the key from his coat pocket. The metal was warm from his body, worn smooth from years of use. He set it on the dresser beside the writ, where she could see it.

A decision, made without ceremony.

Regina watched him closely. She didn't reach for it. She didn't look away.

"I'll be back," he said.

Trevor turned and walked to the door. His pace stayed measured as he stepped into the hall, pulling it shut behind him.

The sound carried along the second-floor hallway. He stood there for a moment, listening to the familiar quiet—the creak of a settling board, the low hum of work continuing in the garage below, the muted presence of people who trusted this place to hold.

His hand went to his coat pocket.

Empty.

The key was still on the dresser, a few steps behind him. Leaving it there had been a choice. He felt it settle now—clean, deliberate, already past the point where it could be taken back without meaning something else.

Footsteps sounded from the stairwell.

Tony came into view, sleeves rolled, black hair pulled back, moving with the kind of ease that came from belonging somewhere instead of passing through it. He slowed when he saw Trevor, his gaze flicking once toward the closed door before coming back.

"You heading out," Tony asked, "or just standing here pretending you're about to?"

"In a bit."

Tony leaned his shoulder against the wall, casual but not careless, lowering his voice without being asked. "Coffee's on. Your sister's up." A beat. "Which means something's already wrong."

Trevor exhaled through his nose. Not quite a smile. "She doesn't need a reason."

"No," Tony agreed. "But she usually picks a better one than sunrise."

His gaze drifted once more toward the closed door, then back to Trevor.

"We finally have a sheriff again," he said.

"I know."

Tony nodded but didn't move right away. His eyes stayed on Trevor a second longer, measuring.

"Timing's interesting," he added. "Depending on what you're planning to do with it."

Trevor didn't answer.

Tony shifted, pushing off the wall.

"You want me to—" He stopped, recalibrating without making it a thing. "You need anything before you go?"

Trevor shook his head. "No. I need to pack."

Tony nodded, easy again. Halfway to the stairs, he paused, glancing back over his shoulder.

"I'll be here," he said. Then, just enough edge to make it his, "You'll want to tell the whirlwind before she finds out another way."

Trevor didn't answer, but something in his posture shifted—small, almost imperceptible.

Trevor watched him go until the sound of his steps faded and the second floor settled again into its careful quiet.

He didn't move right away.

He could have gone up. Tony's loft would have given him distance, oversight, the illusion of control handed off to someone else. He didn't take it.

He didn't go back to his room.

He paused outside it instead, his hand settling briefly against the doorframe before he moved on.

At the washstand at the end of the hall, he turned on the tap and scrubbed his hands until the water ran clear and his skin burned under the cold. The motion was automatic, practiced—something to do with the weight of what he'd already set in place.

He dried his hands slowly, pressing the cloth into his palms as if it might anchor something that had already shifted loose.

Then he straightened and stepped back into the hall.

Around him, the house held.

Shared. Lived in. Trust built into its walls and routines—into the people moving through it without question. It had always been enough. Structure, order, control. A place that didn't bend unless he chose to make it.

He had.

The choice was already inside it now.

Upstairs, a floorboard creaked. Somewhere below, a tool struck metal and rang out, sharp and brief. Life continuing, unaware or unconcerned with the line he'd just crossed.

He stood in the center of it, feeling the shift settle into place—not loud, not dramatic, but final in a way that didn't leave room for revision.

Behind him, a closed door. A key he no longer held.

Ahead of him, a law he could no longer pretend to ignore.

And between them—

he would have to choose which one he was willing to break.

www.ingramcontent.com/pod-product-compliance
Lightning Source LLC
LaVergne TN
LVHW100517110826
845146LV00002B/681